DEATH
DINES
AT 8:30

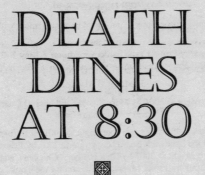

Edited by
Claudia Bishop and Nick DiChario

BERKLEY PRIME CRIME, NEW YORK

DEATH DINES AT 8:30

A Berkley Prime Crime Book / published by arrangement with the editors

PRINTING HISTORY
Berkley Prime Crime hardcover edition / May 2001
Berkley Prime Crime mass-market edition / March 2002

Visit our website at
www.penguinputnam.com

ISBN: 0-425-18442-0

This book is dedicated to our editor,
Natalee Rosenstein,
who loves short stories
as much as we do.

CONTENTS

FOREWORD

When Claudia and I decided to edit this anthology, the one thing we agreed on right from the start was that we wanted to do something special. The field of culinary cozies has really taken off over the past few years, growing enormously in popularity, so we thought it was important for the authors who have found fame (if not fortune) with their recipes to have an opportunity to give a little something back to the community.

Therefore, many of the authors in this collection—and the editors as well—have agreed to donate their royalties from *Death Dines at 8:30* to America's Second Harvest, an organization that feeds the hungry. I say this first and foremost because we can all be proud, including you fine folks, the purchasers of this book, for contributing to an excellent cause.

Here are just a few facts about hunger in America: According to the Congressional Hunger Center, 29 percent of children in the United States under the age of twelve—13.6 million—are hungry or at risk of hunger daily. According to the American Diabetic Association, federal programs to combat hunger and food insecurity reach only about one-third of needy older adults. To quote former President Clinton, "Every day, 25 percent of our food supply is wasted."

America's Second Harvest is the nation's largest domestic hunger relief organization. Through a network of nearly two hundred food banks, they distribute food to twenty-six million hungry Americans each year. Last year, America's Second Harvest distributed one billion pounds of food to needy Americans, serving all fifty states and Puerto Rico. Second Harvest serves nearly fifty thousand local charitable organizations, which operate more than ninety-four thousand feeding programs throughout the country. Their goal is to end hunger in America. We support that effort wholeheartedly and hope you will, too.

Having said all that, I'll take a moment to thank our authors, without whose stories and recipes this book would not have seen the light of day. Some of our authors are well known to the inner circle of homicide-and-food—Claudia Bishop, Tamar Myers, Camilla Crespi, and the incomparable Diane Mott Davidson have been whipping up mysteries and munchies for years. Other well-known contributors are writing their first official culinary mysteries—Ed Hoch, Nancy Kress, and Sharan Newman, just to name a few.

This unusual mix of talent makes for a supremely delicious literary menu filled with tasty treats and succulent surprises. I hope you enjoy reading the stories and testing the recipes as much as I have enjoyed hunting, gathering, and presenting them here à la carte in this most civilized manner, as far as bloody murders go.

—*Nick DiChario*

INTRODUCTION

We were at a mystery convention cocktail party, Nick and I, when a friend we'd known for years staggered up, wineglass in hand, and waved his free hand rather helplessly in the air. Now, this is a friend who is never the worse for drink (and this *was* New York City), so we nodded sympathetically and suggested, "Mugged?"

"Not mugged," he said. "Inundated. Beset. Bemused! By books! What's happened to the mystery?"

The previous hour, he'd wandered into a mystery editor/agent's seminar. Hordes of would-be mystery writers introduced themselves with: "My detective is . . . a cook, a gardener, a motel owner/operator, an architect, a lawyer, a doctor, a monk . . ."

Our friend's bewilderment was clear: "All those *job* descriptions. Aren't private eyes private eyes anymore? Is *everybody* a detective?"

Well, we said, yes. Isn't it wonderful? We're not locked into all the old genre conventions anymore!

"Good grief," he said, "I haven't the slightest clue what to read first. Every book I pick up is a mystery!"

And isn't that the truth? Modern mystery fiction is vital, diverse, and above all, eclectic in style and content. For the first time in the history of popular fiction, there is a mystery for virtually every reader, a detective for every taste, a sub-genre for every proclivity. Thrillers, suspense, cozies, village mysteries, hobby mysteries, techno-thrillers, not to mention my own favorite, and the premise of this anthology—the culinary mystery—the field that has it all. And it is this incredible diversity that drives the selections in this anthology, just as it drives today's "Platinum Age" of the mystery.

Time was—and those of us who grew up reading the masters of the Golden Age of mystery remember it well—when the mystery menu was limited. The detective protagonist was either a professional under a murderous threat in a race to solve a crime, or an amateur compelled to unravel a puzzle. In this new age of the mystery—the Platinum Age—the boundaries of the mystery *begin* with those elements, and there is no end in sight. Today's mystery reader can glory in the amazing explosion of the traditional mystery into exotic and variant forms. As readers, we are limited only by the time available to read; as writers, we are limited only by the need to deal with themes involving law and order.

The mystery has reached an apogee of popularity. And the most significant proof of this is that the short story is back. The genre was created through short stories. As the genre expanded, short stories were often abandoned in favor of novels. But—like seedlings sprouting near the parent tree—the short story's a viable form.

After Poe's orangutan first swung from the stairways of the Rue Morgue in the middle of the nineteenth century, the mystery short story thrived under Doyle and flourished under Chesterton. And then? A desert. A dearth. At the very least, a paucity. The print form receded into a small number of magazines; the concept itself transmuted into radio programs, and later, television drama. All the while the *idea* of the mystery continued to be explored in novels. These explorations led to astonishingly vigorous results. Over a period of fifty years, the mystery field produced Sayers, Christie, Marsh, Hammett, Chandler, Ross Thomas, Ross Macdonald, John MacDonald, Graham Greene, John le Carré, Dickson-Carr, and more. The early writers of the Golden Age are the Galileos, the Thomas Jeffersons of our craft. But they all wrote novels, because the writers needed the time and space that only the novel affords.

The short story didn't disappear, of course. For a while, mystery short stories were written by writers from *other* genres. Anthony Boucher, Roald Dahl, and Isaac Asimov drifted in from science fiction, fantasy, and horror. An occasional classic anthology appeared. Agatha Christie, Dorothy Sayers, and even John D. MacDonald were talked into contributing to collections by their publishers. And, as I suggested above, a good case could be made that radio and later television inherited the short story niche for a time. But that was about it. After Chesterton and Doyle, no writer but Edward D. Hoch made a literary career of them. Most major mystery writers were busy building up the genre through the novel.

Why the novel? Because it's *longer.* The writer has more room to explore his or her themes and tell a story. Is the length of a work all that important? You bet.

The essence of any mystery is crime, preferably with a solution that makes a reader sit up and scream for joy at the cleverness of it all. This intricate plot revolves around the protagonist's struggle with law and order. So by definition, in any mystery, there are always three complex issues that even Mickey Spillane couldn't boil down to short-story form:

- the crime and the criminal
- the activities that lead to the solution of the crime
- the characters' interaction with the forces of law and order that exist in their (fictional) world

The length of a mystery story is determined by other factors. As a mystery novel rises in literary quality, character becomes more integral to plot solution. Character development takes time. And as mystery fiction rises in quality, plots generally become more intricate. And that, of course, takes the most time of all. So writing a short story is a heck of a challenge to the mystery writer. Much easier to spend your time stuffing five pounds of spaghetti into a one-pound sack.

But, lucky us, we had fifteen friends and colleagues who eschewed pasta for prose. In this anthology, you will find some marvelously witty, inventive, delightfully puzzling short stories based on the following invitation:

> A death occurs during dinner at 8:30
> RSVP with short story and recipe
> Donate your royalty $ to good cause!

To our delight, everyone we asked came to the party. The contributors to *Death Dines at 8:30* come from sub-genres, classic, traditional, and new. From Diane Mott Davidson's culinary mystery to Barbara D'Amato and Mike Resnick's takes on the classic noir, we offer you a full course of the best of today's mystery writers.

—*Claudia Bishop*

STEAK TARTARE

BARBARA D'AMATO

If you drive north from Chicago along Lake Michigan, you will pass through several increasingly wealthy suburbs. The first and oldest is Evanston. Then Wilmette, Kenilworth, and Winnetka. Winnetka is one of the richest municipalities in the United States. It may be that the average income in Kenilworth, nestled next to it, is higher than Winnetka, but Kenilworth is so small that it hardly counts.

Basil Stone had therefore been thrilled to be hired as resident director of the North Shore Playhouse, located in Winnetka. It wasn't Broadway, of course, but it was a very, very prestigious rep house. And you rubbed shoulders with nothing but the best people.

Like tonight.

He spun his little red Lexus around the curves of Sheridan Road, which ran right along Lake Michigan and therefore was the Place des Vosges of Illinois, *rue de la crème de la crème,* the street that accessed the highest-priced real estate in an already high-priced area. And the Falklands' mansion was on the lake side of Sheridan, the east, which meant beach frontage, of course, and was far tonier than living across the road.

These things mattered to Basil.

Pamela had given him the street number and told him to watch for two brick columns supporting a wrought-iron arch and elaborate iron gates. And there they were. He swung in, spoke his name into the post speaker, and the gates majestically opened.

God, the place was a castle. The drive wound in a lazy *S* up to a wide pillared veranda. Pamela stood on the lip of the veranda like a midwestern Scarlett O'Hara, framed among acres of flesh pink azaleas that swept away on both sides of the fieldstone steps.

"Welcome, Basil," she said, giving him a quick kiss on the cheek. He pulled back fast, not wanting her husband to see. Although everybody hugged and kissed when they met, didn't they? It didn't necessarily mean anything.

She drew him in the front door.

Basil stopped just inside, trying not to goggle at the immense foyer. A tessellated marble floor flowed into a great entry hall, stretching far back to a double staircase, which curved out, up, and in, the two halves joining at the second floor. The ceiling was thirty feet overhead. The chandelier that dimly lit the hall hung from a heavy chain and was as big as a Chevy Suburban turned on its end.

Basil looked around, found that they were alone, and whispered, "Pamela, I *don't* think this was such a good idea."

"Oh, please!" she said. "Don't be so timid."

Timid! He didn't want her to think he was timid. He was bold, romantic. Still . . . "But what if he guesses?"

"He won't." She patted his cheek, leaving her hand lingering on the side of his face. Just then, Basil heard footsteps coming from somewhere beyond the great hall, and he backed sharply away from her.

Pamela laughed. She touched him with a light gaze, then spun to face the man who had just entered. "Darling," she said, "this is Basil. Basil, my husband Charles Falkland."

Gesturing with his drink, Charles Falkland said, "I know she'll make a wonderful Kate."

"I'm very grateful that she wanted to do the show. With her background in New York. Of course, Pamela is a brilliant actor. And as Kate, she has just the right combination of bite and vulnerability."

"Absolutely," Falkland said, placing his hand on the back of Pamela's neck possessively. "She is extremely accomplished."

Basil studied the room, taking time to answer. Must be cautious here. "Of course, you know we're an Equity house, so all the actors are professional. They'll support her beautifully."

"But why *The Taming of the Shrew*?"

"You'd rather we did a drama? Don't you feel that it's important for the general public to realize that Shakespeare can be light? Humorous? People are so deadly serious."

"Well . . ." Falkland said, drawing the word out, "some issues in life *are* serious, of course. Aren't they?"

"Of course, but—"

"But enough of this. Drink up and let me just mix us all a second drink."

Falkland busied himself with the bottled water, lime, and lemon wedges that the butler, Sloan, had brought in, decanters of some splendid bourbon and Scotch, which the Falklands were too well bred to keep in labeled bottles, but which to Basil's taste in his first drink seemed like Knob Creek or possibly the top-of-the-line Maker's Mark. Not the kind you buy in stores, even specialty shops. You had to order it from the company.

"Here, darling," Falkland said, turning to Pamela. "Basil's and yours."

Pamela carried Basil's drink—in a fresh glass, he
noted—to him, reaching out to put it in his hand. Her fin-
gertips grazed his as he reached for the glass, and her
thumb stroked the back of his hand. Basil's breath caught.
How beautiful she was. He could scarcely believe his luck.
Their affair had started the first day of rehearsals. Seeing
her husband, and this mansion, knowing that she had been
an actress of some considerable reputation, he could imagine that she might be bored in this big house, with a husband who looked fifteen years older.

Pamela left her hand next to his just half a second too
long. Basil resisted pulling back. Surely that would only
make it more obvious. But he thought Falkland had seen.
Or maybe not. He'd been pouring his own drink, rather a
stiff one. But he'd been casually looking toward the sofa,
too, over the lip of the glass. Did he notice? After all, what
would he see? A woman hands a man a drink. Just ordinary
hospitality. Just what was expected.

Abruptly, Falkland said, "Pamela?"

"Yes, dear?"

"I just realized I've not chosen a dessert wine. I have a
lovely Médoc for dinner. We're having a crown roast of
lamb, and the dinner wine should be just right. But we
need something to go with the zabayon and raspberries,
don't we?"

"Yes, I imagine so, dear."

Basil noted that Sloan was waiting near the door that led
from this great room to some unspecified back region.
Briefly, he wondered why Sloan hadn't poured and passed
the drinks.

"Well, go to the wine cellar with Sloan and find something special, would you?"

"Of course, darling." An expression of mild puzzlement
passed over Pamela's face, not rising quite to the level of a
wrinkle along her lovely brow.

"We need something beyond the ordinary for Basil, don't you think? Something that sings. A finale! A last act! After all, he is an artiste."

"Uh, yes, darling. It's just that you usually make the decisions about wine."

"Yes, but Basil is *your* friend."

"Of course."

"Help Mrs. Falkland, please, Sloan," Falkland said.

Pamela went out the door, and Sloan, after nodding to Falkland, followed her.

I t was just a bit awkward with Pamela gone, Basil found. He rose, strolled about, stopping at the French windows facing the back, admiring the lake view, the private dock, and the yacht anchored there, sleek, long, and bright white even in the dying daylight. He tried a few questions about Falkland's line of work, but when the man answered at length, he realized that he didn't know what e-arbitrage was and couldn't intelligently carry on that line of conversation. Pamela was taking entirely too long with the dessert wine. She should have stayed here to protect him. After all, this damned dinner had been her idea. He wondered whether maybe she was a risk taker and liked to skate close to discovery. He'd had hints of that when he saw her drive out of the Playhouse parking lot at highway speed. Perhaps tonight she was teasing her husband. Well, Basil would have to be doubly careful, if so.

Then Falkland quoted, "'And bonny Kate, and sometimes Kate the curst; but, Kate, the prettiest Kate in Christendom; Kate of Kate-Hall, my super-dainty Kate.'"

"You know the play."

"Oh, yes. I was quite a theater scholar once upon a time. In fact, I met Pamela through the theater."

"Oh?"

"I was a backer for one of her shows. She, of course, was the star."

"But she doesn't act outside of rep anymore."

"Oh, I need her all to myself. 'Thy husband is thy lord, thy life, thy keeper, thy head, thy sovereign; one that cares for thee—'"

"Shakespeare has Kate present some good arguments against that point of view."

"Ah, but 'Such duty as the subject owes the prince, even such a woman oweth to her husband.'"

Basil did not respond. How had he gotten drawn into this discussion anyhow? And where the hell was Pamela?

Sloan appeared in the arch between the great hall and the dining room. Basil was startled for a second to see him, and he realized how very soundproof the back regions were. One heard no sounds of cooking, or plates rattling, or glasses clinking.

"Dinner is ready, sir, whenever you are."

Basil had not studied Sloan before, since Basil had been fully occupied with other problems. But now he realized that the man was extremely sleek. His suit was as well made as Falkland's, or nearly so. His cheeks were pinkly smooth-shaven. His hair, thin on top and combed down flat with no attempt to cover the bald center, was rich brown and shiny. Therefore it was a bit of a surprise that, apparently unknown to Sloan, a small tuft, no bigger than the wing of a wren, was disarranged in back. Perhaps he had brushed against something while cooking, if indeed he was the person in the ménage who cooked.

Falkland murmured, "What say you to a piece of beef and mustard?"

Basil winced. He was getting bloody damned tired of Shakespeare. "We should wait for Pamela, shouldn't we?"

"We'll just start on the appetizer, I think," Falkland said.

Basil sat across from Falkland, himself to the right and Falkland to the left of the head of the long table, a wide pond of shiny walnut between them. Candles were the only lights. The head of the table apparently had been left for Pamela, which made some sense, since it put her between them and she was the only woman present. Or absent, as was the case currently. Basil regarded the silver at his place setting with dismay. Why five forks? There were also three spoons, but he was sure he could figure those out. One was likely for coffee. Or dessert? There was a rounded soup spoon. A fellow director had once told him on a shoot, where they were doing a two-shot of the happy couple at dinner, that a small round soup spoon was for thick soup and a large oval soup spoon was for clear soup. But five forks, only one perhaps identifiable as a salad fork? Now that he thought about it, the setup was probably designed to intimidate him. Well, he wasn't going to let that happen.

He said, "Where is Pamela? We'll be done with the first course before she arrives if we're not careful."

"She might be—quite a while. Pamela has always had a difficult time making up her mind."

Basil had no idea what to say to that. He sat unhappily in his chair, wondering why Falkland kept the dining room so dark. It would make a wonderful set for—oh, hell. The kind of atmosphere Falkland had prepared would only be good for a show with a supernatural element. Or a murder. *Gaslight, Macbeth, Deathtrap.*

But, of course, it was just the natural dining behavior of the very rich. For the thousandth upon thousandth time Basil reflected that he should have been born rich. Candles at dinner were probably a nightly ritual at the Falklands'. He'd used them in his production of *An Inspector Calls.*

And of course *Macbeth*. Thank God he hadn't uttered the name of the Scottish play aloud. Very bad luck.

With the darkness crowding his shoulders, and the flicker of the candle flames causing the shadows of his five forks to undulate as if slinking slowly toward his plate, Basil resolved to look upon the whole evening as a set of suggestions for his next noir production. Use it, don't fight it, he told himself.

Sloan entered. He carried two plates of something that surely must not be what it looked like. Surely it was just the low candlelight that made the lumps appear reddish and bloody and undercooked.

As the plate touched down in front of Basil with scarcely a sound, he saw it was indeed raw meat.

"Steak tartare," Falkland said. "A small portion makes a perfect appetizer. As a main dish it becomes a bit much, don't you think?"

"Uh, is he serving just us two? What about Pamela?"

"Oh, Pamela won't be long. As I was about to say, as an appetizer I have Sloan serve it without the raw egg. In these troubled times, people are uneasy about eating raw egg. Although if you can buy fresh new eggs from green-run chickens, there is really no danger. And of course with these new methods of preventing salmonella in chickens, something about the properly inoculated feed, you can be quite confident. Nevertheless, for the sake of my guests' equanimity, I forgo the egg and serve the steak tartare as an appetizer.

"Traditionally, of course, it is chopped fillet steak or sirloin, twice run through the grinder. Then mixed with chopped onions and garlic and capers and raw egg. Salt and pepper. And the patty is shaped with a depression in the center. Into that depression is dropped a perfect golden yolk. It is a beautiful presentation, really, the yolk a deep cadmium yellow, and the meat around it rich red. Well, like this, actually. So fresh it glistens. Do you see?"

"Uhhh, yes."

"Of course," Charles said, steepling his fingers as the manservant stepped back, "it can only be the very, very freshest meat."

"Uh, yes indeed."

"And never, never ground beef from the supermarket." He uttered the word "supermarket" the way another person might say "latrine." The man, Basil thought, should have been an actor himself. He certainly got all the juice out of a word.

"You're not eating. Now, these are the traditional accompaniments around it—capers, chopped onion, and minced parsley."

"Mmm-mm."

"Not used to steak tartare, Basil?"

"No."

"Some chefs mix in cognac as well, and garnish it with caviar. The Swiss even add anchovies. But it seems to me if you're going for the taste of fresh, raw meat, tarting it up with extraneous flavors is a waste. Don't you think so?"

"Uhhhh."

"Still, to revert to our earlier topic, I wonder why it had to be *The Taming of the Shrew*. There are more interesting Shakespeare pieces you could do."

"Uhhh. The trustees, actually."

"The trustees wanted it? Well, then I suppose you're stuck with it. They do hold the purse strings. But I wonder, as time goes on, if you could convince them to do Shakespeare's unappreciated masterpiece. I'm speaking of *Titus Andronicus*, of course."

"Mmm."

"It's reassuring to me, as a Shakespeare enthusiast, that

the Julie Taymor film of it is coming out, at least. But there isn't any substitute for the immediacy of the stage."

"I agree, of course," Basil half whispered.

"Real human beings near enough to touch. And *Titus Andronicus* is so Grand Guignol. It was Shakespeare's breakout play, you know. Made his name. Although at the time people claimed to be upset at all the violence."

"Media violence—"

"Fascinating to think that without it, without all that excess, we might never have known the name Shakespeare."

Basil picked up a heavy Francis the First fork. He touched the chopped meat. It was lumpy and bright red, with tiny flecks of gristle or fat. He wondered whether he could tell anything if he touched it with his finger. If it was warm—? Had it been in the refrigerator, or was it body temperature?

But he couldn't bear to touch it.

Falkland went on. "And what a story. The son of Tamora, Queen of the Goths, has been killed by Titus. For revenge, she has her other two sons rape Titus's daughter and cut out her tongue."

"I know," said Basil in a strangled voice.

"Then Titus, in an antic burst of exquisite revenge, invites Tamora to dinner and unknown to her, serves her a pasty—we'd call it a pot pie, I imagine—made from her two sons' heads."

"I'm familiar with *Titus Andronicus,* dammit!"

"Oh, of course you are, dear boy. You're a director. Terribly sorry."

"Uhhh."

"My word, Basil, you aren't eating."

"Auuhhh—"

"You haven't touched your steak tartare."

It could *not* be what he thought. It could not. How long had they been down in that cellar? And how would Falkland dispose of the—of the rest? But then he recalled the dock, the boathouse. This mansion backed directly onto Lake Michigan. Well, of course it did. It was on the high-rent side of Sheridan. But what about Sloan? Could Falkland possibly have Sloan so much in his pocket that he would do anything Falkland asked?

Inadvertently, Basil glanced up at Sloan, standing silent and lugubrious just left of the dining-room door.

Falkland caught his glance. "Sloan is such a gem," he said. "He's been with me for twenty-three years now."

"Oh, yes?"

"Since I agreed to accept him from the parole board. You see, they would only let him go if he had permanent, residential employment."

"Oh, yes. I see."

"In a home with no children."

Basil stared at his plate. If he so much as sipped a smidgen of water, he would be sick. Staring at his plate was worse. He averted his eyes. But it was too late. Perspiration started up on his forehead and he could feel sweat running into his hair. His face was hot and his abdomen was deeply cold.

Basil threw his napkin down next to the army of forks. He half rose. "I don't think I'm feeling very well—"

"Oh, please. We were so looking forward to this evening."

"I think I'd better go."

He gagged out the words and could hardly understand what he himself had said. It sounded like "guh-guh-go."

The swinging door from the pantry opened. Pamela stood in the spill of kitchen light, holding a dusty glass bottle.

"It's a terrible cliché, I know," she said smiling apologetically, "but I picked out everything else and finally went back to the Château d'Yquem."

"Uh-uh-uh," Basil said, trying to stand upright, but bent by the pains knifing through his stomach.

"Basil! Are you ill?" she said.

Basil ran at a half crouch out of the dining room, through the long hall and the marble foyer, and pushed out the front door into the glorious cool night air.

"Oh, dear," Pamela said, still smiling.

Falkland said, "Fun, darling?"

"Fun. The best we've ever done."

STEAK TARTARE

Steak tartare is not everybody's cup of tea. However, like sushi, if perfect ingredients are chosen, I am told that it is safe. The classic form is . . .

FOR THE PURIST:

One pound best sirloin or fillet trimmed of all fat and gristle. Put it twice through a grinder, *just before serving.* Ground meat is an excellent medium for bacterial growth, so serve it at once. Do not buy ground beef from the store. Mix in:

  1 clove of garlic, minced
  ½ cup of chopped onion
  1–2 teaspoons salt, depending on taste
  1 teaspoon black pepper
  1 egg yolk (you will need 5 eggs in total for a main dish)
  1 tablespoon capers

Shape into patties—four if you are using this for a main course, eight or more as an appetizer. Generally, for a main course, make four flattish patties with a depression in the middle, and into each drop one egg yolk.

Serve with parsley and more chopped onion and capers.

As an appetizer, shape into balls. You may roll the balls in minced parsley or finely chopped green onions. We are also told now not to eat raw eggs. It is possible to omit the egg yolk, but if you can get green-run chickens raised outdoors, many people believe them to be safe.

AND FOR THE FAINT OF HEART:
If all this is too much trouble or too scary, here's another recipe.

For deviled meatballs, mix the chopped beef as above. Form into tiny balls and sauté in a small amount of olive oil very lightly so as not to break up. Then add about ¾ cup of your favorite barbecue sauce. You can make it extra dynamite spicy if you like, since people will only have a small mouthful of each. Serve as an appetizer.

—BD

THE THEFT OF THE
SANDWICH BOARD

EDWARD D. HOCH

The task that had brought Nick Velvet into New York City on a warm Wednesday in June was both simple and profitable, exactly the sort of job he liked. It was only by happenstance that he ended up near dusk in Riverside Park before starting home. The park was a long slender ribbon stretching north from Seventy-second Street along the Hudson to 153rd Street. Though lacking the glamour and ambience of Olmstead's other Manhattan landmark, Central Park, Riverside was still a popular spot for lovers and joggers, dog walkers and derelicts.

He was feeling generous as he followed the path along the river, and when a bleak-looking man with a week's growth of beard appeared ahead of him holding out his grimy hand for money, Nick slipped him a five-dollar bill. That might have been the end of it if the man hadn't looked at the bill and said, "Thank you, Mr. Velvet."

"Do I know you?" Nick asked, peering at the bearded face in the glow of a nearby streetlight.

"Cracken. James Cracken. I used to be an attorney with Bliss and Ryder."

"Of course!" Nick responded. He'd done some work for them five or six years earlier and vaguely remembered Cracken as an up-and-coming young lawyer. "What are you doing here?"

"It's a long story. You don't want to hear it."

A shadowy figure came over a rise and called his name. "Jim! Come on, we're starting to eat."

"I have to go now," the bearded man said, almost apologetically.

"Wait a minute! Are you living here, in the park?"

"I'm afraid so, for the present. It's not bad in the warm weather."

"But—"

Jim Cracken turned to scamper over the rise and join the others. Nick hesitated only a moment and then went after him. Perhaps it was curiosity more than anything else that impelled him to act. From the top of the rise he could see a small campfire burning beneath the pillars that supported the Henry Hudson Parkway or whatever it was called these days. There were four men clustered around it, just starting to eat some sort of meat stew they'd been cooking.

"Who's this you brought?" a heavyset bald man asked, eyeing Nick suspiciously. The other two, another bearded man and a slender smooth-faced chap, were studying him, too.

"I didn't bring him, David. He followed me. I used to know him when I was an attorney. His name's Nick Velvet. He steals things."

Two of the men laughed at that, and the one called David snickered. "We could use a couple of onions in this stew. That the sort of thing you steal?"

Nick decided to play it straight. "As a matter of fact it is, but I don't believe you could afford my price."

"He steals things of little or no value," Cracken explained to the others. "But he charges twenty-five grand for each job."

"Thirty now," Nick corrected.

The others fell silent when those figures were mentioned, perhaps thinking about robbing him. But David merely sneered. "I used to make that sort of money once and I will again. I could make it tomorrow if—" Then he fell silent.

"You fellows always eat this late?" Nick asked, gesturing toward the stew.

"Eight-thirty this time of year," Cracken answered. "We need the daylight for foraging. When the days get shorter we eat earlier." He got himself a plate of stew and they sat down a bit away from the others.

Nick declined the offer of a plate for himself. "How's it taste?"

The bearded man, whose name was Jesse, answered, "Never as good without onions. Nobody was able to get any today."

Nick shifted his attention back to Cracken: "How'd you end up here, Jim?"

A shrug. "Things happen. There was a problem with some clients' fees. Before I knew what hit me I was disbarred. Then my wife divorced me and took the kids. It was all downhill from there."

"I'm sorry."

"I'm not going to stay here forever. I figure I just need one good break to get back on my feet."

Before Nick could respond they were joined by David, carrying his plate of meat stew. "Do you really steal things?" he asked.

"Valueless things only."

"Could you steal something for me if I didn't pay you till later?"

"How much later?"

David thought about it. "The next day?"

"I steal nothing of value. I can't imagine anything valueless that would be worth thirty thousand dollars to you the day after I stole it."

The bald man ate for a few minutes in silence, then said, "I want you to steal the sandwich board standing in front of the Applewhite Theater at Tyler Center."

"What's so valuable about a sandwich board?"

"Nothing. Right now it has an ad on it for the Russian Ballet Company. They're appearing at the Applewhite for the next three weeks."

"Can't you steal it yourself?"

David shook his head. "Not easily. The sandwich board is chained to a lamppost and they bring it into the theater after dark each night. There's a cop on duty across the street because of some construction work causing traffic delays. You can't even drive up to the sign because the street's all torn up."

"When do you need it?" Nick asked. He had already thought of a half-dozen ways it could be done.

"Could you bring it here tomorrow night? Then I could pay you on Friday."

"I usually ask for an advance. What could you give me now?"

The bald man snorted and emptied his pockets. "Seventy-five cents and a subway token. How's that?"

"I'll take it. Jim here will buy your breakfast in the morning. I'll see you tomorrow night with the sandwich board." He went to say good-bye to the other two. The slender one stepped back into the shadows as if he didn't want to be seen too closely.

All the way home Nick wondered why he'd taken on this crazy assignment, which might yield him nothing but grief. The next morning at breakfast, when he told Gloria about it, she agreed. "Want to ride in with me?" he asked.

"Not a chance today. I have to make a tray of my spinach balls for the library meeting tonight."

Gloria had become active in town affairs lately, and Nick encouraged her. There were times when he was away for several days, though this would not be one of them. The theft of the sandwich board would be a simple matter.

Tyler Center was sometimes viewed by cynics as a scaled-down version of Lincoln Center, but in truth the two had little in common. The center was named not for an American president but for Max Tyler, a Manhattan real estate tycoon. The Applewhite Theater was used mainly by touring dance companies. Tyler's intimate cinema, designed for noncommercial films, was more often rented out by Hollywood studios as a screening room. And its art gallery could boast only a few Picassos and Chagalls. The three buildings were grouped around a vaguely triangular plaza, connected to each other by underground walkways.

Driving through the area of street construction and past the buildings, Nick saw the sandwich board at once, announcing the Russian Ballet in a manner that his suburban neighbors might announce a garage sale. He'd rented a small pickup truck and filled the back with orange traffic cones. On both doors he'd placed official-looking adhesive signs reading STATE OF NEW YORK, complete with the state seal. Now, deliberately ignoring the traffic cop at the corner, he made a U-turn and pulled onto the sidewalk next to the sandwich board. From the back of the truck he took a large cardboard sign, wedge-shaped with lettering on each side, and slipped it over the top of the sandwich board, entirely covering it. Nick had spent the morning preparing it with the help of a computer and some photographs.

The sign for the Russian Ballet was now covered by a

message proclaiming YOUR TAX DOLLARS AT WORK, with vague wording about highway improvement and a photograph of the state's governor. Both sides were identical. He got back into the truck and pulled off the sidewalk. He was at the corner, stopped for a signal light, when the door on the passenger side opened and a slender young woman wearing jeans and a man's soiled white shirt jumped in.

"Pretty good," she said before he could do anything. "But you made a bad error."

"Who the hell are you?"

"Your conscience or your guardian angel, take your pick."

"This is an official state vehicle," he told her. "You're not allowed to ride in here."

"Shove it! You're Nick Velvet and you're trying to steal that sandwich board."

Then he remembered the slim shadowy figure at the campfire the night before, the one who'd tried to stay out of sight. "You were there, weren't you? Do the others know you're a woman?"

"Cracken and David know. I'm not sure about the others. It's not always safe for a woman down there."

"What's your name?"

"Heather. Can you believe it? I'm sure my folks had no idea I'd end up with a bunch of homeless guys in Riverside Park."

"So what are you doing here?"

"I wanted to see how you operate. You're something of a legend, you know."

He allowed himself a slight smile. "What was my bad error?"

"This project isn't state-funded. It's all city."

"That doesn't matter. Most people won't know the difference, and the others will just think the state is trying to take credit for something it didn't do. It'll be a day or two before anyone complains, and by that time the sign will be gone."

She lit a cigarette, not bothering to ask his permission. "And the sandwich board with it, I'll bet. Tell me something. Why are you doing it this way? Why not just drive up and take it?"

"A sandwich board seems like a valueless item, yet David is willing to pay a great deal of money for it. There's a cop on duty and I'll have to cut that chain to steal it. The whole thing might be a trap of some sort. So I steal it in stages. First I only steal the sight of the object from its usual setting. If I'm arrested, they can't charge me with theft because the object it still there. Later I return and take it right in front of everyone's eyes, but no one notices."

"I guess that's why you've been so successful."

He shrugged. "You still haven't told me anything about yourself, Heather. How'd you hook up with these people?"

"I came to New York seven years ago, right out of college, with a journalism degree. The first guy I met got me into drugs and I couldn't hold a job. I'm straight now, and I work at a lunch counter. I bring the guys leftover food for their stew. But there's no money for an apartment. It's easier to dress like a guy and live in the caves."

"Caves?"

"Not real caves, but people call them that. They're more like indentations in the hillside. Jim and Jesse sleep in a couple of them, but David sleeps in his '86 Chevy. It's just temporary for me. I want to get back on a paper, or into television. There just aren't any openings unless you've got something to offer."

"Yeah." He drove on up Broadway without asking where to drop her.

"What's David's story?"

"Like mine. He's on the night cleaning crew at the Tyler Gallery, but he can't afford a place of his own yet."

"How do you people get jobs without any address?"

She blew out some smoke. "He tells them he's at the Lexington Avenue Y. I give a friend's address. Nobody bothers to check for those kinds of jobs."

"And that other one? Jesse?"

"He's psych. His big trouble is he won't take his medication."

"Do you think David's going to pay me my fee for the sandwich board?"

"Stranger things have happened." She ground out her butt on the floor of the truck. "Drop me at the next light. I'll see you tonight."

L ate in the afternoon, just after the road crew called it quits for the day, Nick drove his truck back over the curb and parked next to the New York state sign. It took him only an instant to snap the chain with a pair of heavy-duty cutters. Then he folded both the sign and the sandwich board together, lifting them into the back of the truck. He put down a couple of extra traffic cones to make it look like he was doing his job, and then drove away.

Before returning the rented truck he removed the New York state insignia from the doors and transferred the sandwich board to the trunk of his own car. He still had some time to kill before the eight-thirty meeting, so he stopped at a neighborhood bar for a quick beer. He was especially interested in seeing the local news report on television. Nothing was mentioned about the stolen sandwich board or anything else amiss at the Applewhite Theater, though there was an announcement near the end of the telecast that the Tyler Art Gallery was expected to reopen tomorrow after having been closed for the day because of a burst water pipe.

It was still daylight when Nick left his car in a parking area and walked through the grass toward the small gathering under the highway bridge. The man called David was there by the fire, and Jim Cracken was seated on a rock, talking with the other bearded man, Jesse.

"You came back," Jim said. "David was worried that you wouldn't." He motioned toward the other man. "You remember Jesse."

Nick nodded, wondering if this was a world of single-named men, reluctant to pronounce their family names out of a sense of shame.

"We got a chicken for the pot tonight," Jesse announced. "You eating with us?"

"I hadn't planned to," Nick replied, feeling a pang of hunger and wondering why he hadn't ordered a sandwich at the bar. "Perhaps we'd better conclude our business first," he said to David.

"You really got it? Where, in your car?"

"That's right." He led the way to the parking area with the bald man following behind. "Here it is. Where do you want it?"

"I've got a car over here." Nick got a grip on the sandwich board and followed him to the other end of the parking area. He opened the trunk on the rusty green Chevy and Nick slid the signboard in. "I should have the money for you tomorrow."

"Hope so! I don't extend credit for more than a day."

"I just have to see a man." He locked the trunk and they walked back to the campfire together.

"Where's Heather tonight?" Nick asked casually.

David shot him a look. "What do you know about Heather?"

"She was at the Applewhite today when I took the sign. She introduced herself, told me about her drug problem."

"Watch out for her, Velvet. She's trying for a hot news story to get her job back. You might find yourself on the front page of a tabloid."

"What's such hot news about stealing a poster for the Russian Ballet?"

But David didn't answer, and from the campfire they heard Jesse call out, "You coming to dinner, David? It's eight-thirty and we're hungry!"

The bald man chuckled. "I'm the official food taster. If it doesn't kill me, they know it's safe to eat." Jesse handed him a big wooden spoon he'd been using to stir the pot and David dipped it in. "We got onions tonight?"

"Plenty of onions."

David tasted it and made a face. "That chicken tastes like roadkill." He tried another spoonful and stood up. He dropped the spoon and clutched at his chest and stomach. "Poison . . . Max . . . It was Max . . ."

Then he fell to his knees and toppled forward on his face. Nick dropped to the ground next to him as the bald man's body shuddered with spasms. But there was nothing he could do. Within minutes, David was dead.

"What'll we do?" Jim Cracken asked. The blood seemed to have drained from his face.

"Call the police," Nick said as he stood up. "I've got a phone in my car."

Jesse was picking up his things. "I'm getting out of here. I can't afford trouble with the cops."

"Was he saying someone named Max killed him?" Nick asked.

Cracken nodded. "He must have meant Max Tyler of Tyler Center. David was Max's brother."

Before he phoned the police to report a dead man in Riverside Park, Nick carefully removed the car keys from David's pocket and transferred the stolen sandwich board from the dead man's trunk back into his own. After all, he hadn't been paid for the theft. The board was as

much his as anyone else's. He could see that Jim Cracken
and Jesse had vanished from the scene, leaving David's
body lying alone near the smoldering fire. That changed his
intention of phoning the police from a car phone that could
be easily traced. Instead he drove north along Riverside
Drive until he found a pay phone in operation. He reported
a body in the park and then drove on home.

On Friday morning Gloria was up ahead of him, preparing breakfast. "Look at this in the newspaper, Nicky," she
said, directing his attention to a story near the bottom of the
front page.

He hardly thought a derelict's body in Riverside Park
would rate a mention, at least until the victim was identified. But the article in question was something else entirely: CHAGALL PAINTING STOLEN FROM TYLER GALLERY.
The news report stated that the painting, valued at over a
half-million dollars, had been taken from its frame and
stolen sometime Wednesday night. Police were at a loss to
explain how the theft was accomplished, since the building
was locked and patrolled by security guards. Even members of the museum's nightly cleaning crew were inspected
at the end of their shift. Believing the painting must be hidden somewhere in the museum itself, the directors had closed
the Tyler on Thursday while police and staff conducted a
careful search of the entire building. Nothing was found.

Nick finished reading and looked up at Gloria. "Did you
steal it?" she asked.

"You know, I'm beginning to think I did."

He went out to the garage and opened the trunk of the car.
The article had described the painting, a surrealistic view
of the artist at work on a biblical scene, as being twenty-
nine inches wide by twenty-one inches high. Nick stared
hard at the poster for the Russian Ballet, and then felt carefully along its edges. With the help of a putty knife he be-

gan peeling it off. There was another, identical ballet poster underneath, but between the two, covered in protective plastic, was the missing painting.

Gloria had been watching him work. "Are you going to give it back?" she asked.

"Not until somebody pays me for stealing it."

Nick drove back to the city in the early afternoon and parked in the underground garage beneath Tyler Center. He'd called ahead and made an appointment with Max Tyler, saying it was in regard to insurance coverage on the missing painting. After waiting fifteen minutes he was escorted into Tyler's office and faced a short man with thinning hair. Except for his height he bore an obvious resemblance to his brother David.

"I don't quite understand this, Mr. Velvet," Max Tyler said. "I spoke with your home office yesterday and they said a team of investigators would be flying up from Atlanta on Monday."

"Things changed overnight," Nick told him with a smile, taking a seat opposite Tyler's desk. "We've been contacted by the thief, who seems willing to sell the painting back to you for a reasonable sum."

"How reasonable?"

"Thirty thousand dollars. A fraction of its current value."

"I have it insured for six hundred thousand, as you must know."

"Then it's only five percent. A bargain price. And of course my company will reimburse you."

"You want me to pay the money myself?"

"It would speed things along. We could recover the painting by the close of business today."

Max Tyler pursed his lips, as if considering the offer. "There's one thing I haven't told you, Mr. Velvet."

"What's that?"

"I called your Atlanta office after you phoned this morning. They never heard of you."

Nick didn't move. "There's one thing I haven't told you, Mr. Tyler."

"Oh?"

"Your brother David was murdered last night. With his dying words he accused you of killing him."

"He stole it, didn't he? I knew I was asking for trouble when I gave him that job on the cleaning crew."

Nick stood up. "I've just told you your brother is dead. Is that all the reaction you have?"

"David died twenty years ago when he became an alcoholic. Since then he's just been a husk walking around. I was doing no favor by helping him out occasionally, giving him a job." After a moment's pause he asked, "How did he die?"

"He was poisoned in Riverside Park. It was in a stew a group of homeless people had prepared."

"Then how could I have done it?"

"By paying someone, the same as he was going to pay me."

"Pay you? With what?"

"It's not hard to figure out. On Wednesday night he hired me to steal a sandwich board from outside the Applewhite Theater. I agreed to the theft, and that night while working on the night cleaning crew at the museum he stole the Chagall from its frame."

"That's how he repaid me for a job I gave him! But the sandwich board is kept in the lobby of the Applewhite at night, not in the museum," Tyler argued.

"True enough. The buildings are connected underground, though. It was no great task for David to sneak the painting over to the theater, protect it in plastic, and hide it on that sandwich board by covering it with another ballet poster. The sandwich board was put out in the morning as usual, and all I had to do was come by and pick it up. He hadn't a thing to fear walking through security at the end of his shift."

"He was going to sell the painting to pay you for stealing it?"

"Quite likely. Or maybe he was just going to ransom it back to you. But someone killed him first. I suppose it's not too surprising that he thought it was you."

"It wasn't," Tyler insisted. "I had no idea he was planning a mad act like that. I didn't even know he was still living in the park. I thought he was at the YMCA."

"All right." Nick was anxious to be gone. When people talked too long he sometimes felt police were on the way. "What about the painting? It's yours for thirty thousand."

The small man pondered the possibilities, then asked, "Where is it now?"

"Nearby."

"All right. When can we make the exchange?"

"How about this evening? We could meet at Riverside Park." Nick gave directions to the parking spot near the homeless encampment. "Eight-thirty? That's just about dusk. And come alone. No cops."

"You said my brother died in Riverside Park."

"That was last night. Tonight should be safe enough, unless you believe in ghosts."

Nick got there at eight o'clock and pulled into the closest parking area. He was getting out of his car when he saw a familiar figure coming down the hill.

"Hello, Heather," he called to her.

"You've come back!" She was wearing jeans and a man's shirt, as she had the previous day.

"I had to, after what happened last night. David's dead." She nodded. "Jesse told me. How did it happen?"

"They asked him to try the stew first. He didn't like the taste and on the second spoonful he keeled over with convulsions. I tried to revive him but he died in my arms."

"Did he say anything before he died?"

"Yes. He said his brother Max killed him."

She shook her head, as if denying such an impossible suggestion. "Who called the police?"

"I did, from a pay phone. Jesse and Jim took off as soon as he died."

Heather stared hard at him. "You stole that painting from the museum, didn't you?"

"I take only objects of little or no value." He'd started walking toward the site of the campfire, and Heather followed along.

"David hired you to steal the sandwich board. I don't have to be a genius to know that's linked to the stolen painting."

"You're after a story, aren't you?" Nick asked. "You want to get back to being a reporter."

"Sure," she admitted. "Can you blame me? If you've got the painting I'd like to see it. Maybe even get a picture of it. That could mean a good payday for me, a way out of my cave." From her pocket she produced a little single-use camera, the sort sold in drugstores and tourist spots.

As they approached the charred remains of the nightly campfire, another figure came into view. It was Jim Cracken, making his way down the slope toward them. "The police have been out here all day," he announced. "They may be back."

"Did they question you?" Heather asked.

"A little. I didn't tell them I was here when it happened."

"Has Jesse been here?"

Cracken nodded. "I saw him earlier. He's off his medication again."

She turned back to Nick, still holding the camera. "How about it? Can I get a picture?"

"I'll be frank with you. I'm selling the painting back to Max Tyler. It belongs to his museum, after all. He'll be here shortly to collect it."

"He's coming here?"

"That's right." A limousine with darkened windows was pulling into the parking area as he spoke. "Wait here. I'll see if he agrees to a picture."

Tyler stepped out of the car. "All right, Velvet, I have the check. Where's the painting?"

"In the trunk of my car. Let's have the check."

He handed it over. "Thirty thousand, as we agreed."

Nick used the remote control to flip open the trunk of his car. He walked over and lifted out the sandwich board. Heather hurried up with her camera. That was when two men suddenly appeared from the backseat of Tyler's limo, guns drawn. "Freeze, Velvet! Police! You're under arrest."

"What is this?" he asked Max Tyler.

"Just what they said," the short man told him. "I'm reclaiming my painting."

The detective nearest Nick showed his ID and quickly frisked him while the other one peeled the poster off the sandwich board. "There's just another poster underneath," he told them.

Tyler came up to Nick, his face flushed with anger. "Where is my Chagall?"

"Which would you rather have, the painting or your brother's killer?"

"What are you talking about?"

Nick turned to the detectives. "The man poisoned here last night was Mr. Tyler's brother, David."

"We know that."

"And his killer is standing right over there. I'm sorry I don't know her last name."

Heather tried to run then, but the nearest cop grabbed her by the arm.

"You'd better explain all this," he told Nick.

"David Tyler was a homeless man living in the park. His brother here had given him a night job cleaning the art gallery, but David still preferred the park. He hired me to take the sandwich board from in front of the Applewhite Theater. The three others who ate with him most nights heard it. One of them, knowing David worked nights at the museum, must have guessed he was going to steal something. That person poisoned him so she could get it herself."

"Why me?" Heather asked. "Why not Jesse or Jim?"

"They knew I'd brought David the sandwich board. If they wanted the painting they'd have tried taking it from his trunk as soon as he died. I suppose you couldn't quite stomach being present at his death, so you waited till later to try for the painting. But you always brought them the extra food from your lunch counter and you had the best opportunity to poison it in advance. You knew David would taste it first because he always did."

"You'd better come along for questioning, miss," the detective told her. "You, too, Velvet."

Nick merely smiled. "On what charges? Stealing a sandwich board? I didn't think Mr. Tyler would have me arrested for that."

But Max Tyler wasn't giving up that easily. "I want the Chagall back."

"I don't have it," Nick said. "You'll probably find it back in the gallery where it should be."

"How is that possible?"

Nick merely smiled. "I suppose a good thief could return something as easily as he could steal it."

"My check—"

"Was for the return of the sandwich board, and there it is."

"Do you want us to arrest him, Mr. Tyler?" one of the detectives asked.

The short man sighed. "Forget about him. Could someone please put the sandwich board in the trunk of my limo?"

"I'd be happy to do that," Nick said.

✥

GLORIA'S SPINACH BALLS

(Adapted from a recipe in the New York Times *Magazine)*

2 packages frozen chopped spinach, thawed and drained
2 cups Pepperidge Farm stuffing
4 eggs, beaten
½ cup melted butter plus butter for the pan
½ cup grated Parmesan cheese

Preheat oven to 375 degrees.

Combine all ingredients in a large bowl. Form into bite-size balls and place on a lightly buttered cookie sheet. Bake for 20 minutes and serve.

—EDH

8-3-OH

NICK DANGER

The first thing Nathan James saw when he edged his way past the cops into the kitchen was a bloody dead man slumped over the table. The victim's face lay in a plate of stuffed escarole and black olives. Blood everywhere—the floor, the table, the chair, all over the man's silk robe and pajamas. His right hand clutched an artist's ink pen. Beside a full glass of white wine, his large pad of sketch paper was sprinkled with blood. He'd managed to scrawl the time—eight-thirty—across the blood-stained top sheet. The clock on the wall in front of the dead man read five minutes past midnight.

"Who's the victim?" Nathan asked of no one in particular. He wasn't surprised when no one in particular answered. The police force still treated him with the contempt reserved for an outsider, which, in fact, he was. "Dupont, care to fill me in?"

The detective greeted him with a surly grimace. Because of the city's soaring crime rate, murder in particular, the mayor had formed a special Murder Investigation Unit. Nathan was, for the time being, the entire unit. He reported directly to the mayor and was on twenty-four-hour call. If there was a murder anywhere in the small city of Tuscany, New York, Nathan went to the crime scene on behalf of the mayor's office to render whatever assistance and advice he could. The first thing Nathan had learned about police investigation was that if there was one thing the cops hated more than crooks and crime, it was assistance and advice.

"The deceased is Francis Kirkland," said Henry Dupont.

"*The* Francis Kirkland?" Nathan asked. "The cartoonist?"

Dupont nodded. "That's right."

Nathan's surprise lasted only a moment or two. It was probably just as dangerous to be a political satirist these days as it was to be a politician. Kirkland's cartoon character was a homeless man named King who had been on the campaign trail for a dozen years, wreaking havoc among those who took "the oldest profession" seriously. "Do you have a suspect in custody?"

"No."

"Leads?"

Dupont smiled thinly. "Several."

Nathan pulled out a handy little notepad of his own, a lithium-charged Palm Pilot. "What have you got?"

"Slow down, Mr. James. We're still working the crime scene. Why don't you go into the living room and sit down like a good little boy till we're finished, then I'll give you a comprehensive report for the mayor."

Oh, the condescension. At this rate, Nathan would never get any respect from the boys in blue. Dupont, Nathan was sure, thought him a nerd. The policemen dismissed him as a wimp. The other detectives on the force thought he was a spy from the mayor's office.

Nathan slid his eyeglasses up the crown of his nose and stole a closer look at the murder victim. In a sympathetic reflex, he reached up and touched his own throat. Someone had buried a steak knife in Kirkland's neck while the man had been eating dinner. Green strands of escarole gathered at Kirkland's chin, swimming in a tomato-ish blood sauce. A black olive was stuck to his cheek, and a garbanzo bean bobbed at the tip of his nose.

Nathan had been on Mayor Pankowski's Murder Investigation Unit for less than a year. He wasn't yet accustomed to the sight of violent death. Sitting down wasn't such a bad idea. He retreated to the living room, feeling slightly queasy.

About an hour later he retreated from the crime scene, the residence of the deceased, Francis Kirkland, with preliminary notes from Detective Henry Dupont in his briefcase and another open murder investigation to report to the mayor.

"What have the police got so far?" asked the mayor. Most of Mayor Pamela Pankowski's critics figured her for a typical politician. The Murder Investigation Unit was just for show, the press relentlessly accused, something to wave around come election time so she could say she'd done something proactive in the fight against crime. But Nathan knew the mayor wasn't just paying lip service. Pamela Pankowski was honestly concerned about the climbing crime rate in Tuscany, and if she wanted anyone to know she was concerned, it was the Tuscany Police Department.

Nathan tapped through the files on his Palm Pilot until he found Dupont's list of official suspects. "There were three people on the property when Francis Kirkland was murdered. The live-in housekeeper was apparently upset with Kirkland for refusing her request for a leave of absence—apparently she wanted to visit her sick sister in Ireland. His business and financial manager, who also lived at the Kirkland home, hadn't spoken to him in two days because Kirkland had chewed him out over some bad investments in the stock market."

"Easy to get along with, our Mr. Kirkland," the mayor commented.

"A real charmer."

"What about the third person?"

"Kirkland's chauffeur, also live-in. No apparent motive, but a criminal record for assault and bookmaking. And he was the guy who found the body, apparently when he went to the kitchen for a midnight snack. At the time of the killing, they were all in or around the house, and they all had opportunity."

The mayor leaned forward and rolled her pen between her thumb and forefinger. She looked a bit like a librarian with her spectacles hanging down around her neck on a gold chain. "Are the police looking at anyone else?"

"Well, it was no secret Kirkland had plenty of enemies. Just look at the man's comic strip. Political satire is putting it mildly. He insulted a lot of people over the past dozen years. And he's syndicated, of course. Millions of readers every day. In fact, I wouldn't be surprised if Dupont wanted to know where *you* were last night around eight-thirty."

The mayor laughed uneasily.

Nathan continued, "Dupont says he's concentrating on the three suspects in the house. There were no signs of a break-in. Nothing was stolen. Unfortunately the alarm system wasn't set. Anybody might have wandered in and killed him. But Dupont believes that whoever did it knew Kirkland's routine. Dinner at eight o'clock every night, alone in the kitchen, nobody else in the general vicinity. The killer crept up behind him while he was comfortable, stabbed him in the neck with a kitchen knife, and fled the scene. Kirkland didn't die right away. He managed to scribble '8:30' on his sketch pad before he lost consciousness."

"The time he was stabbed?" asked the mayor. "If he was going to write anything, why not just write the murderer's name?"

"He probably never saw the person who stabbed him. Maybe he felt his life slipping away and wanted to give the police some clue, *any* clue, to help them solve the crime. It's hard to imagine what might run through a dying man's mind, but my guess is his last look was at the clock on the kitchen wall, and he thought the time of his death might be important. Dupont doesn't think it's relevant, but I do."

The mayor frowned. She'd been in politics for twenty years; sometimes it showed more than others. "Go back to the Kirkland home and talk to all the suspects yourself. I'll clear it with the chief of police and Detective Dupont. I want your opinion of these people. And I want this crime solved."

"Yes, ma'am."

Nathan put away his Palm Pilot and headed for the door, wondering how well the mayor's interference would fly with the cops, and just how it would affect his sunny relationship with Detective Henry Dupont.

"Like I told the cops, Mr. Kirkland and I argued all the time. It's the sign of a healthy relationship, at least when you're talking about investments. If I were going to kill the guy over an argument, I would have done it years ago."

Carl Stern was Kirkland's business and financial manager. He was a middle-aged man with a sharp haircut, cashmere sweater, dark circles under his eyes, and an expensive smile. Stern's office was elegant but simple: large empty spaces interrupted by two elegant oak filing cabinets, three pieces of suede furniture, a modern wooden sculpture, and a small antique desk with a leather-bound ledger on top of it. There was a faint smell of leather and clean carpeting in the air.

"How long have you worked for Mr. Kirkland?"

"About four years."

"Kirkland hadn't spoken to you for two days," Nathan said. "Was that normal?"

"Normal? He could go a week or two if he wanted. Didn't bother me in the least. Sometimes not talking to him was better than talking to him."

"If he was such a rotten client, why did you stick around?"

"You want to know where I worked before? Ever hear of Sherman and Rowe?"

"The investment firm?"

"Yeah, that's right. When I was working for S and R, I talked to a hundred clients a day, all of them worse than Kirkland, and I made half the money. Anyway, I actually *did* talk to Kirkland in the morning."

"You did? What did you talk about?"

He tapped the ledger on the desk in front of him. "About this. He popped in around ten A.M. to tell me he was canceling our evening meeting. We were supposed to meet at seven P.M. to discuss what we should do about the bond market."

"Did he say why he was canceling?"

Stern shrugged. "Wasn't in the mood."

Nathan glanced at his Palm Pilot for the next question. He wasn't accustomed to interrogating suspects, and he found his tiny technological marvel a wonderful distraction when he needed a few moments to gather his thoughts. "You actually live here, Mr. Stern, is that correct?"

"That's right, although it didn't start that way. At first I

commuted from New York City and stayed one or two
nights a week. When Kirkland became my biggest client, I
was staying three or four nights a week. Soon after that I
left Sherman and Rowe at Mr. Kirkland's request so I could
give him my full attention. One day Mr. Kirkland asked me
to get rid of my Manhattan apartment and move in here. I
didn't really have to think about it. I didn't have any family
in New York. And I like Tuscany. It's quiet and friendly.
Well, until last night, anyway. Pretty scary that somebody
could waltz into a nice place like this and knife a man to
death in his own home."

"Do you know anyone who might have wanted to kill
Mr. Kirkland?"

"Sure, lots of people. Have you ever read his comic
strip?"

Nathan nodded.

"Then you know what I'm talking about. Anyway, I
gave a whole list of Kirkland haters to the police."

"How was Kirkland doing financially?"

Stern smiled like a man who took pride in his work.
"Great, especially since he dissolved the partnership with
his brother."

Nathan tried to hide his shock. *Francis Kirkland had a
brother?*

He couldn't believe that Dupont hadn't so much as mentioned such a crucial detail. Nathan thought about the detective's smirk when he'd first seen Dupont at the crime
scene. His shock turned to ire. It was one thing to treat him
with disdain, quite another to withhold important information about the case. "I didn't know Kirkland had a brother."

"Yeah, his name is Pfeiffer. He lives here, too. Upstairs
on the third floor. But Pfeiffer comes and goes a lot. Like
last night he wasn't home at all. He's got a girlfriend lives
downtown. Anyway, Francis and Pfeiffer had a legal partnership until last summer. I kept telling Kirkland that the

partnership was killing him on taxes. He finally listened to me."

"Why were they partners to begin with?"

"Years ago they started the comic strip together. Francis would draw and Pfeiffer would write. But they argued a lot. Creative differences. After a while Pfeiffer got frustrated. He wanted out. Truth is, Francis had all the talent. Now Pfeiffer owns a computer store in the city."

"Pfeiffer Electronics?"

"Yeah, that's the place."

Nathan held up his miniature computer. "I bought my Palm Pilot there."

"Modern technology. Amazing."

"Why did they remain legal partners for so long after the split?"

"At first the partnership helped Pfeiffer get loans to open his business. After that, who knows? Laziness. Convenience. Didn't want to pay the lawyer's fee. You know, the usual."

Nathan entered the information into his Palm Pilot.

Stern yawned. "Are we almost done, Mr. James? I'm bushed. I didn't get much sleep last night."

"Almost. I have to ask you one last question. Where were you last night at eight-thirty, and did you see or hear anything unusual?"

Stern motioned toward the door. "I was in my room, directly across from my office here. I was alone, watching the basketball game on TNT and surfing the Net. All I saw were slam dunks and stock reports. This place is so soundproof you could probably set off a cannon in the living room and nobody would hear it."

Nathan thanked Stern for his time and told the man to get some rest. He looked genuinely beat.

"Thanks," Stern said. "I'm going to miss that little creep."

Little creep? Nathan knew who the real little creep was. Henry Dupont, that's who. A relative with a motive was about as prime a suspect as anybody could possibly hope for. Dupont was holding out on Nathan so he could solve the murder on his own. Nathan added Pfeiffer Kirkland to the list of suspects he needed to interview. But first, the housekeeper.

Kathleen McKnight, Kirkland's live-in housekeeper, was nothing at all what Nathan had expected. She was a young student at Tuscany Community College, and a star soccer player. Kathleen had shoulder-length hair and healthy pink cheeks. Her eyes were ice blue, and she was wearing a pair of cropped-off soccer shorts and Reebok sneakers. She had the type of Dove-girl appeal that took a man's breath away, and Nathan was no exception.

"I understand that Mr. Kirkland wouldn't allow you to visit your sick sister in Ireland, is that correct?"

"Well, kinda," Kathleen said.

"Kinda?"

"It's my mother who's sick, not my sister. And it's not exactly that he wouldn't let me go."

"What do you mean by 'not exactly'?" Nathan made the correction in his Palm Pilot. *Sick mother.*

"What I mean is, I kinda asked Mr. K to not let me go. I know that sounds strange, but I didn't want to go visit my mom in Ireland. She's *always* sick with something. If I went running home every time she blew her nose, I'd *never* graduate. So Mr. K gave me an out, you know, like, Sorry, Ma, can't get away right now, gotta work."

She flipped back her hair and tucked the cleaning rag in the waistline of her shorts. Nathan had caught her in the middle of polishing brass in the study. There was no hint of an Irish accent in the girl's speech, so he doubted she was an exchange student. When he asked her about it, Kathleen said she'd lived most of her life with her aunt's family only forty miles outside of Tuscany.

"Look, Mr. eh . . ."

"James. Nathan James."

"Right, Mr. James, I kinda liked old man Kirkland. Sure, he had his moods, but the guy gave me a place to live and work while I went to college, even if he didn't pay much. I needed a few more thousand to pay for my last semester, but I never could have covered room and board on top of that."

Nathan nodded. He understood perfectly. He was still paying off college loans of his own that were nearly ten years old. "The alarm system wasn't on. Is that normal?"

"Shoot, no. That was my fault. I usually set the alarm early, but Mr. K had the system updated just yesterday and I didn't have the new code. I was going to tell him I couldn't set it, but I got listening to Pearl Jam on my CD player, really getting into it, you know, so I figured I'd get around to it later. No big deal, right? Only it turned out to be a *major* big deal. I feel awful."

"Don't blame yourself. But I do have to ask you a rather important question. Can you tell me where you were last night at eight-thirty, and when was the last time you saw Mr. Kirkland alive?"

"I was in my bedroom on the second floor. Alone. Almost makes me wish I slept around like all my friends. I might have had a good alibi. Anyway, I didn't see or hear anything other than my anthropology textbook and my CD player. The last time I saw Mr. K alive was in the afternoon, I guess. I wish I could be more helpful."

"That's all right, Miss McKnight. Thank you for your time. Maybe you can tell me where to find Mr. Kirkland's chauffeur, Joe Morelli."

"Sure. He's probably out in the garage working on the

Town Car. It's his favorite pastime. I can take you out there if you want."

"That's okay. I'll find my way."

"Mr. James, you might want to fix your belt."

"My belt?"

"You missed a loop. I wouldn't say anything only it's right in front. Looks a little silly."

Nathan blushed. "Thank you, Miss McKnight."

It was a four-car garage with one automobile and a shiny new Harley Davidson motorcycle. The rest of the building was filled with lawn and garden equipment, trash barrels, car parts, tools, benches, paint cans, motor oil, and cardboard boxes. Nathan was surprised at how neat and orderly it all looked. The hood to Kirkland's Lincoln Town Car was up, but there was no sign of Joe Morelli.

Nathan stepped deeper into the faint smell of gasoline and old lumber. The garage doors were open, casting partial light and shadows across the polished chassis. Nathan was about to call out Joe Morelli's name when he saw something move in his peripheral vision.

He turned just in time to see a wrench and a fist flying toward him. Nathan spun and ducked. The wrench missed the side of his head, but the fist caught his chin and knocked off his glasses. Bright stars filled his eyes. His knees gave way.

A bearded man plodded forward and shoved Nathan to the ground. "You better talk fast, pal. Who the hell are you, and what are ya doin' in my garage?"

Nathan held up his hands and tried to answer, but the pain and dizziness interfered. All he could manage was, "Wait . . . explain . . ."

"Somebody killed my boss last night, and if I find out it

was you, all the explainin' in the world ain't gonna save your sorry ass."

The stars in Nathan's eyes began to clear, and the world snapped back into focus. The feral beast with the wrench leaned over him and grabbed the front of his shirt.

"My name is Nathan James. I'm an investigator with the mayor's office."

"Investigator? You don't look like no investigator. You're too small for a cop. You don't dress like one neither—baggy clothes, old sneakers, nerd glasses. And you sure ain't careful like no cop, the way you walked in here and didn't watch your back."

"Yeah, I see that now. You could have cracked my skull open." Nathan thought he could feel the side of his face beginning to swell.

"Believe me, if I wanted to crack your skull open, your brains would be all over the floor by now."

"Believe me, I believe you. I just came out to ask you about the murder."

"Cops already done that."

"I'm with Mayor Pankowski's Murder Investigation Unit, not the police."

"Got ID?"

"In my wallet."

"Go for it real slow."

Nathan showed the man his ID and said, "Joe Morelli, I presume?"

Morelli nodded and helped Nathan to his feet. "Sorry about the shot I gave ya, but I thought—"

"You thought I killed Mr. Kirkland."

"Something like that."

"Funny," Nathan said. "I was thinking something like that about you."

"Join the club." Morelli was wearing a sweatshirt with

the sleeves rolled up and an old pair of grease-stained jeans. He was a young man, maybe in his mid-twenties, with long arms, rounded shoulders, and a beer gut. He had the apelike appearance of a man who had been too long in captivity. The cobra tattoo on his forearm was so faded, almost completely colorless, that he must have gotten it when he was about five years old. "Cops had me downtown all night. I'll tell you what I told them a thousand times. I didn't kill Mr. Kirkland. I never woulda hurt the guy."

"Why is that?"

"When I was a teenager I used to do yard work for Mr. Kirkland. He'd pay me enough money for smokes and beer, but I got bored with that. Make a long story short, I fell into a job as an errand boy for the mob. I ain't proud of it, but that's the way it is sometimes when you grow up in a foster home. When the cops caught me, nobody in the mob knew my name. Funny how that works." Morelli picked up Nathan's eyeglasses and handed them over. "Don't look busted."

Nathan squinted at them and slipped them on. They were smudged, but otherwise okay. "Thanks. Do they really look like nerd glasses?"

"Sure. Anyway, I did a little time. When I came up for parole, it was Mr. Kirkland who showed up to speak for me. Nobody ever gave a damn about me, but Mr. Kirkland said I was a good kid who fell in with some bad company, and that he had a job waiting for me when I got out. I've been Mr. Kirkland's driver ever since. I owe him a lot. And if I find out who killed him . . ."

"I get the picture."

"Here, you got some grease on your chin." Morelli handed Nathan a clean rag.

"Thanks. Nice hog." Nathan nodded toward the motorcycle. "Yours?"

Morelli smiled. "New credit card. Ain't America grand?"

"Not for Francis Kirkland. Where were you last night at eight-thirty, Mr. Morelli, and did you hear or see anything unusual?"

"I was right here cleaning up the garage. Mr. Kirkland's brother, Pfeiffer, he showed up in the morning and said I had to have the whole place spick-and-span by the end of the day."

"Does he often tell you what to do?"

"Yeah. He kind of runs the household around here. Francis had one of them real creative minds and didn't always pay attention to everyday stuff. Pfeiffer pissed me off, though. Last night was poker night. He made me miss a high-stakes game I been tryin' to get into for a long time."

So much for the reformed Joe Morelli, thought Nathan. "And you live here?"

"I live in a small apartment off the garage. It ain't much, but I like it. It's private and I got my own satellite dish. But I can't see the main house from here, and I sure can't hear nothing."

"No one to verify your alibi?"

"You think I woulda spent all night downtown talking to the damn cops if I did?"

As a matter of fact, yes. Out of the three suspects the police were looking at, Morelli seemed like the only one capable of slamming a knife into someone's neck. "It doesn't look good that you found the body."

"Somebody would have found him sooner or later. Cops would have come for me one way or the other."

"You went to the kitchen for a midnight snack, is that right?"

"That's right. Same thing every night. I don't sleep much, three or four hours a night. Sometimes Mr. Kirkland would be awake and we'd talk, but usually it was just me."

A man stepped into the garage and clicked on an overhead light. "Excuse me, what is going on in here?"

Morelli answered, "Just a guy from the mayor's office, Mr. Kirkland, come to ask a few questions about your brother's murder."

Pfeiffer Kirkland was a tall man with jet-black hair. He was dressed like a male model from *GQ,* but he was too old for the look, and it didn't quite come off. "You should not be talking to anyone, Mr. Morelli, certainly not while the police are still investigating my brother's murder."

Nathan decided to use his ID since it was already out. "It's all right, Mr. Kirkland. My name is Nathan James. I'm with Mayor Pankowski's Murder Investigation Unit. I'm working with Detective Dupont on—"

"What's the matter, the police can't handle the investigation on their own?"

"That's not it at all, sir."

"Oh, never mind. That was rude of me. I didn't mean to snap at you. It's just . . . my brother's death hit me hard . . . and the way it happened . . . well, my brother and I were very close, Mr. James."

"No need to apologize. I understand."

"I should formally introduce myself. My name is Pfeiffer Kirkland."

"Of Pfeiffer Electronics." Nathan held up his Palm Pilot. "I bought my Pilot from your downtown store."

Pfeiffer narrowed his eyes at Nathan. "What happened to your face? It looks like—did that hothead Morelli—"

"No, no," Nathan interrupted. "I slipped when I came in the garage and landed on my chin. No one's fault but my own."

"Hmm, well, follow me. I'll take you to the house and we'll have a look."

"I'm fine, really," Nathan said. But Pfeiffer Kirkland was already off, and Nathan wanted to take advantage of this opportunity to talk to the man who was undoubtedly Detective Dupont's primary suspect in the case, so he nodded farewell to Joe Morelli and followed Pfeiffer up toward the main house.

They strode across the driveway and through the garden, where spring tulips were just beginning to flower. It was an overcast morning, but something about the tulips seemed to bring out the light of an otherwise dreary day. They walked across the back patio and into a Florida room teeming with rich green plants. There was a large white wrought-iron table and chairs set up in the middle of the room. Pfeiffer told Nathan to take a seat, disappeared briefly, and returned with Kathleen McKnight and a first-aid kit.

"Really, none of this is necessary." Nathan suddenly flushed with embarrassment.

Kathleen smiled patiently, opened the kit, and dabbed at Nathan's lip with an antibacterial pad. "No complaints, Mr. James, this will only take a minute."

It would be easier to give in, Nathan decided, if he used the time to ask Pfeiffer Kirkland a few questions. Start slowly. Remember the interrogation manual. Lull the suspect into friendly conversation. "Mr. Kirkland, if you don't mind, I was wondering if you could tell me who might have a grudge against your brother."

Pfeiffer sat on one of the white chairs and crossed his legs. "Where to begin? Have you ever read my brother's comic strip?"

"Yes, I have."

"Then you probably know that he doesn't have a lot of friends."

"That's not the same as having enemies."

"True. The police told me they were looking closely at Joe Morelli. I told my brother—well, let's just say I thought Morelli was bad news. The only reason I haven't fired him yet is because I want him around if the police decide to arrest him for killing Francis. An ex-con. Francis could have afforded a real professional, but no. He refused to listen. Sometimes my brother did things just to annoy me."

Nathan tried to concentrate on something other than Kathleen's soft hands on his chin. "Did you argue a lot with your brother?"

Pfeiffer shook his head. "No. The usual sibling rivalries. But Francis and I got along well enough. I'm a natural organizer. I manage my electronics business and keep the household running smoothly while Francis works on the King strips."

Kathleen applied some first-aid cream to the scrape, and Nathan flinched at the sting. "Sorry, Mr. James."

"That's all right. I'm just being a baby. Mr. Kirkland, didn't you used to work with Francis on the comic strip?"

He nodded halfheartedly. "Yes. But that was years ago."

"Why did you split?"

"It's no secret. We had creative differences. I wanted the strip to go in one direction, and Francis preferred the other direction—always. I finally got tired of arguing with him, so I gave him the strip."

"You gave it to him?"

"Yes. King was *ours,* Mr. James. *We* created him together, Francis and I. Check with our lawyer if you like." He handed Nathan the business card of the most prestigious law firm in town. "The public might have forgotten all about that, but we always knew it."

"You live on the property, too, Mr. Kirkland. Isn't that correct?"

"Francis and I both live on the third floor. Lived, I should say. Past tense. I can't believe Francis is gone."

"And you weren't home at all last night?"

Pfeiffer glanced at his wristwatch and looked suddenly anxious to leave. "I went to dinner at Mama Josephino's

Italian Kitchen with a friend of mine. Her name is Norma Beal. I know where you're going with this. The police already verified my alibi. Norma and I arrived at the restaurant at eight o'clock, went back to her place, and I spent the night there. I have an appointment at the funeral home, Mr. James. I'm sure you'll excuse me."

"Of course."

Pfeiffer left the room. Kathleen stuck a Band-Aid on Nathan's chin and packed the first-aid kit. "I think you're going to have a bruise."

"I'll be fine. Thanks for the medical attention. How did Pfeiffer and his brother *really* get along?"

Kathleen hesitated. A wary expression crossed her face. "Well, I better get back to work. Need anything else?"

Nathan stood. "I was just leaving."

Nathan was looking forward to his meeting with the mayor. Although Dupont hadn't exactly been square with him, Nathan now had a prime suspect and a hunch he expected to play out. He wouldn't bother clueing Dupont in to the angle he was working until it was all over. In the end, Nathan would solve the crime before anyone else. Maybe he was being childish about the investigation, but it was Dupont who had started it by withholding information.

The mayor sat down at her desk, said something vague and grumpy about meetings and subcommittees, and told her secretary to hold her calls. "All right, Nathan, what have you found?"

He pulled out his Palm Pilot. "I'll give it to you straight. I discovered that the live-in housekeeper, Miss McKnight, liked working for Kirkland just fine and didn't want to go to Ireland to visit a sick sister, a sick mother, or a sick anything else. I discovered that Carl Stern, the investment man, gave up a high-powered job at Sherman and Rowe because Kirkland paid twice as much and was a piece of cake to work for compared to his other clients. And I discovered that Joe Morelli, Kirkland's driver, was crazy in love with the man for giving him a job right out of jail and caring about what happened to him when nobody else did."

Mayor Pamela Pankowski's expression didn't change, but her shoulders slumped almost imperceptibly. "Doesn't sound promising. What about that bruise on your chin?"

Nathan explained what happened in the garage, adding that in spite of Morelli's violent nature, he didn't believe the man was guilty. "But there's someone else. The victim's brother. Man by the name of Pfeiffer Kirkland. Dupont didn't mention anything about him, but Pfeiffer also lives in the mansion. He's got a pretty good alibi, but he's also got one helluva motive—jealousy over the King comic strip. If I can just get one or two more pieces of evidence—"

The mayor's secretary buzzed. "I'm sorry to interrupt, but I have a call for Nathan James. It's the coroner's office, an important message."

"Ah, that's the report I've been waiting for. Mind if I take it?"

Mayor Pankowski handed Nathan the phone. The coroner didn't tell Nathan anything unexpected about the cause of Francis Kirkland's death. The knife in the neck had done the trick. But that wasn't what Nathan had been waiting to hear. It was the *time* of death that made him smile when he hung up the phone.

"You're grinning," the mayor noted.

"My hunch. Forensics says the time of death might be anywhere between seven and nine o'clock at night. That cracks my suspect's alibi. I've got to give Dupont a call. Do you mind?"

"Be my guest."

Dupont, Nathan learned, was at the Kirkland residence, performing some perfunctory follow-up investigation work. Nathan dialed Dupont's beeper and left the mayor's phone number. He told the secretary to put the next call straight through. The phone rang a few seconds later, and Nathan answered it on the first ring. "Mayor's office, Nathan James speaking."

"This is Dupont. What do you want?"

"Are you still at Kirkland's place?"

"Still here."

"Are all the suspects there? And Pfeiffer Kirkland, too?"

"Yes. Why?"

"I think I've broken the case. Keep everybody in the house until I get there." Nathan hung up the phone.

The mayor looked amused. "Broken the case?"

"Well, all right, I admit it's a little corny, but all I need is one more piece of evidence, and I think I've got Pfeiffer Kirkland right where I want him."

When Nathan arrived, everyone was waiting for him in the living room. Joe Morelli looked like a guy who'd been chewing his fingernails and answering questions all night. Kathleen McKnight had slipped into a Tuscany Community College soccer outfit and sat comfortably on the arm of the sofa, the flesh of her leg distracting every male in the room. Pfeiffer Kirkland had changed his look from *GQ* to English gent, complete with turtleneck, loafers, and a brandy snifter. Carl Stern looked half asleep, but gamely sat up straight in the reclining chair when Nathan entered the room. Two police officers stood silently in the corner.

Henry Dupont stared at Nathan with the annoyed expression of a man who had been fishing all day without a catch. "Well, look who's finally here."

"I'm sorry I'm late, but I had to stop at the county clerk's office before I came," Nathan said.

Pfeiffer stood behind the wet bar in the corner of the room. "This had better be worth the wait. You have no idea how many details I need to take care of before the funeral. What would you like to drink, Mr. James?"

"Nothing for me, thank you. And I assure you it will be worth the wait." He pulled out his Palm Pilot and slid his glasses up the bridge of his nose.

Morelli looked just about ready to snap. He stared at the two police officers. "What's goin' on here? If you're gonna arrest me, get it over with."

Nathan moved to the center of the room. "I don't think we're going to arrest you, Mr. Morelli. Not after I explain why Pfeiffer Kirkland killed his brother."

Pfeiffer looked appropriately shocked. The guy was one hell of an actor. "Don't be ridiculous. Why would I kill my brother?"

Nathan walked over to the bar. "You killed Francis because he dissolved your partnership agreement. The partnership didn't mean anything on paper anymore. Neither of you needed it. But it meant a great deal to your pride, Mr. Kirkland, didn't it? The partnership was the only remaining evidence that you had contributed anything at all to the comic strip that made your brother famous. Francis dissolving that agreement was the same as him saying that you didn't matter anymore."

"That's nonsense." Pfeiffer swallowed a sip of brandy, and Nathan noticed the man's fingers trembling.

"I don't think so. You had motive and opportunity. You knew your brother's routine. You waited until he was alone in the kitchen—"

"I already told you that I was at Mama Josephino's Italian Kitchen when my brother was killed. The police checked my alibi."

"Yes, you had an alibi for eight-thirty. But forensics is a tricky sort of science. The coroner reported that your brother could have died at seven o'clock. That would have given you plenty of time to kill him, pick up your date for the evening, and get to the restaurant by eight P.M. You also went to the trouble of ordering Joe Morelli to stay home and clean the garage. You needed to have a handy suspect around the house at the time of the murder. An ex-con like Morelli fit the bill perfectly."

Pfeiffer made a scoffing noise deep in his throat. "That's a nice theory, Mr. James. But my brother scratched '8:30' on his sketch pad. Why would he write that if it weren't the time of his death? The coroner's report is obviously wrong."

Nathan stepped to the center of the room. He had been nervous a few moments ago, but now he was beginning to enjoy himself. "I wondered the same thing. But I believe Francis Kirkland knew his killer."

Even Carl Stern was paying attention now: "Then why write '8:30' when he could have written the name of the killer?"

"Because Mr. James doesn't know what the hell he's talking about," Pfeiffer Kirkland sneered.

Nathan shook his head. "It's a bit more complicated than that. Francis was dying quickly, and he knew it. But he was an artist after all, a creative thinker, and who can say what might have been running through his mind. With the life draining out of him, knowing full well that motive would be important to convict, he wanted to tell us *why* he was killed."

"And the *why* was the partnership agreement?" Detective Henry Dupont sounded only slightly impatient.

Nathan took this as encouragement to press on. "Yes. It was my visit to the county clerk's office on my way here that finally convinced me. I accessed their computers and looked up the date the partnership was officially dissolved. What was that date, Mr. Kirkland? Do you remember?"

Kirkland slammed his brandy snifter onto the bar. "If you intend to pursue this, I'll have a lawsuit for false arrest against you and the mayor and this city so fast it will make your head spin!"

"The date was August thirtieth. The ink smudged on Francis' sketch pad, but I believe he was trying to write '8/30,' with a slash not a colon. I'm fairly certain it will hold up in court."

Henry Dupont snickered. It wasn't the sort of response Nathan had been hoping for. "No, it won't hold up in court. You've got nothing but circumstantial evidence and a theory that any law-school student could puncture with a thumbtack."

"That's right," Pfeiffer said indignantly. "Save yourself a lot of trouble, Mr. James, and if you're lucky I won't get you fired. Francis' killer didn't care anything at all about the comic strip. All he cared about was money. Isn't that right, Mr. Stern? You were embezzling from one of my brother's investment accounts, diverting interest payments into a dummy account that only you could access. It wasn't easy to track because you handled a lot of money for Francis, but I noticed it and brought it to my brother's attention."

Carl Stern's eyes narrowed. He seemed to shrink into the sofa. "Even if that's true, I had nothing to do with the murder."

"I think you did. I think my brother confronted you about it, and that was why you weren't speaking to each other. Then I think you kept your seven P.M. meeting with him on the evening of the murder and begged for another chance. When he said no, you came back later and stabbed him in the neck. Francis knew his killer, all right, and he wasn't scribbling the time of his death on the sketch pad. Eight-three-oh was the account line on his ledger sheet where the discrepancy was first noted. Line 830. Isn't that right, Mr. Stern?"

"You're crazy," Stern snapped. "You can't prove any of it."

"Oh, I will, Mr. Stern. If the police can't handle it, I'll hire my own private investigator, and there will be no place in the world for you to hide—"

Suddenly Carl Stern laughed. It was a laugh so shockingly out of place that it made Nathan's skin crawl. "You're *all* crazy. If it's the numbers on the sketch pad you're looking at, none of you are considering the most obvious suspect. Do you really think it was mere coincidence that Miss McKnight *forgot* to turn on the alarm?"

Nathan was beginning to get a headache. He switched off his Palm Pilot and stuffed it in his pocket. "Are you saying that Kathleen McKnight purposely left the alarm off? She said she didn't know the code."

"And you believe her? Of course she knew the code. She was here the day the system was upgraded. If the alarm had been set, only the people in the house would be suspected of Mr. Kirkland's murder. With the alarm off, there might be thousands of suspects. Much better odds for the killer, wouldn't you say? Mr. Kirkland told me that Miss McKnight asked him for three thousand dollars to pay for her last semester at Tuscany Community College. Kirkland always believed in paying one's own way. He was going to work out a loan and payment plan for Kathleen. Maybe that made her angry enough to want him dead."

"That's ridiculous!" Kathleen said.

Stern smiled triumphantly. "Not when you consider that the only people who knew the new code were you and Francis. I just learned this morning from the alarm company that the numbers were eight, three, and zero. Think about it. It doesn't take a genius to figure if Kirkland was trying to say anything at all with those numbers on his sketch pad—"

"I would never hurt Mr. K!" Kathleen objected. But she looked pale, and there was fear in her voice.

Suddenly Joe Morelli stamped his foot. "Jeez, you guys are all idiots! I can't believe a moron like me has to tell a bunch a smart guys like you that eight-three-zero was Mr. Kirkland's lottery numbers."

"Lottery numbers?" Nathan heard everyone say it at once, even the two uniformed cops.

"Yeah. *Eight-three-oh.* He played them every Tuesday and Thursday at the A&P. Look, I can prove it." Morelli dug into his pocket and pulled out a lottery stub. "This here is the winning ticket—twenty grand, my friends. The money kept rollin' over, man, like five weeks in a row without a winner until Kirkland got lucky and hit the jackpot just two days ago! This baby here is the winning ticket!"

Everyone stared silently at Joe Morelli.

Finally Henry Dupont stepped over to him and said, "And how did you come by that ticket, Mr. Morelli?"

More silence, until Morelli's face turned slightly red, his lips twitched nervously, and a thin line of sweat glistened on his brow. "Uh-oh."

"Uh-oh, indeed," Dupont said. "Boys, let's put those handcuffs on Mr. Morelli, shall we?"

Later that night, Nathan went to Mama Josephino's Italian Kitchen and ate dinner alone. He ordered a large portion of stuffed escarole in honor of the late Francis Kirkland, only to discover he couldn't eat it when he pictured Kirkland's face swimming in a bloody casserole dish with a knife stuck in his neck.

Joe Morelli had murdered Francis Kirkland for his winning lottery ticket, a twenty-grand motive. It seemed so ridiculously simple.

Nathan ordered a glass of wine. He pulled out his Palm Pilot and tried to figure out where he'd gone so horribly wrong with his investigation. The fact that Joe Morelli had been Henry Dupont's prime suspect right from the start didn't help Nathan's mood. The clues were all there: Morelli's criminal past and violent nature, his new motor-cycle and high-stakes poker game, the late-night chats he'd shared with Francis. Nathan had been hoping for a more glamorous resolution to the case, and that had blinded him to the obvious truth.

But the one thing Dupont couldn't come up with on his own was motive. The lottery ticket. He probably never would have been able to move on Morelli without it. In a roundabout way, Nathan had provided that last piece of damning evidence. Tonight he'd be completing his own comprehensive report to the mayor, and that was one very important detail he'd make sure to highlight. This job, he decided, had its moments.

STUFFED ESCAROLE FROM MAMA JOSEPHINO'S ITALIAN KITCHEN

Well, all right, so maybe my mother's name is Josephine.
And maybe she gave me this recipe. So what about it?
I dare you to try it . . . and tell me you don't like it . . .
and tell me you wouldn't have robbed the recipe if Josephine
was your mom.

1 large head of escarole
Italian-style breadcrumbs
Salt, pepper, California-style garlic salt
grated Parmesan cheese
1 can black olives, quartered
Olive oil
½ cup chicken soup (Swanson if using canned soup)

Separate escarole leaves.

Wash and rinse escarole several times to remove dirt and sand then drain in colander.

In large oblong casserole, layer several escarole leaves, pressing them down.

Sprinkle lightly with salt, pepper, garlic salt, black olives, cheese, breadcrumbs, and olive oil.

Be sure not to use too much salt or too much olive oil.

Continue doing this till all leaves are used.

Pour chicken soup over top of escarole.

Cover and bake for 45 minutes in 350 degree oven.

—ND

CHICKEN CATCH
A TORY

TAMAR MYERS

At precisely 8:30 P.M. on a warm Tuesday evening Ophelia Rumpp gasped, lurched forward, and fell facedown on her generous serving of chicken cacciatore. I was not surprised. Frankly, I was rather annoyed that the splattered sauce had ruined a perfectly good tablecloth. Lest I come across as coldhearted, it is imperative that I recount the events of the two days that led up to Miss Rumpp's dramatic demise.

In order to do that properly I must first introduce myself. My name is Magdalena Yoder and I own and run the Penn-Dutch Inn, a full-board establishment snuggled in the hills just outside Hernia, Pennsylvania. I am a Mennonite woman of Amish descent, and am related by blood to virtually every Amish person in America. My cook, Freni Hostetler, is Amish, and we are double second cousins once removed. The branches of my family tree are so tangled that I am, in fact, my own cousin, and require only a sandwich to make it a family picnic. But that is a different story. My point here is that I am a simple woman who lives by the Golden Rule.

Not that it is any of your business, but I am unmarried and have reached the midpoint of what I expect to be a very long life. Incidentally, my marital status has nothing to do with my looks. I may be tall and bony with the sort of face that inspires love in horses, but don't think for a moment I haven't had my share of suitors. I merely prefer a life in which, next to the Good Lord, I am in command. My detractors have been known to say that I am opinionated and have a tongue so sharp it could slice cheese. They are, of course, full of nonsense.

But speaking of potentially lethal linguae, surely none can compare with that belonging to Miss Ophelia Rumpp, the English tour guide who arrived with her little group Sunday evening past. I had always thought the English to be a civilized people, given to circumspection, and, above all, polite. Ophelia Rumpp opened my lobby door, opened her mouth, and changed that perception.

"What a dump," she said.

I stared at the woman, too dumbfounded to glare. She was a bit on the dumpy side herself. Short and thick of build, she had unruly red hair turning to gray, wore smudged wire-rim glasses, and had somehow managed to cram herself into a cheap dress which was at least two sizes too small and which gaped at the bosom.

"I beg you pardon?" I said when I finally found my voice.

She tapped a brochure with a thick, freckled finger. "This says 'quaint.' I'd hardly call this quaint. Run-down is more like it."

I willed my tongue to behave. Miss Rumpp had in her tow a band of five mortified British tourists. By the looks on their faces, they would rather be pushing up daisies in merry old England, than be in Ophelia Rumpp's charge.

"It only looks run-down because I haven't had a chance

to cut the grass this week." I pretended to scan my register. "And who might you be?"

I knew quite well who the abrasive woman was. I'd been expecting the party of five English tourists and their guide. But I'd been *hoping* for a Miss Marple clone and maybe a nice little hostess gift, like a jar of homemade marmalade or possibly some crystallized ginger. I had not anticipated Genghis Khan in polyester.

"Ophelia Rumpp here. With two *P*s."

"Gotcha." I looked inquiringly at the others.

Before any one of them could respond, Ophelia Rumpp began barking off names. "Maypole, Perry, Birdsong, and Reese-Jones-Pendergast."

I nodded at each in turn. An experienced hostess, I long ago learned to associate people's names with some peculiar aspect of their physiognomy.

Marjorie Maypole was indeed tall and thin as her surname suggested. It was a wonder she could stand so straight, given the weight of her jewelry. The ancient Israelites could have made *two* golden calves from the bangles on just one arm.

Jonathan Perry had unusually narrow shoulders for a man and unhealthy skin the color and texture of small-curd cottage cheese. No association there. But it was a warm June day and he was wearing a turtleneck sweater and hugging himself like it was winter at the North Pole. Admiral Perry came to mind.

Gloria Birdsong was, and I say this charitably, a fat woman. An ebullient fat woman. Although she had yet to say a word, she looked as if she were on the verge of bursting into song. Perhaps even birdsong.

It was harder to associate George and Annette Reese-Jones-Pendergast with their mouthful of a last name. He was a dapper, well-groomed man about my age, and she perhaps a few years younger, as stylish as any matron to pass through my door. They looked like a couple, which of course they were, but you know what I mean. A single word association would suffice for both. I decided that the diamond solitaire pendant that hung around her upper-class neck would do the trick. Pendant—*Pend*ergast. If I forgot the Reese-Jones part I would just mumble a few words as a preamble.

"Welcome everyone," I said. "Welcome to an authentic Pennsylvania-Dutch experience. Like it says in your brochures, you may add to your experience by enrolling in ALPO."

"We can read," Ophelia Rumpp snapped. "What exactly do those initials mean?"

I smiled patiently. "Amish Lifestyle Plan Option. For a mere fifty extra dollars a day you have the privilege of making your own beds, cleaning your own rooms, and helping with the farm chores—you know, milk the cows, gather eggs, that sort of thing. Just like a real Amish person would do. Now, how many of you are interested?"

Everyone put up a hand except for the obnoxious Miss Rumpp. I wasn't surprised. There is no limit to the amount of money folks will pay for abuse as long as they get to view it as a cultural experience. ALPO has helped to make me a very rich woman.

Ophelia clenched her fists. "That's ridiculous. We're not about to pay a premium to act as your charwomen."

Jonathan Perry cleared his throat. "Actually, neither George nor I would qualify as charwomen. All the same, I think milking cows would be rather fun."

The tour guide snorted and turned to me. "Check to see that your cows have udders when he's through."

"I beg your pardon?"

"He may seem like an earnest young man," she said as if

he weren't even there, "but he's been arrested for picking pockets."

"Both charges were dropped," Jonathan Perry said through clenched teeth, his once cheesy complexion now as red as Freni's beet pickled eggs.

"Well," I said, totally flabbergasted. "I'm sure that's none of my business."

"Oh, you haven't heard anything yet. This bunch," she said, and wagged that freckled finger at the group, "this bunch is nothing but losers."

"Well, aren't we all in some way or another?" I said kindly, and hurriedly checked the group in before one or all of them murdered the old bat right there in my lobby. Blood can stain natural hardwood floors, you know.

Thank heavens I saw very little of the awful woman for the next two days. She stayed in her room, preferring to eat from a tray, while the others scurried about, delightedly performing a myriad of chores. I even persuaded the Reese-Jones-Pendergasts to sweep out the henhouse, a task that I personally loathe.

Between jobs I got to visit with and come to know the English tourists. My particular favorite was Gloria Birdsong. True to my intuition, she was a burbling fountain of vocal energy. She trilled, warbled, and sang, rather than spoke, which under normal circumstances I would have undoubtedly found annoying. But in light of Ophelia Rumpp's outlandishly rude behavior, I was inclined to be generous.

"Tell me, dear," I said, "why do you folks put up with her? Why don't you just ditch her and travel about on your own?"

We were sitting in the parlor, where I was trying to teach the woman to quilt. I keep a work in progress in there at all times and encourage my guests to try their hand at it. With any luck they can be taught to produce a decent stitch and I get to sell the finished product for a king's ransom over in Lancaster. If their handiwork is inferior, I rip out the stitches at night after they've gone to bed and redo them myself.

Gloria's giggle sounded like a mockingbird drunk on overripe holly berries. "On our own? We couldn't possibly travel on our own, Miss Yoder. We don't know America." She paused to giggle again. "It's so big!"

"Indeed it is, dear. But this rude Rumpp woman, she knows it?"

"Oh, yes. She's been here many times. In fact"—she paused now to glance around the room before chirping—"she's half American."

"You don't say! That explains everything."

Gloria nodded. "Besides, we wouldn't get our money back if we bailed out now. Not a farthing. I've already checked."

I pointed to Gloria's latest stitch. "You can do better than that, dear. It looks like a chicken walked across your side of the quilt."

She grinned and burst into song. "You have such a charming way with words, Miss Yoder."

"Do I?" I patted my bun, over which I wear a white organza prayer cap. "Still, I don't know how you manage to put up with that woman. I think if I were you—and were it not against my faith—I'd sue to get my money back."

"Oh, we plan to. As soon as we get back safely to British soil I'm seeing my solicitor. I've already stopped payment on my check." She glanced around the room again, and seeing no one but ourselves began to warble softly. "I must admit, though, that this trip has been anything but boring. Miss Rumpp seems to have researched us all thoroughly. She knows *everything* about *everyone.*"

Gossiping is, of course, a sin. On the other hand, lending a sympathetic ear to the lonely and verbose is a form of virtue. I decided to take the high road.

"Do tell!"

"Well, not only does she know something scandalous about each of us, but she's been trying to blackmail us each in turn."

I arched an eyebrow in disbelief. "You don't say."

"Oh, but it's true!"

"*Each* of you?"

She nodded vigorously. "We've compared notes, you see. It's not like some of us have anything to hide anymore. Miss Rumpp can't help herself. She's become very frustrated that no one will capitulate and has taken to mentioning our supposed sins publicly. You heard what she said about young Perry."

"Indeed I did."

"Wait, there's more." She paused, and I obliged her by leaning forward in mock anticipation. "Well, as you know, young Perry has been in trouble with the law before. More than just picking pockets, too, if I understand correctly. Drugs, I hear. I imagine that's why he wears those sweaters in this beastly hot weather."

"Drugs make one cold?"

Her laughter made the jay outside the window shriek in annoyance. "Oh, no, not that I know of. But needles leave marks on the arms. Still, a turtleneck is hard to understand."

I arched my other brow. "Picking pockets, while surely a sin, is not a major crime. And as for the drugs—well, our own president admits to experimenting in his youth. Does Jonathan Perry plan to run for Parliament?"

Gloria's giggle was better, sounding more like a flock of chickadees. "Oh, no, he comes from a very wealthy family, but he hasn't any ambition. He's a country vicar."

I'd read enough English novels to know what a vicar

was, but I couldn't believe my ears. I jiggled a pinkie in both just to make sure they were in working order.

"He's a man of the cloth?"

"Some cloth! If exposed, he stands to be both defrocked and disinherited."

"And the others?" A responsible innkeeper can't know too much about her guests, if you ask me.

"Well, I hate to say this, but I have to agree with Miss Rumpp. This lot is a bunch of losers. Take Marjorie Maypole, for instance. She has the morals of a Trafalgar Square pigeon. To hear Miss Rumpp tell it, Marjorie has slept with every able-bodied man in London, but still somehow managed to keep it a secret."

"From whom?"

"Her husband!" Gloria trilled merrily. "Marjorie is married to a famous London barrister. They have two children. If he finds out—well, she could lose the children."

"Surely the Pendants—I mean, Reese-Jones-Pendergasts have nothing to hide. They look so normal."

"They're bloody rich!" she warbled. Fortunately, at the time I didn't know "bloody" was a swear word, or I would have scolded her soundly. I allow no profanity in my establishment.

"There's nothing wrong in being rich, dear. It's the *love* of money that is the root of all evil, not the green stuff itself."

"Yes, of course. But Miss Rumpp claims he made his fortune fleecing the poor of Manchester."

"Did he?"

She shrugged. "He's been giving a lot of the money away to charities. I know that. Rumor has it he's hoping for knighthood."

"*Lord* Pendergast?" I gasped.

"That would be Sir George," she chortled, "only it will be just plain 'mister' if the Queen were to find out about his wife's past."

"Annette? What has she done?"

Gloria dropped her needle to clap her pudgy little hands. "*This* I didn't get from the old Rumpp. This I know on my own." She paused to build suspense. "In fact, I'd wager even her husband doesn't know it."

"Well?" I finally said, after ripping out a dozen of her stitches and replacing them with neat ones of my own. It was the first time I'd ever been driven to do such a thing in front of a guest.

"Well, Annette Reese-Jones-Pendergast is a prostitute. An ex-prostitute, of course."

"How do you know?"

"Annette is—well, was—a friend of mine. We were in the same business."

My gasp, which deprived the parlor of half its oxygen supply, seemed to amuse, rather than offend the ebullient woman. Her eyes twinkled.

"So now you know the rest of my story, as your Paul Harvey likes to say."

I pointed to her needle, which was poised in the air, accomplishing nothing. "Idle hands are the devil's playground, dear." Then I blushed as I thought of all the places her hands might have played given her former profession. "So what is it you do now?" I asked quickly.

"You mean you don't know who I am?"

"Of course, I do. You're Gloria Birdsong. A plump little woman—"

"The diva."

"Don't be so hard on yourself, dear. The Lord forgives everyone who truly repents."

Her mouth opened and closed silently several times, like a baby bird begging to be fed. Then she laughed. I managed ten more stitches before she got a real word out.

"I'm an opera singer," she said, still laughing. "I'm actually very famous in the U.K. But"—even her sigh was musical— "I'm not recognized much over here. That's one of the reasons I decided to tour the States with the evil Miss Rumpp and IPANT."

"I what?" I asked anxiously. I hoped this wasn't yet another sexual detail. My spinster's heart had all it could handle for one day.

"Intimate Portraits of Alien Nations Tours. That's the name of her agency. They claim their clientele is especially selected from the elite. You actually have to compete to qualify. At any rate, I thought I could enjoy myself incognito. I wasn't counting on blackmail."

"'Be sure your sins will find you out,' dear. That's from the Bible, you know." I stood. "I've got to talk to my cook, Freni, about supper. Do you like chicken cacciatore?"

"Love it," she cooed.

I tried not to smile. I doubted if there was any dish a woman of her girth didn't love to eat.

Freni Hostetler is more than just my cook. As I said, she is a cousin of sorts, and she is also my friend. If she weren't, I wouldn't tolerate the fact that she has quit her job a grand total of ninety-three times.

You have every right to ask why a woman seventy-five years old—a grandmother, no less—would continue to work at a job she apparently hates so much, and why I put up with her. The answers are simple. I put up with Freni because she is the best cook this side of the Alleghenies, and she puts up with her job because she can't stand to be at home. You see, Freni's son, John, and his wife, Barbara, live with her, and Freni feels about Barbara the way I do about spiders. She won't admit it, of course, because she's a pious Amish woman, forbidden by both Bible and creed to hate. I, however, know better.

"So, dear," I said, "did you find that recipe for chicken cacciatore?"

Freni, a stout woman, stared at me through glasses dusted with cake flour. "Yah, but the English give such strange names to their recipes. Chicken with tomato sauce, that's what we call it in Dutch." To the Amish, everyone not of the faith is classified as English. The fact that we had *real* English guests staying at the inn meant nothing to her.

"Good. Do you want to kill the chickens, or shall I?" I know that might sound harsh to some, but it is a lot kinder to kill the birds first.

"Ach, I will kill them," Freni said. She said it with so much enthusiasm, I shuddered. Thank heavens I hadn't named any of the chickens Barbara, or Freni might well be about to commit a sin.

"How about Desdemona? She hasn't been laying regularly anymore."

"Ach, it is a wonder any of them lay. The English you sent in there yesterday to rake out the straw, they fight like cats and rats."

The woman is metaphorically challenged, so I felt compelled to correct her. "That's cats and dogs, dear."

Freni waggled a stubby finger at me. "Too much noise, Magdalena, no eggs. You know that."

"But the Reese-Jones-Pendergasts seem like such a happy couple!" I wailed.

"Ach, these were two women, Magdalena."

"Are you sure? What did they look like?"

She shrugged. "All the English look the same to me."

"Well, in any case, we're going to need two hens. Do you have any suggestions for the second?"

"Yah, Jezebel. That is a mean hen, Magdalena. She pecks at my ankles."

"She pecks at anything, dear. Last week I saw her pecking at her reflection in the water dish. It's a wonder she didn't drown."

Freni nodded. "Yah, Jezebel is a good choice. And she, too, has stopped laying."

"Since when?"

"Yesterday no egg. Today the same."

"Then to the guillotine with Jezebel!" I cried.

Freni shook her head. To her I am only slightly less bewildering than the English. At times like these, I may as well be a Presbyterian.

Ophelia Rumpp finally put in an appearance in the dining room. To say that she looked like something the cat dragged in would have been to pay her a compliment. But since she at least kept her mouth shut, so did I. The others, thank heavens, had spruced up nicely.

I demand that my guests bathe and change for dinner, and I do the same. I was wearing a new dark blue broadcloth dress and a fresh prayer cap, and felt rather spiffy. Marjorie Maypole was dressed in a black velvet sheath and still dripped gold. Gloria Birdsong looked larger than ever in a red iridescent gown, and around her mere suggestion of a neck hung an opera-length string of pearls. Jonathan Perry still looked pasty, but surprisingly presentable in a dinner jacket over a black turtleneck (he wore pants as well, of course). George Reese-Jones-Pendergast looked remarkably handsome in his full tuxedo and his wife, Annette, absolutely splendid, if somewhat immodest, in an off-the-shoulder pink silk gown with a slit up the skirt. She wore no jewelry except for her wedding ring.

We all had steaming plates of chicken cacciatore in front of us and I was just about to say grace—something I insist on—when Freni came flapping in like a chicken with its head cut off. At first she was just as coherent as the afore-mentioned fowl.

"Not now, dear," I said kindly. "Am-scray."

"But, Magdalena—"

"Shhhh! We're about to pray."

"Yah, but this is important."

I gave her a stern look. "More important than thanking the good Lord for this food?"

"Ach, maybe."

That shocked me to my feet. I grabbed one of Freni's flailing arms and steered her into the kitchen.

"This better be good, dear. Those are *real* English in there. I doubt if they're even Presbyterians. And you say this might be as important as praying?"

Freni colored but stood her ground. "Maybe not as important as praying, Magdalena. But very important."

"Then out with it!"

"This afternoon when I cut up the chickens I put the giz-zards in another pot for later. Tomorrow I will make soup."

"And *this* is what is so important? Soup?"

"Ach, no! So now I take a moment to wash and clean the gizzards, yah? Well, in one of them, I find this." She opened her hand to show me what she'd found.

"Well, well, well," I said, and pocketed her discovery.

"Is important, yah?"

"Yes," I said, patted her broad back, and returned to my guests.

A moment later, as I was saying grace, Ophelia Rumpp pitched forward into her plate.

Melvin Stoltzfus, another cousin, happens to be Her-nia's chief of police. Unfortunately the man is the world's most incompetent law enforcement officer, and I say this with a charitable Christian tongue. No doubt his ineptitude is due to the fact that he has the physiognomy of a praying mantis, and the IQ to match. He once *mailed* his favorite aunt a carton of ice cream. Need I say more?

While we were still dressed in our finery, Melvin made us file into the parlor. There we sat for hours while he and his only slightly less incompetent sidekick Zelda Root, along with Hernia's eighty-seven-year-old coroner, Doc Shafer, processed the crime scene. Fortunately I had had little to drink that day. Nonetheless, that evening gave birth to my new philosophy of life: *Tinkle whenever you get the opportunity*.

At any rate, just before midnight Melvin threw open the parlor door and strode in with all the theatrics befitting a high-school drama student. He had that "aha" look he invariably gets just before he makes a fool of himself.

"Ladies and gentleman," he began. "Welcome to this great country of ours, the United States of America. In our system of jurisprudence—"

"Cut to the chase, Melvin," I said kindly.

His left eye fixed on me while his right continued to scan the room. "There's been a murder, Yoder. They need to know how our justice system works."

"Murder?" I asked. If jumping to conclusions was a valid form of exercise, Melvin Stoltzfus would be the fittest man on the planet.

"That's what I said. *Murder*."

"Doc performed an autopsy already? In my dining room?"

Melvin shook his bulbous head.

"Ach, not in my kitchen," squawked Freni.

"Don't be silly, Yoder. An autopsy will, of course, be performed, but in the meantime Doc has made some very interesting medical observations."

"About you?" I asked innocently.

"About the deceased," he hissed. "Miss Ophelia Rumpp most likely died from a sharp blow to the back of the neck, just at the base of the skull." Both eyes now scanned the room. "Of course one of you already knows that," he said accusingly.

"Don't be ridiculous, Melvin. We were all sitting there with our hands folded, praying, when she took the cacciatore plunge." I didn't mean that to sound disrespectful. Honest.

Melvin arranged his mandibles in a sneer. "Doc says a blow like that can cause a blood clot that can hang around for days, and then later suddenly break lose and kill someone within minutes."

"That's all fine and dandy," I said, "but it doesn't prove anything. Maybe Miss Rumpp fell."

"Maybe. But when most people fall that hard, they fall forward. And when they do fall backward, they're likely to hit the back of the head, not the base of the skull. No, Doc says it's likely Miss Rumpp was struck from behind, or pushed and fell against something. The autopsy will tell us more." The mandibles clattered a few times in what approximated a chuckle. "It might even tell us what a chicken feather was doing in her hair."

"This is all quite interesting," Annette Reese-Jones-Pendergast said, stifling a yawn. "But I fail to see what it has to do with us."

"Really," Gloria Birdsong trilled. "It is well past my bedtime."

"And mine," Marjorie Maypole whined. What with the late hour and the weight of her gold bangles, she looked more like a gilded candy cane than a maypole.

"Perhaps I can shed some light on this," I said helpfully. "I happen to know that everyone here—except for Freni and me—had a motive to kill the deceased." I pointed in the direction of the dining room, now a morgue.

You should have heard the gasps.

"Bloody rubbish!" Jonathan Perry bellowed. A fine clergyman he'd make.

"Slander, I should think." The would-be knight, George Reese-Jones-Pendergast, mopped his forehead with a linen handkerchief.

"Not if it's true," I said.

Melvin glared at me with his left eye. "I don't need your help, Yoder."

"Oh, but I think you do. I think I may know who was present when Miss Rumpp fell in the chicken yard."

"I didn't say she fell in the chicken yard, Yoder."

"But suppose she did. Suppose that's how she got the feather in her hair. Suppose there had been a tussle first and—"

"Yoder—"

"Let me finish, Melvin. Suppose Miss Rumpp had attempted to blackmail everyone in this room—except for Freni and me, of course—and suppose they'd all given her the brush-off. All except one, whose secret even her husband doesn't know."

"You can't prove it!" Annette Reese-Jones-Pendergast clapped a well-manicured hand over her mouth.

"Ah, but maybe I can." I fished into the pocket of my broadcloth dress and removed the object Freni had found in Jezebel's gizzard. "Some chickens will peck at anything, dear. Why should diamond pendants be the exception?"

Annette paled. "I want to speak to a solicitor. It was an accident, you know. I didn't push her. She tripped. You can't prove she didn't. Besides, she deserved it. The old hag—"

Melvin turned to me. "Yoder," he said, without a trace of sarcasm, "I think your chicken caught a Tory."

CHICKEN CACCIATORE

2 young freshly killed hens, plucked and cleaned (although supermarket birds will suffice)
2 cups sliced mushrooms
1 large onion, finely chopped
8 ounces tomato puree
½ cup dry red wine
3 tablespoons olive oil
1 teaspoon dried oregano
¼ teaspoon dried basil
1 teaspoon salt
¼ teaspoon black pepper
Dash cayenne pepper

Wash chicken, pat dry with paper towels, and cut into serving pieces. Meanwhile heat oil in large skillet (cast iron preferred). Brown chicken in oil. Add mushrooms and onions. Mix tomato puree with wine and spices. Pour liquid over chicken and vegetables and bring to boil. Cover, turn down heat, and simmer for approximately one hour or until chicken is tender, adding hot water as necessary to keep from sticking. May be served over cooked pasta or rice. Serves 8.

This dish may also be prepared in the oven by placing browned chicken and other ingredients in a large casserole or glass baking dish and baking at 350 degrees for 1 ½ hours.

Note: while the chicken cacciatore is cooking, examine the gizzard for diamond pendants. If you find one, contact me in care of the publisher. The gem belongs to me.

—*TM*

A PASSION
FOR THE COOK

ELIZABETH DANIELS SQUIRE

Here in Monroe County, folks said Helen was too pretty for her own good. Our Helen's face had never launched a thousand ships and caused a Trojan War, like that gal in history. But I knew Helen's problem went more than skin deep. I didn't realize that my friend who wrote the food column for *The Weekly Word* could cause murder.

Actually, you wouldn't believe all you learn working for a rural weekly newspaper. You cover the story of some triumph or disaster, but then—because people all tend to know each other here—you learn what happens next, the final outcome. Which is often almost beyond belief.

Helen came into the office Friday morning, bringing her food column. Her eyes were wider than usual. They're green eyes, with long black lashes, and seem absolutely electric set in her heart-shaped face. Helen's skin is soft and fine like an orchid. She's slender but curvy, and there's something vulnerable about her that makes you feel you should protect her.

On Friday morning she was trembling as she sat down

in the chair across from my desk. Luckily, Friday is our most laid-back day, since the paper comes out on Thursday. I had time to listen. "You're alone, Peaches?" she asked, looking all around.

Yes, I explained. Martin, our trusty editor, was out covering a fire, and our advertising gal was out selling ads. That's all of us on this paper except Tamara, our occasional photographer, who snaps pictures when needed. I think of her as Tamara with the Camera.

Helen clenched her hands in her lap to stop the trembling. "I'm afraid Charon is going to shoot me," she blurted.

Charon was her third husband, as arrogant as a baron, but, God help me, he had seemed like an improvement. Alfred, husband number one, had been so jealous he beat Helen up, always carefully so the bruises were covered by her clothes and didn't show, and for a while we didn't even know. But he did agree to a divorce and then went to California. Harold, husband number two, not only beat her up, but after the divorce and a court order to stay away, he'd still stalked her. Luckily for Helen, but not for him, he followed her across Eller Creek Road without looking both ways, was hit by a cattle truck, and killed.

But Charon, who filled third place, was a nationally known artist with pictures in the Guggenheim and other museums. We were impressed with ourselves when he moved to Monroe County—to be closer to nature, he said. That went with his rugged good looks. When he married Helen, we were pleased because we thought he got the violence out of his system on canvas. His pictures in shades of red and orange and purple and yellow were arresting and original. One critic said they gave a foretaste of the end of the world, but in a way that kept you looking.

As she sat by my desk, Helen was as pale as if she expected the end of the world. She toyed nervously with the cup of pens next to the box of bookmarks to promote my book on memory. I'd just brought the bookmarks back from the printer.

"Why on earth are you afraid that Charon might shoot you?" I asked. That was the worst possibility yet.

"It's because of the food column," she announced, twisting her hands.

"Then stop writing it," I said. "Folks will miss the great recipes you find around the county, but they'll miss you more if you get shot." I knew she wrote mainly for her own pleasure. *The Weekly Word* doesn't pay worth a darn. Helen taught second grade to earn dependable money. She was also my longtime friend. She used to live near me in Buncombe County. Yes, I live in one county and work over the line in the next.

She said: "I mustn't stop doing anything I always do. I mustn't make any change that could get the wind up. Charon doesn't really like me doing the food column. He doesn't like the attention I get. But if I make any change in my life he has to know why, and if he finds out what's been going on—well, Charon gets wildly jealous, and he's been getting worse."

I sighed. It seemed all her husbands got worse, the longer she was married to them.

"So exactly what's wrong?" I asked. But before she could answer, our trusty editor, Martin, came back from covering the fire and bloomed with pleasure to see Helen. Normal male reaction.

He said, "That chocolate-indulgence-cake recipe from the mayor's wife was positively sinful. My wife made it, and I think we both gained ten pounds." He lit a cigarette, waved, and went in his office. A relapse. Last week he'd given up smoking.

Helen beamed. Even scared white, she still loved to be told how folks enjoyed her column.

Then she said, "You know, I could use some air, Peaches. Would you be willing to go for a walk?"

She plainly didn't want a soul, including Martin, to hear what she was going to say. By now, I had to know. So I drove her down the river road to a little park where there's a walk by the water. Flowing water calms the mind.

She didn't say a word on the way—composing her thoughts, perhaps. The road is so lovely, with a rugged rock cliff on one side, now festooned with vines of little white flowers, and the broad rolling river on the other, that I was quiet, too, enjoying the ride.

We parked in an empty parking area and walked down past a sign that said we'd go in the water at our own risk, past picnic tables to a bench near the water—water almost as musical as a fall, and muddy brown from the last night's rain. We sat down on a bench near the grassy edge of the river where a bloodred wildflower shared space with yellow daisies. Somebody, perhaps a child, had left a pile of yellow and white pebbles on the end of the bench.

Helen sighed. Then she began to talk in a rush. "It all began with that column about the peppermint sheet cake from Lou-Anne Penland, the president of the Hobbs Creek Extension Club."

Helen flicked away an electric-blue dragonfly and slowed down. "Peaches, I did like I always do. I tested the recipe in my kitchen. People do occasionally leave out ingredients. I called Tamara and told her when I expected to have the cake frosted and ready to photograph. I had invited Lou-Anne over to be in the picture. But before they arrived, just as I had that cake finished, the phone rang. It was some woman who said I'd won a bearskin rug in the church lottery. Well, that was interesting, and I couldn't be rude. I had to take the time to tell her I was thrilled."

Helen paused and looked me straight in the eye. I could tell she was coming to the dramatic part.

"When I went back to the cake, would you believe somebody had come in my kitchen and decorated it with red candy hearts and put a card with a red heart on it right by the cake? The card said, 'You're going to be mine.' It wasn't signed. I was scared silly."

A blue van drove into the parking lot above us. Oh, dear, I hoped someone wouldn't come close and shut her up.

"What did Tamara and Lou-Anne think of that?" I asked.

"Do you think I'm out of my mind?" she demanded. "I hid that card quick and pretended I'd put the candy hearts on the white frosting to make a better picture. If Charon had heard about that card, he'd have gone ballistic. That was three weeks ago."

I could see this was going to be complicated. Luckily, the person by the blue van was taking his time, letting his dog mark every bush, and staying at a distance.

"The next week," Helen said, "I locked all the doors, and I told nobody what I was going to do. I made lemon-sesame chicken, the recipe donated by Mattie Belie who works in the library. She hates to have her picture taken, so I said I'd just use a picture of the chicken beside a pile of books. Nobody knew when Tamara was coming to take that picture, except Tamara, of course.

"I arranged the chicken and the books on the dining-room table. The doorbell rang, and I went to let Tamara in, but she wasn't there. I looked both ways and called her. No Tamara. Then I noticed a package on the doorstep. I opened it and there was nothing inside. So I ran back to the dining room, and there by my chicken thighs was a page torn from an old book about medieval chastity belts. You know, those nasty metal belts that a man could lock on his wife as he went off to the Crusades to make sex impossible until he got back with the key."

Yes, I knew. I had always wondered how a chastity belt could be the least bit sanitary.

The blue-van man was walking toward us with his dog, past the cement picnic tables. But he was not close yet.

"There was a note, too," said Helen. "The note said, 'I want you just for me.'" Angrily, she took a pebble and threw it in the water with a splash.

"Did the handwriting look at all familiar?" I asked.

"It was written on a typewriter or a computer, I guess. On plain white paper like anybody could get." Helen threw another pebble hard into white water where the river flowed over a rock.

"But how did someone get in my house? How did they know my schedule?" Her voice rose in panic. "The doors were locked. My God, suppose Charon saw that note? Or saw the man who brought it? Charon was right over in his studio behind the house, lost in his work the way he gets. If he saw the note he'd think—he'd be sure—I'd been with that guy.

"And when he wasn't painting, Charon spent the week cleaning his guns. He'd given up smoking, I'd been begging him to do that, but it made him nervous. At least when Martin quit he didn't clean guns, did he? Charon made me very nervous."

I could tell. The water sound was not enough to soothe her.

The man with the dog had luckily stopped a good ways off, for the dog to do his business against the sign that told what was not allowed in the park.

"Who has a key to your house?" I asked.

"Nobody but my sister and my cleaning woman, and I trust them both absolutely. Sis has six kids and sometimes she has to get away. She can come to my house anytime and sit down and read a book. She sits in the kitchen. She says she likes the way my kitchen smells." Helen allowed herself a small smile. "Sis wouldn't make me trouble."

"But either one could have left that key where someone could copy it," I said. Helen's twin sister looked almost like her and yet she wasn't as sexy. She had a sturdy air that made you think she could take care of herself. I had to admit she was not the type to leave a key where someone could copy it. And her sister's husband was dependable, too. "Dull but kind" Helen called him.

Now the man from the blue van came right toward us, walking a German shepherd. Ah, yes—Alfred Battle, our white-haired and rugged retired county commissioner. I remember he once winked at me, pointed at his white hair, and said, "When there's snow on the roof there's fire in the furnace." Not too much, I hoped. He stopped and glowed with pleasure to see Helen. He was polite to me but I saw where his attention went. "What a lovely surprise to see you-all here," he said.

We chatted a moment and then I said, "We're just taking a brisk walk." We got up and left him looking startled at our getaway. We headed toward a path that went off into the wooded part of the riverbank.

"He has the same cleaning woman I do," Helen said. "And he's a friend of my sister's. Oh, this is awful. Now I'm going to suspect everybody I know!" Sunlight through the leaves above us dappled her face.

"Your valentine man may be somebody who has been watching you from a distance, someone you don't know," I told her. "Why didn't you tell me the column was getting dangerous, right off?" Poison ivy climbed a tree that edged the water. Somehow that seemed appropriate.

"I didn't tell anybody," she said. "I was so afraid Charon would find out. And if a stalker can't get to you one way he'll try another. By this week I was really scared. So I made coupe Bugatti."

I didn't see the connection, but I waited. We passed a gently sloping place—obviously for boats and rafts to be pulled in or out of the river. Fortunately, at 10:00 A.M. there were no boats.

"This week I've written about Lawrence Whittaker, a writer who once interviewed Ettore Bugatti, the great car designer and maker. Lawrence got the recipe from a millionaire collector of cars who he also interviewed in connection with the story. Hey, pretty uptown for Monroe County, don't you think?"

That obviously still pleased her, scared or not.

"Now, this recipe is so simple and quick that I figured I could throw it together and photograph it so fast that the man who's bothering me wouldn't have time to make trouble," she said. "I'd be done when he thought I had just started."

Helen stopped and rested against a tree that leaned out over the water. Luckily, no poison ivy there. "All I needed was the best coffee ice cream, dark rum, simple syrup, whipped cream, and shaved bitter chocolate," she said. "And Lawrence Whittaker said I didn't even need to make the simple syrup. That would have taken a while, boiling it up and waiting for it to cool. He said his shortcut was to use pale clover honey instead, and the taste was virtually the same." That did sound good.

"I told no one what I was going to do, except Tamara, who had to take the picture. I mixed the honey with one-third as much rum. That took two minutes. I put two scoops of ice cream in each of two tall coupe glasses, and put the glasses in the freezer compartment. One minute. No problem so far. When Tamara arrived, I planned to pour some rum syrup over each coupe. I then planned to do something sacrilegious to the memory of Bugatti, but I was doing this to photograph, not to win a gourmet prize. I did not whip heavy cream myself. I planned to use the kind that comes in a pressurized can, and make a mound of whipped cream on each coupe. I grated the bitter chocolate in a little grinder I have, and planned to put a generous sprinkle on each portion. Total time, ten minutes. No interruption from that crazy man. The doorbell rang. I hoped that this time it would be Tamara and I thought, *Hoorah,* I'm home free!" Helen threw one more pebble she'd brought with her into the water. They were her exclamation points.

"But Tamara was holding a bouquet of yellow roses and she said, "This was hung on your mailbox. There's a card.'

"I was angry. 'Some nut has been pestering me,' I told her. 'Please, for God's sake, don't tell anybody. Charon gets jealous.' Well, I had to tell her something." Helen was so upset she couldn't stand still. We hurried on. She couldn't stop talking, either.

"After Tamara left, I read the card: 'I'll pick you up in front of your house right after you test the recipe next week. You can put a sign in the kitchen window, which says YES or NO as you start to cook. If you don't come I'll kill you and then kill myself. Our bodies can be in the picture on page one.'" She turned and faced me so suddenly that I almost bumped into her. "What will I do? This sounds too crazy and I'm scared."

I grabbed a young tree and got my balance. "Maybe it's an ugly joke," I said hopefully. "But I think you need to call the sheriff, right now."

"I wouldn't dare! Then Charon would certainly hear about it. You know Charon is so talented. But most great artists are a little unbalanced."

I figured that was an exaggeration, even if Vincent van Gogh, whose work now sold for millions, did cut off his ear.

She stayed planted in front of me. "And Charon has told me that if I'm ever unfaithful he'll shoot me."

I was appalled. "Helen," I said, still holding on to my

tree, "forgive an old friend's bluntness, but you need some counseling. If you marry a destructive man once, that can be a mistake. But you've done it three times. You need help." For the first time I noticed the cicadas, like a loud buzzing in my ears.

She didn't even get mad. She said, "All right, if you'll help me through this without the sheriff, I'll do it. Help me find out who this man is who's sending me notes, and if this is a real threat or a joke. Help me to do it before Charon finds out."

"Call the sheriff," I said again. I know how stubborn Helen can be, so I knew she wouldn't.

"Listen," she said, "the sheriff is the worst one. He hugged me at the Fire Company fund-raiser last month. Charon had fits."

I sighed. "All right," I said. "I'll think about what you can do."

Now, Helen would be better off if she weren't so sexy and I'd be much better off if I weren't so inventive. Because the idea of setting the trap came to me, as if the sound of rushing water could inspire my thoughts. And the trap seemed like such an interesting idea that it would be a sinful waste not to go ahead and do it. I should have refused to help.

"Are you sure you want to take the chance that this nut won't do something dangerous and unexpected?" I asked Helen. "Why should he wait for next week?"

"Because he's obviously fixated on the cooking column," she said. She began to walk again. "Maybe it's the man who got so mad when there was a typo and he put a tablespoon of salt in the chicken salad with white grapes and pecans, instead of a teaspoon. Everybody else had enough common sense to know it must be a typo. But he did it and doubled the recipe for a family reunion. Oh, he was mad."

And suddenly I thought, Why, it could even be a woman

who was mad at Helen and trying to make trouble, maybe a woman who wanted Charon for herself! Man or woman, my idea would show that person up!

I sat down on a boulder and Helen sat down uneasily beside me. I said, "You know, I have a recipe that I've put on bookmarks advertising my *How to Survive Without a Memory,* now that the paperback edition is out. I went to the printer to pick up the bookmarks on my way to work this morning. The recipe is for cookies you can forget but not burn."

She gave me a "why are you wasting my time?" glance.

"Next week, you can run my recipe, and we'll catch your tormentor with it," I said. I had one of the bookmarks in my pocketbook. I read it out loud.

"They sound good," she said, only a little impatient. "But how could they be a trap?"

So I explained. "What I don't say in the recipe is that you can leave these cookies in the oven a long time, even twelve hours. You can really forget them, and they'll still come out fine. So you don't have to photograph these cookies at the time the stalker will expect. You can creep around and stalk him and find out who he is."

I regret to tell you Helen's eyes sparkled. She enjoys risk.

Of course, I worried about her when she went home. But even if I called the sheriff myself, what could he do? He didn't have the staff to shadow Helen all week.

After work, I drove past her house. All peaceful. I parked down the road in the mouth of an old wood road, out of sight of the main road, and walked up the mountain in back of her house. The top of the first rise overlooked her kitchen window. Pretty quick, I found a spot with a fallen log to sit on and a lot of cigarette butts scuffed out near it. I looked at a butt. Camels. Good Lord, Martin smoked Camels. But he would never—would he? From where I sat, a watcher's presence would be masked by bushes, but binoculars would have picked out Helen's every move in the kitchen. I shivered.

I noted the lay of the land. Charon's studio was separate from, and in back of, the white clapboard house. The house looked 1920s. The studio was natural wood and modern with large glass skylights on the north side. The watcher from the hill could have seen Helen in her kitchen as clearly as if he stood right outside the window, and see Charon if he left his studio. He could not have seen a car parked in front of the house, but he could have seen Tamara's car drive up.

I heard crashing through the bushes, and froze. Thank goodness it was only a black dog with wagging tail. But it made me aware I shouldn't hang around near a place where a possibly deranged chain-smoker felt at home.

On Tuesday, Helen was set to test the recipe. No further communication from the valentine man.

I told Tamara not to go take a picture, but if anyone asked her if she was going, to say that she was.

Helen put the cookies in the oven and a "yes" sign in the window and then came out into a spot that you couldn't see from the mountain log-and-cigarette place, and we hid across the street in the bushes.

That's when everything went wrong. We saw a blue Volvo park in front of the house. "That's Sis's car," Helen said, amazed. "Would she pull a joke like this? No, she has a book under her arm. She's coming to my house to get away and read! Oh, help!"

We ran after her into the house. But not quick enough. We heard two shots before we reached the kitchen. In the kitchen we found Sis shot in the heart. Oh, Lord, this was dreadful! Sis who looked just like Helen, with a book on gardening still clutched in her hand. Helen screamed with horror and put her arms around her dead sister lying on the floor. Frantically I looked around for the killer. We could be next.

I found him outside the shattered window. Charon lay still with a pistol in his hand. He'd shot himself in the neck. Didn't he know enough to shoot himself in the ear so he'd die instantly, or did his hand slip? There was blood all over the place, raw red as one of his pictures. He was alive, though barely. "I knew she cheated. I proved it," he half gasped, half gurgled, and then he stopped breathing.

I can't tell you how desperately I wished that he'd merely cut off his ear.

Or how desperately I wished I had somehow persuaded Helen to call the sheriff. Or figured out that Charon hadn't really given up smoking. It was Charon who cheated. He'd slipped off and smoked while he spied on his wife. I shuddered. My friend Deputy Wynatt says I'm murder-prone—and he's right. If someone is going to get killed, I'm going to be there. That negative thinking was not going to help. At least sometimes I prevent a death. I had saved Helen. I could feel good about that. I had not saved her sister.

As for Charon, the seeds of his own destruction were in him, I think. I was sorry. He would have been pleased, however, at the obituaries that called him a true original and a great artist. He would have loved the way his work went up in price.

The most amazing part of this story happened next. Helen mourned for Sis and Charon both. She said it was her fault for not noticing that Charon was heading for a breakdown. She should have figured out a way to help him. The excellent Asheville shrink she visited had a hard time talking her out of obsessing about that.

But she decided she would marry her brother-in-law. "He's dull and that's what I need," she told me. "And he's kind, and he needs a mother for those kids. And furthermore," she said, "raising six children should keep me so busy I won't get into trouble." I prayed that was true.

Of course, Helen never wrote the food column about the cookies. We were so upset about Charon and Sis that we forgot and left the cookies in the oven all day. But when Helen remembered and took them out, they were just fine. She put them in a cookie tin. They keep.

Three weeks later she came by the office and presented us with the tin of cookies. "I can't bear to eat these," she told me. "Because everything else went so desperately wrong the day I baked them. Only the cookies turned out right."

I bit into one with my afternoon coffee. It was crunchy, spicy, and absolutely delicious.

■

SPECIAL OCCASION GINGER COOKIES

(That You Can't Forget and Burn)

2 egg whites
⅔ cup sugar
1 teaspoon vanilla
1¼ cup roughly chopped pecans
½ cup chopped crystallized ginger

Preheat oven to 350 degrees. Beat egg whites almost stiff, add 2 tablespoons of the sugar. Beat very stiff, then slowly add the rest of the sugar, then vanilla, while continuing to beat. Fold in the ginger. Then fold in all but about 2 tablespoons of the nuts. Drop by spoonfuls onto cookie sheets covered with foil or waxed paper. Sprinkle cookies with reserved nuts. Put cookie sheets in oven and TURN OFF THE OVEN.

Cookies are done when they are firm enough to come off sheet in one piece. Don't open oven to test for at least two hours, as oven will lose heat. Makes 2 dozen.

—EDS

JUST ONE BITE WON'T KILL YOU

VALERIE WOLZIEN

"She's trying to kill me."

"Vanessa, how can you say that? Mother may not be a sweet little old lady all the time . . ."—he chose to ignore his wife's "harrumph" and continued with his statement—"but she is not a murderess. She would never even think of killing anyone."

"Ha! Every time we accept a dinner invitation from her, we risk death. Fried chicken. Gravy. Mashed potatoes. String beans cooked for hours until they're brown in bacon fat—bacon fat! And apparently she can't make a salad without adding tons of mayonnaise. Mayonnaise and bacon fat can kill you."

"Bacon fat and mayonnaise are not strychnine and cyanide, Vanessa. But if you're worried, you don't have to eat it all. Just take the skin off the chicken and pass on the mashed potatoes and gravy. The beans really won't kill you. And ask for your lettuce without any dressing."

"Iceberg."

"Excuse me?" He put his foot on the brake and peered

through the windshield at the road ahead. There didn't seem to be any upcoming hazards, but Roger was a careful man, despite his inherited eating habits.

"Your mother serves iceberg lettuce."

"Iceberg lettuce is perfectly fine food. People ate iceberg lettuce for decades before some smart farmer started promoting all those bitter little leaves you and your friends think of as salad." He took a deep breath and then continued: "And I have to say, Vanessa, that I really didn't appreciate your behavior last night."

"My behavior last night? I don't believe I did anything wrong last night."

"You never believe you do anything wrong. But how do you think I feel eating dinner while you criticize my mother from the appetizer through espresso?" He didn't say from the hummus through the tofu casserole to the decaffeinated swill that his wife and her friends chose to consume on festive occasions, but he would have been accurate if he had. "I found it very upsetting." Then he had another thought.

"And, anyway, what makes you think your friends don't eat food exactly like my mother makes? Donna and her husband are both pretty chunky for a couple who claim to be vegans."

His wife was quick to leap to her friends' defense. "Donna has a slow metabolism. She's been seeing a health practitioner about it for the past few months. And as for David . . . Well, everyone knows it's impossible to control what your husband sticks in his mouth."

He knew a nasty gibe when he heard one—he should have, he'd heard enough of them in the three years they'd been married. He also knew it was better to ignore them than to get into a fight. There was no reason to argue with her. Not now. Besides, he never won. He spoke more softly. "I still don't think there was any reason for you to spend so much of the evening criticizing my mother's cooking. You actually had Donna and David laughing at her."

"Dear, it's impossible not to laugh at someone who offers salad and then brings out a dish of cherry Jell-O, maraschino cherries, pecans, and tiny marshmallows."

"Well, you won't get that today. She only serves that at Christmastime. It's the middle of the summer," he muttered in his mother's defense.

"Of course she serves it for the holiday. It goes so nicely with that awful sticky fruitcake and those dried-out cookies she serves then, too."

"No one insists that you eat dessert." Roger spoke through gritted teeth. The last time they'd made this drive he had ground his molars so hard that a piece broke off. His wife, naturally, blamed his mother's cooking rather than her own whining.

"You know I don't want to hurt her feelings."

Since yelling "liar, liar" would have been a bit immature, Roger just kept his mouth shut and his eyes on the road. With any luck, his wife had vented enough about his mother and would soon start on another subject—like why they couldn't afford a bigger house or when was he going to take her on the Parisian vacation he had promised when they got engaged. Since Roger had only one answer for either question—lack of money—both topics engendered rather one-sided conversations.

But Vanessa seemed to feel the need to talk about this very subject. "We need money. Admit it, you barely make enough to buy the necessities . . ."

But there was a limit to how long even the meekest person could remain silent. "Most people think of necessities as food, clothing, and shelter, not supporting every damn health-food store on the East Coast!" Roger exploded.

"Most people would include medical care as a necessity. Especially their wife's medical care."

"Quackery. It's not medical care. It's quackery. And it's eating up every single extra dollar we have!"

"We would have more extra dollars if your mother would help out a bit," his wife broke in. "Other people's families help them when they're just starting out. Why, Jackie Turner's in-laws bought them a house."

"Al Turner's family is wealthy. Mother is not. We're lucky, in fact. Mother is self-sufficient and many parents are not." He had a thought and added, "You might start thinking that we're fortunate we don't have to worry about taking care of Mother as she gets older." Roger regretted the words as they were coming out of his mouth. Vanessa would certainly not let his comment pass without serious disagreement. He glanced over at his wife and was surprised to see a smile flickering on her usually stern face.

"What are you smiling about?"

"I was just thinking that you're right. That we won't have to worry about your mother when she gets older. And, of course, about the surprise I'm bringing your mother."

"Vanessa . . ."

"What? What do you mean, saying my name in that tone of voice? I'm not doing anything wrong. I'm contributing to a family meal. It's the right thing to do!"

"Van . . . honey . . . Mother likes doing all the cooking herself. She always does all the cooking herself."

"Well, she'll just have to adapt a bit, won't she?"

Roger bit his lip and shut up. Neither his mother nor his wife was famous for her flexibility. Maybe he'd be able to catch Mom alone for a few minutes and explain. He could tell her that Vanessa was on a diet . . . but then his mother would end up making comments about skinny women that were definitely unflattering . . . And Vanessa would think that he had been criticizing her . . . No, there had to be another way. He thought he had a solution, but . . . did he dare? Keeping one hand firmly on the wheel, he felt for the small vial in his pocket.

They were both silent for the rest of the trip. Roger, never a confident driver, concentrated on the road and on his problem. Vanessa seemed uncharacteristically nervous, occasionally caressing the casserole in her lap, her eyes on the road ahead, one foot tapping the floor mat.

They had just passed a familiar landmark—the elementary school Roger had attended for seven miserable years—when his wife spoke up.

"Maybe you're right. Maybe I shouldn't have brought this. I . . . I could leave it in the car."

But Roger—who had just remembered that the spelling bee he had won in fifth grade was decidedly the high point of his early years if not in his entire life—had become more generous. "No, bring it. Maybe you're right. Maybe it's time Mother loosened up a bit."

"If you think so . . ."

"I do. I really do. Dear . . ." Roger added the last word and glanced at his wife to see if she noticed.

But Vanessa was staring out the window. The casserole was clenched in her hands. And her foot kicked almost violently against the floor of the car.

Roger turned the steering wheel and the car started up the long driveway to the home where he'd grown up.

"No fond feelings here," his wife muttered, and he didn't disagree with her. "You know what I think?"

He didn't, but he also knew he wouldn't need to ask to hear them.

"I think your mother plans on outliving us."

"What?"

"I think she plans on outliving us. That's why she won't even loan us money. And why she refuses to talk about her will or . . . or discuss plans for her old age."

Roger ran out of anything resembling patience. "I cannot believe you would say . . . or even think . . . about something like that. It's almost as though you were just waiting for Mother to die." He was so angry he slammed his foot down on the brake. Vanessa grabbed her casserole protectively.

"I don't know how you could say anything so horrible about me," she said, getting out of the car and smiling up at the old woman standing on the front steps. "Mother Applegate. You're looking well."

"I may be looking well, but I'm exhausted. I barely made it to the basement to get the beans."

"She's serving us canned beans," Vanessa hissed at Roger as they followed the remarkably energetic old woman into her house. "We must have passed a half dozen farm markets on the way here and we get canned beans!"

"Vanessa! *Shh*—"

"What did you say, dear? Are you talking about my beans? You can smell them, can't you? I made an extra large pot of them. My stomach's been bothering me a bit and so I may not have much chicken. I know what you're always saying about fried food and my old age, and you may be right. But beans are different. Beans settle the stomach, don't you think?"

"You may be right, Mother Applegate. You may be right. I . . . I brought this casserole. You've made so much food for us over the years, I thought maybe it was time I contributed."

"Why, aren't you sweet. We'll put it on the table right now. Come on into the dining room. I brought out your grandmother's tablecloth. It looks lovely, doesn't it, Roger?"

"Yes. But it's so much work to wash and iron. I thought you saved it for special occasions, Mother."

"Anytime my son and his dear wife visit is a special occasion. You know I always say that."

"Yes, Mother, you always do."

They sat down at the table.

"Now, there's a platter of fried chicken, and the mashed potatoes are in the covered dish, there's a Jell-O salad as a special treat, and, of course, the beans. Take a big helping of beans, Vanessa. I know how you healthy types like to get your greens. I'll just run to the kitchen and get the gravy. I was just keeping it warming in the oven . . ."

"You sit down, Mother. I'll get it."

"He's a wonderful son, my dear." She pushed a chipped blue-and-white willowware bowl toward her daughter-in-law. "I'm lucky to have a son so wonderful."

"Yes, Mother Applegate. He's a wonderful son." Vanessa piled the beans on her plate.

"They were dead? When they were discovered all three of them were dead?"

"Yup. Look at the photos. I've never seen so much vomit on a hand-crocheted tablecloth . . . my mother used to make 'em." The older cop explained about crocheted tablecloths to the younger. They were sitting at a table piled high with reports from doctors, coroners, and various experts in poisons.

"Guess we'll never know whether his mother killed his wife or if his wife killed his mother or if he killed 'em both and then committed suicide or what," the younger said. "Not from this stuff."

"You're not reading the clues correctly."

"I don't—"

"Look at the garbage in their bodies. What a mess that is . . . the wife is full of strychnine and arsenic. The husband has some strychnine and some cyanide and even a bit of arsenic. The mother is full of cyanide—no strychnine, no arsenic.

"And look at this report. You can tell who ate what. The fancy tofu casserole was laced with cyanide. The fried chicken had strychnine in its tasty, crunchy coating. There was arsenic in the gravy—and in the little pill container in the husband's pants' pocket. Not enough to kill anyone, though. There wasn't enough cyanide to do much either. And the mother's idea of lacing something with strychnine is almost a joke. There wasn't really enough of any poison to kill anyone on that whole table. What an ineffectual group of attempted murderers!"

"But . . . but they're dead," the junior officer stammered.

"Damn right they're dead! Botulism will kill you quicker than any of that stuff they write about in English mystery novels. And let that be a lesson to you, young man. Never, ever eat old home-canned beans."

❖

VALERIE'S MOTHER'S NONLETHAL SOUTHERN-FRIED CHICKEN AND GRAVY

1 fresh chicken cut into serving size pieces
Flour, salt, pepper
Lots of bacon fat
¼ cup tasteless salad oil
1 cup of milk

Sprinkle salt and pepper liberally on chicken pieces. Find a good-sized paper bag and pour in flour. Shake each chicken piece in flour and lay out to dry slightly. Pour bacon fat in heavy, flat-bottomed frying pan. Add ¼ cup of tasteless salad oil. (This is to help prevent spatter, not for health reasons.) When oil is almost, but not quite, smoking, arrange chicken pieces in pan. Cover immediately. Fry for

10 to 15 minutes before taking off cover and turning pieces once. Fry for 10 minutes more then remove cover and allow chicken to "crisp up" for a minute or two. Remove chicken from fat in order of size—smallest pieces first. Drain on paper towels and keep warm in oven.

To make gravy, pour off all but a few teaspoons of fat. Turn heat down under pan and add ¼ cup of flour. Make a roux. Slowly add a cup of warmed milk, scraping the bottom of the pan to incorporate all the tasty bits of fried skin and crisp coating. Add salt and pepper according to personal taste. When gravy is the correct consistency, serve with the chicken and mashed potatoes.

—VW

DEAD AND BERRIED

CLAUDIA BISHOP

The *Canandaigua Lady* bumped peacefully at the municipal boat dock. The sky was blue, the lake bluer, and a gentle August breeze stirred Sarah Quilliam's hair. Apart from the erratic *whack-clang* of cutlery flung against the sides of the little paddle wheeler and the shrieks of her sister Meg, little disturbed the quiet of the upstate New York resort town of Canandaigua.

"Capers!" Meg yelled, pulling her right arm back for another pitch. "Dammit!" She threw underhand, a relic of her days as the best softball pitcher on the Connecticut High School Girls' Baseball team fifteen years before. The long stainless-steel braising fork missed the bulwark, and splashed a mallard scavenging for breadcrumbs under the pier. The mallard's squawk and Meg's fury were indistinguishable.

"Fine. Just fine!" Doreen said bitterly. Their housekeeper folded her arms under her skinny bosom and poked her head forward like an irritated rooster. "That's twenty dollars' worth of stuff in the drink, missy."

Doreen, Meg, and Quill herself stood on the gangplank

leading to the smartly painted *Lady*. Doreen and Meg glared truculently at one another. Quill gazed thoughtfully into the serenity of the countryside.

Meg made a noise like "nnnyah," but she held her fire and sat down abruptly at the edge of the dock. She banged a spatula idly against the oak edge and stared broodingly at the water.

"Are you finished throwing stuff?" Quill said.

Meg tugged at her short dark hair. "I can't do this. I can't *cook this pasta dish without Greek capers!*"

"The realtors will be here in two hours. They asked for a thirty-minute open bar, that's two and a half hours until the starters are served, and close to three until the entrée's due. We have plenty of time to find the Greek capers."

"Greek!" Meg scowled. "Not Turkish."

Quill sighed. The Upstate New York Realtors Association (Southern Tier Chapter) were paying them a lot of money to put on their annual banquet. Stuart Gray and Louise Guildenstern (vice president and secretary, respectively) had both spent vacations at Quill and Meg's Inn as guests. Mr. Gray in particular was a favorite of Meg and Quill's. When he had asked Meg to cook in a strange kitchen, it had been hard to say no.

It didn't hurt that the offer had come when the Inn was temporarily closed for a few necessary plumbing and electrical repairs. An all-expenses-paid weekend on one of the most beautiful freshwater lakes in the world seemed like a good idea. And in fact, the day had gone really well until Meg discovered Bjarne the assistant chef had purchased Turkish capers instead of Greek.

"You shoulda said." Doreen's stance was truculent. "You just asked for capers. How was Bjarne to know! And if he don't know, how's he supposed to tell me? You get specific, you get what you want. You don't get specific . . ."

"All chefs know the difference! The Turkish is fat and

squashy. The Greek is small and pungent. Only an idiot would confuse the two!" Meg jumped to her feet and stamped down the gangplank to the little ship. The plastic grocery bags Doreen had given her bumped theatrically against her leg. She turned and flung over her shoulder, "Well, *find* them, dammit. Or the whole dish will be spoiled."

"Fine!" Doreen shouted. She stamped off toward the parking lot, where Quill's ancient Oldsmobile lay rusting.

"Fine!" Meg yelled back, and disappeared into the bowels of the ship.

Quill looked from the hot expanses of the asphalt parking lot to the delightful rocking of the ship. She could go with Doreen on the caper search, and soothe her down. Or she could finish the menu cards. Quill decided her time would be better spent writing out the menu cards for the dinner. She'd set up her calligraphy equipment topside.

For an hour or more, Quill sat peacefully in the sunshine, black ink flowing in a satisfyingly elegant way from her pen. The sun slipped peacefully down the western horizon, flooding the placid lake with amethyst light.

"The Chosen Spot," someone said in her ear. Quill jumped, the terminal *a* in *Pasta Quilliam* skidding into puddled incomprehensibility.

"I'm so sorry!" A thin, tall elderly man patted his suit pocket in a distracted way. He pulled out a handkerchief, crouched, and dabbed at spilled ink on the deck.

"Mr. Gray," Quill said, pleased. "I didn't hear you come up. It's so peaceful up here . . ." She shook hands with him, noting with concern that he seemed thinner than ever. And there were purple shadows under his mild gray eyes. She knew he had recently returned from his retirement in Florida to take up his career again, and asked after his wife, Amaryllis.

He looked gravely out at the water and ignored her question. "It is very beautiful up here. Yes. It's why the Onandoga call it 'the Chosen Place.' Chosen by the gods for its beauty, you see."

"I do. Is that why you decided to come back here?"

He flushed with embarrassment, "No, I . . . well, there was some trouble with my pension. The only thing I have left from it is a decent life insurance policy. And Amaryllis . . . the doctors don't give her a great deal of time, Quill."

Quill put her hand lightly on his arm. Mr. Gray's eyes filled with tears and he muttered somewhat incoherently, "Not at all, not at all."

There was a short, uncomfortable silence. Quill glanced at her watch. "My goodness! I had no idea it was so late! Your friends will be arriving soon."

"I am a little early," he apologized. "But my daughter insisted I get out of the house to relax. She came down from Rochester for the day to sit with Amaryllis so that I could come to the banquet, and there wasn't any other place to go, so I thought perhaps I could watch Meg at work. If I may. I promised to give Amaryllis every last detail."

Quill smiled. "My sister usually loves an audience. Especially if she can stage a temper tantrum."

"Meg is a true artist," Mr. Gray said. "A volatile temperament is the sign of a highly creative mind."

Quill, with one painting on permanent display at the National Gallery in London and another at MOMA, thought briefly that it would be really nice if she could stage a temper tantrum now and then. But she said, merely, "I've got one more card to finish, and then we'll go see what Meg is up to, all right?"

She finished the final *Entrée—Pasta Quilliam* with a

flourish and waved it in the soft air to dry. Then she and Mr. Gray descended two decks to the galley to find Meg scowling into the crème fraîche.

The galley was surprisingly spacious, but every surface was filled with trays and bowls of food. Meg's response to special locations like the *Canandaigua Lady* was to create meals that were assembled rather than cooked on-site. The only actual cooking was the pasta for the main entrée. The breads were already baking in the two ovens. Two of the sous chefs were preparing plates for the avocado grapefruit salad, the shrimp appetizers, and the chilled pepper mousse. Bjarne, the Finn who was Meg's chief assistant in the kitchen, chopped sun-dried tomatoes with a large cleaver. Meg herself prepared the crème fraîche for pasta Quilliam, an incredible concoction of a white sauce, fresh mushrooms, sun-dried tomatoes, and capers.

"You're using Turkish capers, I see," Mr. Gray said with a great deal of interest. He poked a long finger at the bowl standing on the stainless-steel counter.

"Greek," Meg said, her scowl deepening. "Even Mr. Gray"—she addressed the hapless Bjarne severely—"knows the difference between Turkish and Greek."

"I know perfectly well the difference between Greek and Turkish!" Bjarne said with wounded dignity. "You, Meg. You did not specify which was which. So naturally, I chose the caper with the more aggressive flavor. Pasta Quilliam is a somewhat bland dish, after all. If you had listened to me when you developed the recipe, you would have seasoned with much greater style. It's *boring*."

Meg breathed through her nose like a short, brunette dragon.

Bjarne picked up the bowl and popped a caper into his mouth with a defiant air. "Just right!" he proclaimed, his Finnish accent more pronounced than usual.

Quill winced at this blatant provocation.

Meg grabbed the bowl from Bjarne. Punctuating the air with empathetic waves of her arms, she began to yell. Capers flew through the air. So did Finnish imprecations. Quill settled back against the wall with a sigh, almost squashing the people trying to enter the galley behind her. She turned with an apology to find Louise Guildenstern and Allan O'Brien, the president of the Upstate New York Realtors Association. Both disregarded Quill's apology and observed Meg with awe. Meg shrieked. Bjarne cursed. Small squashy capers flew through the air and stuck to the floor, the walls, and Meg's chef hat. Mr. Gray watched it all with a faint, happy smile.

"You'll both want to check out the arrangements for the dinner," Quill said firmly. She shepherded her guests out of the galley and up one deck to the lounge, where Quill had ordered the bar set up. Mr. Gray trailed wistfully in their wake.

"Is she always like that?" Allan O'Brien asked. He was a big-bellied, florid-faced man with white leather loafers and green-yellow plain trousers.

"Yes," Mr. Gray said proudly. He smoothed his narrow silk tie. "She is a great artist." He cocked his head slightly. "Ah! The rebellion is over!" And indeed, the shouting from the kitchen had been replaced by Meg's off-key rendition of Mozart's "Rondo alla Turka." Someone—probably Bjarne—kept time by banging on a kettle. "I'll go down and see her finish the dish, if I may." With a courteous inclination of his head, he disappeared back down the stairs.

"Maybe we can get your sister to throw something at Brose." Louise Guildenstern settled onto a bar stool with a gloomy thump. Like all of the real estate professionals Quill had met so far, Louise was well groomed and not too fashionable and not too stodgy. She wore a colorful suit

jacket, a navy skirt, low-heeled shoes, and tasteful gold
jewelry. Quill thought this was the sartorial equivalent of a
new three-bedroom Colonial.

"Throw something at Brose?" Quill repeated.

"Brose Carmody. Our guest speaker." Louise drew a
compact from her black clutch purse and stabbed blusher
on her cheeks with a disgruntled air. She clicked the compact shut with a snap. "Brose is a snake."

"Brose is a lawyer in town," Allan O'Brien said. "Just
got his broker's license. And yeah, Louise, I'd have to
agree. Brose is a snake."

"Hmm," Quill said. She sighed heavily. She had more
than a passing acquaintance with business dinners ending
in one sort of fracas or another. She wasn't anxious to en-
dure another one, and passed over the tempting issue of
why the Upper New York State Realtors Association had
chosen a snake for a guest speaker. "Did you want to check
the bar supplies, Mr. O'Brien? I sent in some Shiraz, and
we're pretty well stocked with Chardonnay, but you might
want to make sure we have everything you need."

Allan O'Brien nodded happily. Quill left him to the bottle count and guided Louise down to the water level deck,
where waiters from the Inn had already set up the tables for
dinner. Louise's sour expression brightened perceptibly.
There were six tables seating eight diners each. Quill had
separated them into groups of three, each table at a right
angle to another. The overall seating plan wasn't quite as
pleasant as Quill wanted, so she had taken extra effort with
the table decoration, to act as an optical diversion.

Provençal colors set the banquet theme. The tablecloths
were a soft butter yellow. The flowers were a mixture of
gentians, miniature iris, and creamy freesia. Doreen had
carefully packed up the peacock dinnerware Quill stored for
casually elegant events, and it had been worth the effort.

"The biggest problem," Quill said to an admiring

Louise, "was setting tables so that they would cover the ballast hatches, but still have people able to talk to each other in a friendly way."

"Huh?"

"The *Canandaigua Lady* has these hatches, for ballast," Quill explained. She bent down and drew aside one of the table cloths. "There are six of them, three on each side of this room. See?" She grasped a handle set into the carpeted floor and tugged. An empty cavern loomed beneath their feet. "It's for storage, I think," she said vaguely, "but I had to place the tables over the handles, or people would trip on them. And I wanted to avoid a sort of regimented look, you know, placing the table like soldiers standing exactly apart, so the best I could come up with is this sort of angly thing."

"It looks gorgeous," Louise said. "If Brose Carmody were in jail instead of getting paid to speak tonight, it'd be perfect."

Quill tugged violently at her hair to keep from asking the next question, then gave in to the curiosity that had previously led her and her sister to investigate seven cases of murder. "What's wrong with Mr. Carmody?"

"MLS," Louise said darkly.

"Oh, my," Quill said. "I'm so sorry!"

"No, no. I'm not talking about a disease, Ms. Qulliam. Unless you consider Brose Carmody a disease. He's a lawyer in Canandaigua. He's started multiple listing of properties on the Internet for five hundred dollars apiece. MLS. Multiple listing service. It's when property—"

"I do know what multiple listings are," Quill said a little eagerly.

"Then you know that the broker's fee is six percent of the selling cost if the broker sells the listing he's listed. And three percent if the broker sells a listing someone else has listed. But Brose is hacking the heck out of things by charging a flat fee of five hundred bucks. Then he'll handle closing costs for another five hundred and cut the broker out altogether. It stinks. Why, I've had three clients alone in the past month go straight to *realtor.com* and find their own homes, which is great for business, but if the homes are listed with a snake, I mean a guy like Brose, it undercuts all our careers. And he flatly refuses to work with us when he's representing a client on the other side of the table." Louise fiddled with her purse in an agitated way. "Stuff like that has the potential to wreck Allan's whole business, and mine, and everyone else with a real estate license in the whole upstate New York area. I mean, God, Quill. I'm a divorced mom with three kids. In Canandaigua. Where am I going to find another job that'll pay like this one?"

"Oh, dear," Quill said inadequately. "The net seems to be causing a lot of businesses trouble."

"Somebody," Louise said darkly, "ought to take that turkey out."

"Um," Quill said. She sympathized with small business owners, having been taken out more than once by super-shark Marge Schmidt back in Hemlock Falls. "Well, perhaps Mr. Carmody will be so pleased with the dinner that he'll—"

"What? Repent? Not likely." Brose Carmody clattered down the short steps into the lounge, teeth flashing white in his tanned face. "Wave of the future, guys! Best you can do is go with the flow. Hey, Louise. What's happening?"

Carmody was dressed in a three-piece seersucker suit, a concession to the August warmth that also maintained his status as a professional. Patches of sweat under the arms belied the lawyer's easygoing, "hail fellow well met" attitude. Carmody was as thin as Mr. Gray, but where the realtor's slenderness seemed due to a natural abstemiousness, Carmody was skinny like an underfed hound. He air-kissed a reluctant Louise Guildenstern and thumped Quill on the back.

Quill, pleading more calligraphy, made her excuses and retreated topside, where she stayed out of everyone's way until the chatter of guests swarming the gangplank recalled her to managerial duties.

Everything seemed under control, for once. Doreen had found Greek capers at the local Wegman's grocery. She talked Allan O'Brien out of serving flaming rum drinks on the advice of ship's Captain Lucas. Bjarne had apologized to Meg. Meg had apologized to Bjarne. And Quill introduced Louise to a likely widower.

The *Canandaigua Lady* cast off promptly at seven thirty-five, all guests on board and shrieking happily at one another in the comfortable lounge. A half hour later, the little boat bumped and lurched as the guests trooped to the lower deck and seated themselves at dinner.

Everything went well with dinner, too. Quill's sense of unease disappeared altogether. Just before dessert, she sent most of the kitchen and wait staff back to the hotel. Meg turned the dessert and coffee service over to Bjarne, and the two sisters went to the top deck to wait for the party to wind down.

They sat in the moonlight, sipping at a quarter inch of brandy and idly discussing the high points.

They'd run out of the Japanese shrimp (marinated in a peanut soy sauce), the chilled asparagus and prosciutto, and of course, the pasta Quilliam itself. It was always better to have guests demanding more of a dish. It encouraged returns.

Meg had fended off six requests for recipes, the inebriated demand of a twenty-two-year-old broker-in-training to father her children, and accepted a round of applause from the satisfied diners with charming modesty. Quill had handed out a number of the Inn's cards and lined up at least two promises of conventions at the Inn during the off-season. Their business manager, John Raintree, would be very happy about that.

Relaxing in the soft air from the lake, Meg and Quill sat contentedly as the little paddle wheeler chugged up and down the water. "And no bodies!" Quill said. "I'm so thankful that it didn't end in bodies."

"Brose up here?" Allan O'Brien's bald head rose from the starboard stairwell like a dim half-moon.

Quill set her brandy glass on the deck next to her chair and got to her feet. "Mr. Carmody, you mean?"

"A-huh." O'Brien tapped impatiently on the railing, then emerged to stand on deck. His tie was askew. "*Great* dinner, ladies. Just great."

"Thank you," Quill said. "About Mr. Carmody?"

"Sum-a-bitch has to give his speech. 'Our Future on the Internet.' Some sort of garbage like that. Thought he might be up here."

"Maybe he's in the men's room?" Meg suggested with a bored yawn.

O'Brien shook his head dolefully. Quill realized he was a little drunk. "Nope. Not in the head. Looked there. Not in the galley. Looked there. Not in the pilot cabin. Looked—"

"When did you last see him?" Quill cut in, fearful that the list of where Mr. Carmody wasn't would prove exhaustive.

O'Brien squinted painfully. "Drinks?" he said hopefully.

"He's had enough," Meg whispered.

"I think he means in the lounge," Quill said. "Do you mean you haven't seen Mr. Carmody since seven o'clock when you were having drinks in the lounge?"

Mr. O'Brien beamed. "Thass *right*! Part of the reason why it was such a great dinner!"

They found Carmody's body eventually, of course. Quill remembered the hatches in the dining room at one o'clock in the morning. And that's where the body was discovered, curled in the recesses of the forward hatch by the men's room, or "head," as Allan O'Brien insisted on calling it.

"Which means it could have been anyone," Meg said. She peered over her sister's shoulder into the upper lounge. They were standing at the stairwell leading to the galley. The local sheriff and a tired-looking deputy were busily taking the names and addresses of the exhausted realtors. Quill had replenished the coffeepot at least twice, and Mr. O'Brien, for one, seemed on the edge of a caffeine jag.

"Strangled," Quill said thoughtfully. Her eyes went to the corpse, shrouded now in a body bag and waiting for the coroner. "Which argues a man, don't you think?"

Meg shrugged. "It was a thin wire. Didn't require a lot of strength. Just somebody quick."

Quill leaned against the bulkhead. "So it could have been a man or a woman. Carmody arrived here around seven. Allan O'Brien was alone in the lounge. I left Louise alone in the dining room. And I went topside. The wait staff was on shore, having coffee."

"And all the kitchen staff was in the galley."

"And Mr. Gray was in the kitchen with you," Quill said.

"Nope. He left when you took O'Brien and Guildenstern away."

"He didn't come back?"

"Not that I noticed."

Quill didn't make too much of this. When Meg was cooking, World War III could break out and she wouldn't notice.

"Mr. Gray had a motive, though," she said reluctantly. "He mentioned that he had to go back to work because of something about trouble with his pension. Amaryllis is sick, and he needs the realtor's commission he makes."

"So does Louise," Meg said. "You told me she's a single mother raising three kids. And Allan O'Brien's entire life is his business."

"Oh, dear." Quill looked out at the lounge. The sheriff hadn't allowed them to clean up, and the usual after-dinner detritus met her eye. Crumpled napkins. Empty glasses. Food on the floor. "Food on the floor," she said aloud. "Oh, yuck. Come here, Meggie."

She walked over to the corpse, which was guarded by the sleepy deputy sheriff. "The bag," she said. "Could I open it? I mean . . . there's a clue we might have missed."

Without waiting for the deputy's response, she drew the zipper down, took a deep breath, and stared at the unlovely remains of Brose Carmody. She skipped over the distorted face and protruding tongue. "Here," she said. "You see that?" She pointed at Carmody's collar.

"Hands off, miss," the deputy ordered, somewhat belatedly.

"That's a caper," Meg said.

"The caper's murder," the deputy said.

"Yes," Quill said. "I mean no. It's a caper caper, Deputy."

"So Carmody must have been killed after the entrée was served," Meg mused. "And we're looking for a sloppy eater."

"Not after," Quill said. "Before. What kind of caper is it?"

"Oh, nuts." Meg blinked. "Turkish. And the only person in the kitchen before I threw out the Turkish capers . . ."

They turned to look at Mr. Gray. He sat with his hands lightly clasped between his knees, his gaze on the water lapping quietly under the moon. He turned his head slightly. Perhaps he had caught the intensity of Meg and Quill's gaze from the corner of his eye. He nodded at them. For a moment, he looked intensely sad. "All I have left is the life insurance policy," he'd said.

He leaned over and tapped the sheriff politely on the shoulder. "I believe, sir, that you are looking for me."

❖

PASTA QUILLIAM

*Meg's recipe for Pasta Quilliam is truly sensational—
whether you use Turkish or Greek capers is up to you.*

1 pound fresh baby artichokes, or 10-ounce package frozen
   artichoke hearts (not canned marinated artichokes)
¾ pound pancetta (fresh Italian bacon), cut into ¼" dice
2 cloves garlic, minced
1 medium onion, diced
½ cup sun-dried tomatoes in oil, drained and diced
½–1 cup Italian dry white wine
½–1 cup heavy cream (or a combination of heavy cream and
   half-and-half)
salt and pepper to taste
1 pound orrechiete pasta

Prepare artichokes: trim stem to ½ inch, cut off top half,
pull off any tough outer leaves, cut longitudinally into thin
slices, drop into acidulated water (1 tablespoon lemon juice
to one quart of water). Bring a large pot of water to a boil
while you prepare the sauce.

In a large, heavy frying pan, sauté diced pancetta over
medium-low heat until just beginning to brown on the
edges. Add garlic and onion, sauté until soft. Pour off all
but 2–3 tablespoons of the fat, add drained sliced artichokes, and continue to sauté over medium heat until they
are just browning on the edges. Add the white wine and
simmer until reduced to ½ cup. Put the pasta in to cook in
the large pot of boiling water.

To the sauce, add the cream and reduce heat to medium-
low or low, stir until slightly thickened. Add drained diced

sun-dried tomatoes, stir until heated through. Keep the sauce warm while the pasta finishes cooking—check frequently and cook just until al dente. Drain the pasta and turn into a large heated dish, pour the sauce over, and toss to coat the pasta. Serve immediately, offering freshly grated Parmesan cheese.

—CB

Chocolate Moose

Bill and Judy Crider

Sheriff Dan Rhodes didn't go to the Round-Up Restaurant often, but not because the food wasn't good. He didn't go because the food was *too* good.

The portable sign out front told the story with black letters on a white background:

ABSOLUTELY NO CHICKEN
FISH
OR VEGETARIAN DISHES
CAN BE FOUND
ON OUR MENU!

What could be found were huge chicken-fried steaks and mashed potatoes smothered in cream gravy; big, soft rolls served with real butter; cooked-to-order T-bones marbled with fat on a plate beside a gigantic baked potato slathered with real butter, sour cream, and bacon bits; hamburger steaks with grilled onions piled high, along with a mound of french fries or, if you preferred, hand-cut and battered onion rings. And, for dessert, there was a choice of peach or cherry cobbler with vanilla ice cream on top. If you didn't like cobbler, there was chocolate pie, with the best, the richest, the sweetest filling that Rhodes had ever tasted under its inch-thick meringue.

In other words, the Round-Up served good, solid food that stuck to your ribs, put a smile on your face, and, according to many leading physicians, filled your coronary arteries with substances whose effect on your health it was better not to think about.

Which was why Rhodes rarely ate there. His wife, Ivy, had him on a low-fat regimen that was taking inches off his waistline and, she claimed, adding years to his life.

As Rhodes pulled the county car into the Round-Up's black-topped parking lot, he wished, in spite of the risk to his longevity, that he were going there to have a big slice of chocolate pie, or, failing that, maybe one of those baked potatoes. But he wasn't. He was going to see about a man who'd been killed by a moose.

The Round-Up's parking lot was full of people milling around and talking in the eerie light of the sodium vapor lamps. The crowd moved reluctantly out of the way as Rhodes drove the county car as close to the front door as he could get. Rhodes stopped the car and got out.

Sam Blevins was standing there waiting for him. The owner of the Round-Up, Sam, was six feet tall and thin as a ten-penny nail. Either he didn't eat at his own restaurant or he had a better metabolism than Rhodes did. He wore a white western shirt, starched and ironed jeans, and low-heeled boots.

"There wasn't any need for you to come, Sheriff," he said. "It was just a terrible accident."

"That's what Hack told me," Rhodes said. Hack was the county dispatcher, and he'd taken the call. "But since it involved Mack McAnally, I thought I'd better have a look for myself."

Blevins nodded. "I can see why. Nobody liked Mack much."

That was an understatement, Rhodes thought. Not only did nobody like Mack McAnally, most people in Blacklin County despised him if they knew him at all. Even people who didn't know him despised him.

McAnally was, or had been until only a short while earlier, a bully. He had a small income from some gas wells, and he didn't have a regular job. He spent his time working in his yard and harassing any animal that happened to stray onto his property. He had a pellet gun that he used to shoot at dogs and cats and, rumor had it, even the occasional human. When he was driving, he would sometimes swerve out of his lane in an attempt to run over a squirrel or family pet. In the local stores, he would deliberately bump into anyone he thought was in his way, including old folks on walkers. When he backed out of a parking spot, he never looked to see who might be in his way, and he'd been involved in a number of minor accidents, some of which had had legal repercussions. He attended every meeting of the Clearview City Council, often arguing loudly with council members and calling them idiots or worse. But he wouldn't be doing any of those things any longer.

Rhodes went inside the Round-Up, with Blevins at his heels.

"Where is he?" Rhodes asked.

"Right in his usual spot," Blevins said. "He comes . . . *came* in three nights a week—Monday, Wednesday, and Saturday—and he always sat at the same table. One night there was somebody already there, some farm equipment salesman from out of town who didn't know about Mack. He'd asked if he could sit there when Tom was seating him, and Tom just didn't think. Mack came in and grabbed a handful of that salesman's jacket and yanked him right out of the chair. Nearly threw him across the room and into a waitress. She dropped a tea pitcher, and I had to give the salesman a free steak to calm him down."

You're supposed to call them servers these days, not waitresses, Rhodes thought, but he didn't say anything.

The Round-Up was a big building, spread out over a large area and divided into several rooms. Rhodes didn't know where Mack's usual spot was. He asked Blevins to show him.

"Right through here," Blevins said, leading the way.

Rhodes looked around as they went through the main dining room. The walls were festooned with deer antlers of all shapes and sizes. In the spaces between the antlers there were old metal advertising signs covered with images that were no longer commonly seen: Mobil's flying red horse, an RC cola bottle, Speedy Alka-Seltzer, Reddy Kilowatt.

There were only a few diners still seated in the room, and none of them was eating. Rhodes didn't blame them. He doubted that they even heard the song playing on the jukebox that Blevins had stocked with decades-old country music. Hank Snow was telling the world that the gold rush was over and the bum's rush was on.

"I'll unplug that thing in a minute," Blevins said. "Mack's just around the corner."

Rhodes and Blevins went into another room, smaller than the one they'd left, but still large. There were no diners in it, unless you counted McAnally, who was seated at a table by the wall.

Well, Rhodes thought, *seated* wasn't exactly the right word. McAnally was in the chair, true, but he was also facedown in a large piece of chocolate pie, held there by the moose head that had fallen from the wall.

"Got that moose up in Alaska three years ago," Blevins said sadly, shaking his head. "He was a big 'un."

He certainly was, Rhodes thought. Must have weighed fifteen hundred pounds, to judge by the head and antlers, which had a spread of more than four feet. If it had fallen much farther, and if the solid wood tables in the Round-Up had been any less sturdy, the table would have collapsed to the floor.

As it was, when the head had fallen off the wall, the tremendous weight of the antlers had tilted them downward, and they had struck McAnally before the head reached him, with one of the points going right through his neck and cracking the tabletop slightly. The head now rested atop McAnally's body, with most of its weight leaned against the wall.

The antlers had hooked themselves on the cord of an old Dr Pepper clock on the way down and pulled the cord out of the wall outlet. The clock was stopped at exactly eight-thirty, and McAnally had been just about finished with his dinner.

There was blood on the table, seeping into the crack, and chocolate pie filling had splashed up on the moose head. Rhodes didn't think he wanted any pie now.

"How much do those antlers weigh?" Rhodes asked.

"About ninety pounds," Blevins said. "It's all my fault."

Rhodes thought that Blevins was showing a reckless disregard of possible lawsuits, but the restaurant owner was probably on safe ground. As far as Rhodes knew, McAnally didn't have any relatives. Nobody would claim to be his kin.

"I should have anchored that thing to the wall better," Blevins went on. "I thought I'd done a good job, but I guess I was wrong."

Rhodes looked around. There were other trophy heads,

mostly mountain goats, affixed to the wall in this room, mixed in with more metal advertising signs that advertised things like Hadacol, Burpee's seeds, and Red Chain feed. Everything seemed firmly in place.

Rhodes was looking up at the spot where the head had pulled out of the wall when he heard the wailing of the ambulance from the Clearview Hospital.

"Go out there and ask them not to come in yet," Rhodes told Blevins.

The restaurant owner turned and left the room, his boot heels thudding on the floor. He had forgotten to unplug the jukebox, and now Don Gibson was drifting away on the sea of heartbreak.

Rhodes looked to his right. The jukebox was sitting up against the wall only about ten feet from McAnally's table. It appeared to be a reproduction of a classic Wurlitzer, with air bubbles floating through the tubes of liquid colored by the bright lights behind the plastic panels. The bass notes thudded with an authority that Rhodes could feel through the soles of his feet, and he wondered if the subwoofer's vibrations could have dislodged the moose head.

Probably not. Rhodes had a look around the room. There were tables scattered here and there, but none too close to McAnally's regular spot. Rhodes figured that Blevins had arranged things that way.

The door to the rest room was about twelve feet from McAnally's table in the direction opposite the jukebox. There were no tables between McAnally's regular spot and the door. It seemed like a waste of space to Rhodes, but, again, he figured that Blevins had deliberately moved a table in order to give McAnally plenty of room and to keep other customers away from him.

Blevins came back in about that time, to the accompaniment of Merle Haggard, who was reminiscing about having turned twenty-one in prison.

"There's a justice of the peace out there with the ambulance," Blevins said. "He wants to declare Mack dead."

"Mack can wait," Rhodes said. "So can the JP. I want to have a look at that wall."

"The screws just pulled out," Blevins said. "You can see that from here. I thought everything was fine. Heck, I grabbed hold of those horns and swung from them when I mounted that thing up there. I was sure the screws would hold."

"Where's your stepladder?"

"Out back," Blevins said. "I'll go get it."

When Blevins was gone, Rhodes walked around to the side of the table opposite McAnally and pulled out the empty chair. Rhodes thought about standing in the chair and then getting up on the table instead of waiting for the ladder. He put a hand on the chair and tried to shake it. It seemed steady enough, so, avoiding the antlers, he tried the table. When he did, he accidentally knocked over the saltshaker, which spilled a few grains out onto the table.

"Bad luck," Rhodes said aloud, reaching for the shaker to set it upright.

When he moved it, he noticed a couple of shapes like elongated circles near the edge of the table where the shaker had been standing. There was a thickly folded paper napkin nearby. He picked up a few grains of salt and threw them over his left shoulder. He hoped that was the correct procedure. Maybe he should have thrown them over his right shoulder, but it was too late now.

He set the saltshaker upright and looked at the screws that had held the moose head to the wall. There were ten of them, heavy-duty screws, at least four inches long, and they had been screwed solidly into the thick wooden wall. There was still a bit of wood stuck in the grooves near the tip. The heads of the screws showed signs of fresh silver, indicating that a screwdriver had been applied to them fairly recently.

Blevins came back with the stepladder and opened it out. It was plastic, Rhodes noticed. No chance of getting a shock if you accidentally touched a live wire with it.

Rhodes climbed up on the ladder and had a look at the wall. The wood was splintered for about a quarter of an inch at the top of each hole where the sharp ends of the screws had ripped through the wood as they tore loose.

Rhodes climbed down the ladder as Johnny Cash was explaining that he didn't like it, but he guessed things happened that way.

"Has that farm equipment salesman been around lately?" Rhodes asked.

"Not likely," Blevins said, looking over at McAnally's body. "Not even after that free steak I gave him."

"What about the server?"

Blevins looked at him. "Server?"

"Waitress," Rhodes said. "The one McAnally threw the salesman into."

"Oh," Blevins said. "Her name's Julie. She was okay after a day or so. The pitcher landed on her foot, and it was pretty heavy. The pitcher, I mean. It sprained her foot pretty bad, and it left a big bruise. She thought for a while that the foot was broken, but it wasn't. It didn't cripple her or anything. Not permanently at least. It hurt her like hell, though."

"What time did she come to work today?"

"She didn't. She quit right after that. One of the best waitresses I had, but she said she didn't want to wait on Mack ever again. I can't say as I blame her."

"Anybody else on your staff have a grudge against McAnally?" Rhodes asked.

Blevins looked at the man whose face rested in the chocolate pie and nodded.

"Just about all of them," he said. "Why?"

"Because I think one of them killed him," Rhodes said.

The Round-Up had been cleared of customers, and the moose head had been lifted away from Mack McAnally's body and put on the floor near the table.

McAnally himself had been removed to Clyde Ballinger's funeral home, where he would be prepared for his final resting place.

There was still blood on the table, however, and the moose head was still splattered with the chocolate that had spurted up from the pie when McAnally's face smashed into it.

And the jukebox was still playing. Blevins must have completely forgotten about it. Tex Ritter was begging his darlin' not to forsake him, and Rhodes was standing there looking at the restaurant's employees.

All the servers were young women dressed in short red western-style skirts with white fringe, white shirts, red vests with white fringe, flat-crowned red western hats that they wore at a jaunty angle, and roping boots.

All the kitchen employees, cooks, and busboys were male, ranging in age from around eighteen to sixty-five. They were all dressed casually in jeans, sneakers, and cotton shirts, except for the greeter and cashier, Tom Jenks, who was wearing western garb a lot like the outfit sported by Blevins. Jenks wasn't as thin as Blevins, who was standing next to him, however, and the western look didn't seem quite as natural on him.

One of the servers, Frances Abbey, had been assigned to McAnally's table that evening. She was short, with black eyes and dark hair showing under her hat. Rhodes asked if McAnally ever gave her any trouble.

"All the time," she said. Her voice was low, almost a whisper. "He says rude things, and you can never do anything to suit him." Her voice got stronger. "He always complains about the food and the service, and he never leaves a tip."

Rhodes wasn't surprised. "Did you notice anything odd about the moose head tonight?" he asked.

"Not really," she said. She had her hands clasped tightly in front of her.

"What does that mean?" Rhodes wanted to know.

"Well, you know how it is," she said. "It's like, I've worked here for two years now. I know the moose head's there, but I never look at it anymore. I don't remember even looking up at it tonight."

She shuddered slightly as if thinking about what might have happened to her if the moose head had come crashing down while she was standing by the table taking McAnally's order.

"So you don't know if it was tilted away from the wall?"

"No. I never noticed."

"Did anyone notice?" Rhodes asked, addressing everyone there.

No one had. Rhodes hadn't thought anyone would. He was sure the killer had been counting on the same thing.

Rhodes sent the servers home. He didn't think any of them had been involved in McAnally's death, though it was possible. On the jukebox, George Jones was explaining why his old lover thought he still cared.

When the servers had left the room, Rhodes looked over the male employees, all of whom were sitting as far as they could from McAnally's table and looking very uncomfortable, shifting their bodies in the chairs, shuffling their feet on the floor, and avoiding Rhodes's gaze. They all looked guilty to Rhodes, all but Blevins and Tom Jenks, the cashier, who was smiling confidently. So Rhodes decided to start with him.

"What time did you close last night?" he asked Jenks.

"About ten," Jenks said. "We never have any customers much later than that except on weekends."

"Who closed up?"

"Well, I guess you could say I did. Sam always clears the register, and I go around and make sure all the floors are cleaned and the doors are locked."

"Do you have a burglar alarm?"

Jenks looked at Blevins and then back at Rhodes as if the sheriff might have taken leave of his senses.

"What for? There's nothing in the register, and who's gonna steal knives and forks?"

"Just wondering," Rhodes said. "Anybody stay here late, after closing?"

"No," Jenks said. "Everybody was gone. Sherman and Larry do the floors, Toby and Hank and Gene take care of the kitchen. When they're done, they go home. That's when Sam and I finish up."

"The two of you left together last night?"

"That's right. We went through and checked the place, like we do every night. Then we cleared out."

"All right," Rhodes said. "I'd like for everyone to go back to the kitchen except for Mr. Blevins."

The employees seemed more than eager to get out of Rhodes's sight, and they left while Eddy Arnold told the story of the Tennessee stud on the jukebox. Rhodes waited until the room was cleared and then asked Blevins whether McAnally's table was where it always sat.

Blevins turned around and looked.

"You know," he said, "it's not. It's usually a couple of feet down toward the restroom door, exactly halfway between the jukebox and the door. Do you think—?"

"That somebody moved it?" Rhodes said. "Yeah. So it would be right under the moose head. Then someone loosened the screws."

"How do you know that?"

"Because of the way the wood's been ripped," Rhodes

said. "Those screws were just barely into the wood when the head fell. Do you use this room at noon?"

"Sure. We have a good crowd then."

"What about McAnally's table?"

"Well, I've told Tom not to seat anyone there if he doesn't have to. Just in case Mack comes in. He does, or he did, now and then."

"Okay. So who back there is the happiest that McAnally's dead?"

Blevins had to think about it.

"None of them liked him," he said finally. "Tom, especially."

"But he left with you last night."

"That's right. What difference does that make?"

"Whoever loosened those screws must have done it after you were gone. It wouldn't be possible during the day. He'd have been seen. But someone could have stayed inside, maybe in the rest room, and then come out and done the job. It would be easy to get out, since there's no alarm. You'd never know anyone had been here."

"You're right," Blevins said. "Well, there's also Larry Barnes. Mack ran over his dog a week or so ago, or so Larry claimed. Gene Tobin said that Larry spit in Mack's mashed potatoes one night after it happened."

"And Larry's still working here?"

"I'm not sure he really did spit in the potatoes. In fact, I'm sure he didn't. He and Gene don't get along, and Gene's always coming to me with stories and trying to get him fired."

"Which one was Larry?" Rhodes asked.

"The short one. He was sitting right over there."

Blevins pointed to a chair, and Rhodes said, "I don't think he loosened the screws. Too short. Tell me about Gene."

"He was dating Julie," Blevins said. "Maybe he still is. He was really mad about what happened when Mack threw that salesman into her and hurt her foot. I wouldn't be surprised if he'd spit in the potatoes and blamed it on Larry."

"Is he tall?"

"He sure is. The tallest of the bunch. Why?"

"Whoever loosened those screws stood on the table," Rhodes said. "I'm not sure I could reach that high, and I'm six feet tall."

"Well, Larry's got four inches on you. But if he did it, how did he get the head to fall?"

"Let's go to the rest room," Rhodes said.

They walked down to the door, and Rhodes asked Blevins to open it. It opened much too easily.

"I need to check the pneumatic closer," Blevins said. "Next thing you know, that door will be slamming shut. People don't like that."

"Try slamming it now," Rhodes said.

"Huh?"

"See what happens when you shut it as hard as you can."

Blevins opened the door, then shoved it shut from the inside. When it hit the frame, the whole wall shuddered. He opened the door and looked out at Rhodes.

"You think that's what did it?" he asked.

"I'd bet on it," Rhodes said.

"Wouldn't people notice?"

"With that moose head falling off the wall on McAnally at the very same time? Not a chance."

"I guess you're right," Blevins said.

Rhodes nodded. "Probably. Let's talk to Gene and find out."

Gene Tobin was probably eighteen, and he was at least six-four. Maybe more. He had unruly hair and long, thin arms that would easily have reached the highest of the screws. He wouldn't meet Rhodes's eye.

"I don't know what you're talking about," he said when Rhodes told him what he thought.

"You probably didn't mean to kill him," Rhodes said. "You probably just wanted to scare him. Is that right?"

"I didn't want to scare anybody. Or kill them, either. What are you talking about?"

"I just told you. You fixed the head so it would fall, and then you made it happen."

"I'd be crazy to do something like that," Gene said. "How could I know it wouldn't hit somebody else?"

"You couldn't," Rhodes said. "But hardly anyone ever sat there, so you weren't taking much of a chance. Just like you weren't taking much of a chance that anyone would notice the moose head was leaning. And like you figured no one would notice the folded napkin you put under the mounting to keep the head as straight as possible."

"I didn't do any of that," Gene said. He still wouldn't look at Rhodes directly.

"It's easy enough to prove you didn't," Rhodes said.

"How?"

"Let me see the bottom of your shoe."

"What for?"

"To prove you didn't do it," Rhodes said. "Come over here."

Gene walked over to where Rhodes was standing, and Rhodes pointed to the top of the table where McAnally had sat.

"See those little flattened circles?" Rhodes said. "Someone put them there when he stood on this table. I think it was you. So have a seat, and we'll take a look at your shoes."

Gene looked down at his feet, at the pair of ragged old white Adidas shoes he was wearing. Then he turned and ran.

Rhodes wasn't nearly as young as Gene, but he was still quick, and he caught the younger man before he got to the front door. When Gene felt Rhodes's hand on his shirt, he quit running, as if he knew he didn't have a chance. His thin shoulders slumped.

"I didn't mean to kill him," he said. "Even if he was a bastard. I just wanted to scare him, that's all."

By that time Blevins had caught up with them.

"The hell you didn't mean to kill him," Blevins said. "You moved the table, Gene, for God's sake."

"He won't be wanting you for his defense attorney," Rhodes said.

As he took Gene out to the county car for the ride to jail, Webb Pierce was wailing on the jukebox in the background, but Rhodes couldn't quite make out the words.

⬛

WORLD'S BEST CHICKEN-FRIED STEAK

Enough round steak (about a half inch thick) to cut into eight
    pieces of 5 or 6 inches in diameter.
3 eggs
3 tablespoons of milk
Flour
Salt and pepper
Cooking oil

Combine the eggs with the milk and beat the mixture with a fork. Combine the flour with the salt and pepper. Pour the oil in a heavy skillet (a big, black, well-seasoned iron skillet if you have one). The oil should be about a half-inch deep. Heat the oil at a moderate to hot temperature.

Dip the pieces of steak into the egg mixture and then into the seasoned flour. Shake off the excess and then dip the steak into both mixtures again. After each piece is dipped the second time, put it straight into the hot oil. Whatever you do, don't let the coated steak sit around before you start frying it.

Cook each piece of steak until the batter is crisp on the bottom side. Don't touch it or disturb the coating. When it's done, turn it very carefully and cook the other side. When that side's done, take it out of the pan and drain it on a paper towel.

Since chicken-fried steak is nothing without thick gravy, here's the gravy recipe. For eight pieces of steak, you'll probably need two cups.

◼

WORLD'S BEST CHICKEN-FRIED STEAK GRAVY

2 or 3 tablespoons of cooking oil
2 or 3 tablespoons of flour
1 cup of warm milk
Salt and pepper

Drain the extra oil from the skillet after you've fried the steak, leaving any of the crispy brown bits of the coating that might have fallen off and approximately 3 tablespoons of oil (2 tablespoons if you want slightly thinner gravy). Add the salt and pepper and the 3 tablespoons of flour (or 2 if you want the slightly thinner gravy). Stir the mixture and cook it until the flour starts to turn brown (not too brown, whatever you do). Then add the warm milk and cook and stir the mixture until it thickens. Serve the gravy over the steak and pour it on the side dish of mashed potatoes, which you should also cook. Chicken-fried steak without mashed potatoes is like a day without sunshine.

—BJC

THE FIXER

CAMILLA T. CRESPI

Edwina Culver nearly fell off the stool when Henry Culver strode in her upstairs sitting room.

"*You* scared me, Henry."

"I came home early." He held up three letters, one of which he had opened. "Pray tell, Edwina, what is the meaning of this?"

Edwina shuddered, as if suddenly chilled. "Maria, the waist on this gown is far too tight!"

"I shall fix it, signora," the seamstress said, knowing full well the waist was a perfect fit.

Henry stepped closer. He was a tall, heavyset man in his forties, with a heavily lined face that was still handsome. "I'm due at my club, Edwina, and I would appreciate an answer."

Edwina met her husband's gaze with difficulty. It had once been brimming with love for her. Now his expression was filled with loathing she had done nothing to deserve. The unfairness of it gave her courage to speak out.

"Please understand, Henry. We cannot possibly give a dinner tomorrow night, as Mrs. Maguire has taken sick and

Molly can barely boil an egg. I took the liberty of writing to our guests to postpone the dinner. Hartford was to deliver the letters immediately."

Henry pulled a face. "It's fortunate that I came home early and stopped him. It's bad form to cancel at the last minute. You will agree we cannot announce publicly that we have been stymied by a cook who eats herself sick."

Edwina reached for Maria's hand. It's roughness was reassuring. "How do you know it was something Mrs. Maguire ate? Dr. Bailey said it was her heart."

Henry came closer, his eyes grazing the pewter-gray charmeuse slip over which Maria was fitting a shorter two-tiered pale gray chiffon gown.

"This fashion may be the latest rage in Paris," he said, "but you are far too thin and shapeless for Monsieur Poiret's straight style. Mrs. Maguire, on the other hand, is as large as the biggest water tower in Gotham, and growing. If she does not restrain herself from eating sweets, she will kill herself. Find another cook, Edwina. I will not have this dinner postponed." Henry turned on his heels and left, the letters now in his pocket.

His departure brought no relief to his wife. "Please unbutton me, Maria," she said. "There is no hurry for the gown now."

Maria did as she was told. "It is finished except for the hem."

"It is a beautiful gown. Thank you." Edwina stepped down from the stool and out of her dress. She wouldn't find a cook. She would become ill herself before she would allow Mrs. Foley to enter her home, sit in her drawing room, eat from her table. Mrs. Foley was a trollop!

Wearing the latest inventions of ladies' fashions—a brassiere and the new straight corset that locked her in down to her knees—Mrs. Culver, in Maria's eyes, looked like a young bird caught in a trap. After only three years of marriage, a desperately unhappy bird. Pretty in the pale watercolor way of most blondes, Mrs. Culver was also spoiled and willful. If only she had listened to her father and not married Henry Culver.

"I will cook for you," Maria offered. She had been devoted to Mrs. Culver's father, who had given her her first job in this new, terrifying country she had come to from Naples only four years ago. Judge Ashton had made her study hard, saying the future would be closed to her if she did not know the language of the land. When he had died six months ago, he had left her enough money to set up her own dressmaking business. In turn, Maria had promised herself she would help his daughter any way she could. "I am good at cooking when I give my heart to it."

"Thank you, but no." Edwina lowered herself down in a blue brocade armchair that matched the color of her eyes and fought tears of humiliation. The entire sitting room was blue and stuffed with knickknacks: ormolu clocks, silk flowers, stuffed birds in glass cages, gilt-framed mirrors that caught your every movement. It gave Maria a headache. She knelt beside Mrs. Culver. "Forgive me, signora, I know it is not my place to say, but I will say it. It is not by making more anger that you will win back Mr. Culver's love."

Edwina pressed her handkerchief to her mouth, her large eyes widening with anguish. "Does the whole world know, then?" Tears scurried out of her eyes, leaving tracks on her powdered cheeks. "Oh, Maria, Papa was so right."

"Do you love your husband?"

"No! He has revealed himself to be a horrid man, but my greatest fear is that he will divorce me. I couldn't stand the shame of it."

"If he does, you will finally do as you wish. Do not forget that your father has left you a rich woman, signora. You will not have to answer to anyone."

"Oh, Maria, you don't know the ways of society. All doors will be closed to me."

Maria stood up, her cheeks burning with anger. "Why do you let society tell you how to live? This is a free country, is it not? That is why I and millions of others like me have come to America. It cannot be that the privilege of democracy is enjoyed only by the immigrants. You are young, pretty, rich. Let Mr. Culver divorce you if that is what he wishes. Begin again with your head held high. Let us immigrants be an example to you. We are poor, perhaps. We have made mistakes, as you have perhaps, but there is no shame in wanting a better life for us."

"A divorced woman has no life," Edwina said, and wept.

Maria bent down to dry Mrs. Culver's tears with her own handkerchief. "Will not your society close the doors on Mr. Culver, too, if he divorces? He has an important career as a lawyer, no?"

"For a few years perhaps, but the rules are more lenient for men. Divorce or not, Henry will not leave that woman. He is besotted by her. She is far more beautiful than I."

"What you need, signora, is not more beauty, but a plan."

"What plan do you mean?"

"Start with the dinner. I will cook for you a fine dish. Pasticcio di primavera. A springtime cake made with strands of dough as fine as angel hair. It is Italian cooking, but give it a French name and your guests will be very admiring."

"What good will it do?"

Maria allowed herself a rare smile. "It will give us time." She stood up and gathered the gown. There was much to do. Hemming, shopping, kneading, questions to be asked. "Do not worry, Mrs. Culver. Maria is a good seamstress. She will fix it."

Edwina looked at the expression of calm strength on

Maria's plain, square face and suddenly felt filled with optimism.

Mrs. Maguire lay in her bed, her carrot-red hair covered by a ruffled cap that made Maria think of a gigantic jar of marmalade.

"For you," Maria said, dropping an embroidered satin pincushion on Mrs. Maguire's vast chest. The cook picked up the cushion between two fingers and studied it as though it were a mushroom that might prove to be poisonous.

"Why, thank you, Miss Maria, much obliged." She didn't sound one bit obliged, Maria noted with good humor. Mrs. Maguire made her suspicion of foreigners very clear, in particular "Eyetalian" women foisting themselves on lonely widower gentlemen who then up and died and left the foreigner with more money than the cook.

Maria settled herself on the ladder-back chair without waiting to be asked. She meant to stay awhile in Mrs. Maguire's comfortable fourth-floor bedroom.

"You are feeling better, I hope? What does the doctor say?"

"I need my rest, I do. It was awful."

"I'm so sorry. Everyone downstairs misses you very much. The house isn't the same without you." Maria meant what she said. Mrs. Maguire was a superb cook, but most importantly a kind woman underneath her bluster. "I hope your suffering is over." Mrs. Maguire seemed somewhat mollified by Maria's obvious sincerity. "A few more days of broth and toast. I might even lose me a few pounds. Now, wouldn't that be a laugh?" The bed shook with Mrs. Maguire's chortling.

"Mr. Culver is most upset," Maria said.

"Mr. Culver's only worried about his fancy dinner."

"Important, is it?"

"Two of his partners in the law firm are coming. Mr. Stafford and Mr. Gibson. There's bad blood between them."

Maria leaned forward. "Bad blood?"

"Hartford heard it from Mr. Stafford's butler." Hartford was the Culvers' butler. "Mr. Culver is deep into debt because of that woman's extravagances."

"Mrs. Culver?"

"No, no!" Mrs. Maguire's bosom rose in protest. "He hasn't been buying her anything since the mistress inherited her own money. He's miffed that the Judge left it so that he can't touch her money, which is a good thing the way things are going." The bed creaked as Mrs. Maguire leaned over. Maria could feel her hot breath on her face. "I was talking about"—her voice sank to a hoarse whisper—"the other woman."

Maria made a clicking sound with her tongue and tried to look suitably horrified.

"The partners in the law firm are most upset, is what I hear. Mr. Stafford's butler overheard talk of them asking Mr. Culver to leave the firm."

Maria clucked again and wondered why Mr. Culver had invited Mrs. Foley to the same dinner with his partners. Was he defying them, convinced he did not need them anymore? Was he counting on her beauty to disarm them or was he so in love he no longer saw reason? "I'm sure that will not happen, Mrs. Maguire. Now, I came to hear about you. How did you get sick? You have always had good health."

Mrs. Maguire's dimpled face darkened into a scowl. "Dr. Bailey says it's my heart, but what does he know after drinking half a bottle of my cooking sherry? My heart's made of iron, it is. It's my stomach that done me in.

"Last week Mr. Culver came home with a box of chocolate-covered cherries for the mistress. Usually she'll gobble them up as quick as a wink she likes them so much, but I suppose this time Mrs. Culver was too upset over that woman coming to her home. Yesterday morning, down she comes to the kitchen—it's not often that happens—and offers the box to me and Molly.

"'Now, aren't you the kind lady,' I said to her, and popped two in my mouth. Half an hour later I had to run and—never you mind what I had to do." Mrs. Maguire fell back on her pillow and crinkled her eyes shut. "Awful it was!"

Maria pulled her chair closer. "It must have been terrible."

"Thank the good Lord I only ate two. I might have been dead otherwise. The mistress sent for the doctor right away. She was crying and praying. Devoted she is to me."

"What happened to the rest of the chocolates?"

"I had Molly bring me the box. It was empty! I only ate two chocolates, I'll swear to that in a court of law. Now, mind you, Molly was so scared seeing me in that state, she probably flushed them down the toilet. That's what I would have done. I told Mr. Culver to keep a lookout. No sense anyone else getting sick."

"Did you warn Mrs. Culver?"

"How could I? She was the one who gave them to me. She was upset enough as it was."

"Are you sure the chocolates made you sick?"

"It was that little bit of liquor in the chocolate, is what I think. Foreign 'bonbons,' they were. From Paree. What's wrong with Made in America? I hope you don't mind my saying so, Miss Maria."

"Not at all. You are a very lucky woman to have been born in this country." Maria stood up, said good-bye, and promised she would send Molly up with tea.

Down in the kitchen, Molly, a thin weed of a girl, told Maria that she got hives from chocolates.

"And I'm not stupid. Those chocolates are too expensive to throw in the toilet!"

"Did you see anyone take them?"

"How could I? My eyes were too busy takin' in the sight of poor Mrs. Maguire on the floor throwing up her heart."

Hartford swore he had not even seen the chocolate box. Edith, the parlormaid, had nothing to add. Yesterday had been her day off.

Maria put on her cloak and her bonnet. The disappearing chocolates frightened her. Mrs. Culver was either a very foolish woman or in grave danger.

The next morning Maria carefully hung the thin strands of pasta she had just made over the kitchen chairs to dry. She had slept little the night before. Try as she might, she could not come up with a way to help Mrs. Culver. She doubted that Mr. Culver would divorce his wife now that she was rich, and Mrs. Culver certainly did not have the courage to divorce him and face the ensuing scandal. What was left?

"Isn't Molly helping you?" Edwina Culver asked from the doorway.

"Molly has taken breakfast to Mrs. Maguire," Maria said, continuing to hang the strands of pasta. "I am used to working alone. I prefer it. By the time you explain, it can already be done."

Edwina took a few hesitant steps into the dark basement room. Maria looked up. "What is it, signora?" Mrs. Culver looked dreadful. Her long curls were disheveled, her eyes red and swollen. Her blue silk bathrobe was covered in wrinkles, as if it had been wrung dry.

Maria lifted the angel-hair pasta from the back of a chair and pulled it out from under the table. "Please sit down. Let me make you some coffee."

"Please no, you have enough to do." Mrs. Culver sat down, her head held between her hands, as if overnight it had become too heavy for her neck to bear. "Do you have a plan yet?"

"Give me more time, signora. When I cook a dinner as important as this one, I cannot think of anything else." Maria went to the sink and began to snap off the ends of string beans. "Forgive my back, but I must keep working."

Edwina was grateful. Not having to look Maria in the face allowed her to speak more easily. "I have a plan. It came to me last night after my visit with Mrs. Maguire. You will think it a foolish, sinful one, but please listen and please do not interrupt me."

Maria continued to snap.

"Mrs. Maguire told me you had gone to see her, then she told me about the chocolates. My heart shattered. I would have eaten the entire box if I hadn't been so upset! Instead, I almost killed Mrs. Maguire, who has never done me any harm." She clenched her jaw to stop herself from crying. She was filled with fear and horror, but also with an odd exhilaration.

"Please, Maria, I want you to do me this one enormous favor. If not for me, for the memory of my sweet papa."

Maria turned round. "I owe the Judge all that is good in my life. What is it you want from me?"

Edwina looked away, at the copper pots and pans gleaming on the far wall of the kitchen. "My husband has tried to poison me. Now I ask you to buy me a poison. I ask you to put it in the springtime cake this evening. I ask you to mark where you put the poison and tell me what the mark is so I will not make a mistake when Hartford serves me. You may not know that the hostess is always served first so the guests' food does not grow cold waiting for me."

Maria said nothing.

Edwina reached inside the pocket of her bathrobe and took out a folded sheet of paper. "I have already written to Mr. Culver." She held out the sheet to Maria, who turned back to her string beans. "Don't you want to read it?"

"It is difficult enough to listen."

Edwina unfolded the letter and read it out loud: "Dear Henry, I do not wish to live without your love. Since you wish me to be gone, I set you free, and leave you a rich man. Both will make you happy. With all my devotion, your loving wife, Edwina."

She was crying again. Did she have the courage to do such a sinful thing? Could she bear the pain?

"You will do this for me, Maria? Something quick."

Maria came over with a damp dishcloth and washed Mrs. Culver's face. A silly woman, was Mrs. Culver, thinking she wouldn't understand. A woman full of wounded vanity that did not allow her to see beyond her pretty upturned nose. But Judge Ashton had loved his daughter deeply. "Poison is always painful, signora. Mr. Culver has a revolver in his desk drawer, I believe. You put the barrel in your mouth, pull the trigger, and it is over. That would be best."

Mrs. Culver pushed Maria's hand away. "You sound so heartless!"

"What you are asking me to do is heartless, signora, but I understand. In the south of Italy, where I come from, the suffering of the heart is always dramatic and the cause of desperate gestures."

Edwina pressed her handkerchief to her nose. "My husband wanted me dead by poison and that's how I shall die."

"As you wish." Maria untied her apron. Perhaps Mrs. Culver's plan was not a terrible one. "I will go to find Peppe,

the Sicilian. He lives next door to me on Mulberry Street
and knows everything about plants *and* their poisons. I
promise on your father's memory, signora, I will help you."

A fresh burst of tears fell from Edwina's eyes. This time
from sheer relief.

"I am very sad to hear of Mr. O. Henry," Mrs. Foley was
saying as the guests entered the dining room. "I enjoyed his stories so."

"His death was quite sudden, it seems," Mr. Culver said.

Edwina placed her hand over her heart to quiet it. Let it
be sudden, she prayed silently as she surveyed the dining
table. The silverware flickered underneath the hundred candles of the chandelier. The Meissen china gleamed. The
pink peonies shined brightly against the white linen tablecloth that had been part of her dowry. Maria had taken many
hours to embroider it with white forget-me-nots. Blessed
Maria, always there to help.

Edwina sat down and watched Mrs. Foley take her place
between her husband's partners. They had both looked dis-
pleased when Henry had introduced the woman to them,
but now, Edwina noted, they could not keep their eyes
away. Neither could their wives. The woman was wearing
an outlandish gown in eye-blinding Oriental colors—green,
yellow, orange. On her head a jeweled circlet sprouting an
osprey feather dyed purple, of all colors! Edwina heaved a
great sigh of relief. Soon her eyes would never see that
woman again.

Hartford approached and lay Maria's pasticcio in front
of his mistress. It was a truly beautiful dish. A cake of fine
dough ribbons intertwined with the hopeful colors of spring
vegetables. Maria had already cut the poisoned wedge, a
subtle marking that only she, Edwina Ashton Culver, could
see because she knew what to look for.

Edwina plunged the knife into the soft center of the cake, releasing a deliciously mouthwatering odor. She lifted the wedge. The pasta was filled with asparagus spears, bits of string beans, slices of mushrooms, flecks of tomatoes, and the best part—black dots she knew were the seeds of the English yew that Peppe the Sicilian had sold to Maria. The pain would start in one or two hours at the most. It would be over quickly, Maria had promised.

After carefully placing the serving of pasta on the dinner plate before her, Edwina looked up at her guests. Could they not hear the hammering of her heart?

"It looks marvelous," Mrs. Foley exclaimed.

"It's the latest rage in Paris," Edwina said. "They call it bonté du Printemps. Now, you will excuse my breach of etiquette." She could barely bring the words out, her mouth was so dry. "As it is a new dish in our home"—she handed the dish to Hartford—"I would like to give the honor of the first taste to my dear husband."

Henry's eyes gleamed a smile across the table. "You flatter me, Edwina, but I fear that tonight I can only watch the rest of you eat." He raised his hand to stop any questions that might come. "A slight stomach upset. Nothing to be concerned about."

Hartford stood nearby, his face impassive, his glove hand holding up the plate, waiting for new instructions.

"If you don't mind, my dear," Henry said, "why not let our new guest have the first taste?"

Edwina felt a moment's despair, then she looked at Mrs. Foley preening like a peacock. A far too beautiful peacock. In the hallway, the long case clock chimed eight-thirty.

Edwina sat taller in her chair. "Please serve Mrs. Foley first, Hartford."

The ormolu clock on the upstairs sitting-room mantel chimed eleven. Mrs. Culver paced the room. Less than an hour before, with dinner over, she had led the ladies to the withdrawing room. Before they had a chance to sit down, Mrs. Foley had turned quite pale and hastily excused herself. Edwina had almost blurted out the truth, but Maria had warned her that nothing could stop the poison. There was nothing anyone could do. Why hadn't she snatched the plate from her? She would never forgive herself. Thank God at least Henry was safe. How stupid she had been to think she had the stomach for murder.

It was a tragic mistake, she would tell the police. "The poison was meant for me! I wanted to die!" Now she really did want to die. It was the only honorable way to free herself from Henry. It was the only way to atone for killing Mrs. Foley. Maria would help her again. She had already written the suicide note. Where was it?

Edwina checked the pockets of her bathrobe, the drawers of her secretary. She lifted pillows, knickknacks. Where had she put it?

The click of a door opening made her look up sharply. Someone was in the bedroom. Whoever it was must have come in through the hallway door. "Molly, is that you? Maria, are you still here?" She noticed the door that led to her bedroom was ajar. "Henry?"

"I'm here, Edwina."

Edwina spun around with a gasp of surprise. Henry was filling the second doorway, the one that led to the hall. He reeked of cigars and port. She would have to tell him now. To delay would be suspicious.

"Henry, did you just come from my bedroom?"

"I've come up from the library to tell you the dinner was delicious. Do thank Maria. She must not take Mrs. Foley's indisposition to heart. These things happen, as I well know."

Edwina fluttered her hands in front of her face.

"What are you upset about, dear? Didn't Molly bring you your tea? You look as though you might need it more than ever."

Edwina walked over to the pie crust table in the corner. She'd forgotten about her nightly camomile. It might help. If nothing else, it would give her time.

The cup rattled against the saucer in her hand. "Henry, something dreadful has happened. I don't know how to begin."

"Sit down, drink your tea, and then you'll tell me all about it."

Mrs. Culver sat in a gilt-framed armchair and took her first sip. She swallowed with a grimace. "It's cold and needs sugar."

"Shall I ask Molly to make another cup?"

Edwina shook her head.

"Well, drink up, then. I'm all ears to hear what you have to say that is so dreadful." Henry lowered his large frame on the chaise longue and watched, in the cheval glass, his wife struggling to finish the rest of the tea. She was used to obeying.

Mrs. Culver placed the empty cup and saucer on the table at her elbow. Tears came easily. "Henry, I've been so unhappy, I meant to kill myself tonight."

Henry roared with laughter.

Edwina widened her eyes. "My wishing to die amuses you?"

"Did you actually think your dumb scheme would work? Maria came to me, as well she should, and told me what you were up to. She believed you really did want to kill yourself and was quite distraught. That woman adored your father and wouldn't let you come to any harm. You should have considered that. But then you have never had the brains to consider anything, have you?"

Edwina felt her heart cave in. "I did want to kill myself. Maria made a mistake in the marking. That's how Mrs. Foley got the poison."

"You cannot fool me, my dear. You wanted to kill me and there *was* no poison."

"But I saw it! Black seeds."

"Peppercorns, Maria said."

"But Mrs. Foley—" Perspiration beaded on Edwina's forehead. Her stomach suddenly cramped. "She became ill!"

"I'm sure that biting into peppercorns is not particularly pleasant, but Mrs. Foley's indisposition and hasty retreat was my idea."

A slash of pain cut across Edwina's stomach. She doubled over from the sharpness of it.

"Injecting something nasty into the chocolates was another silly idea. I might have lost an excellent cook."

"A few drops to make her sick. No more. I didn't want that woman—" Edwina gasped. The cramps were coming fast now. "Henry, help me." She dropped to the floor. "Henry, please, I'm in pain!"

"What did you use? Your father's heart medicine? I was planning to use it myself on you, but being such an obvious suspect, I hesitated. But tonight you gave me the golden opportunity. You must forgive me, dear Edwina, but Mrs. Foley has very expensive tastes and I cannot live without her." A shadow seemed to fall over Henry's eyes at the possibility of life without Mrs. Foley's stunning red-haired beauty by his side. "Truly I cannot."

Edwina could only protest with a rending stomach growl.

Henry drew himself up straight, the shadow gone. "Bear the pain, dear. In an hour it will be over."

"The tea!" Edwina screamed, and lashed out at the teacup, which fell on the flowered Chinese carpet.

Henry chuckled. "Made with the leaves of the yew. I prepared your tea and gave it to Molly. That plant is a veritable arsenal of poison. Seeds, bark, leaves, they'll all kill you, Maria told me. Useful woman. Her friend Peppe the Sicilian was quite obliging. Nasty-looking fellow."

"H-e-e-nry!" Edwina rocked, clutching her stomach.

"Calm yourself, dear wife. There isn't anything you can do. I have poisoned you and you will die." Henry leaned forward in his armchair, his joviality gone. "Where's that suicide note you so conveniently wrote?"

The door to the bedroom swung open without a sound. "There is no note, Mr. Culver," Maria said.

Henry snapped to his feet. "What do you mean?"

Edwina started whimpering.

Maria stepped aside to reveal a stump of a man with tar-black hair, a hawk nose, and bushy whiskers that hid his mouth. His eyes were hidden behind dark glasses. "Mr. Culver, you already know Peppe il Siculo."

Peppe bowed his head.

"Peppe was a gardener in Palermo before coming to this country. Now he still has a devotion to plants, but also to his new duty as a sergeant in the New York Police Department."

Henry lunged toward the door that led to the hallway. "My wife has tried to kill herself. I must call a doctor." Peppe reached the door before him, a Smith & Wesson .38 Special in his hand.

"Let Mr. Culver make his telephone call, Peppe. He cannot go far with the house surrounded by your colleagues."

Peppe stepped aside to let Mr. Culver pass.

"I am dying!" Edwina cried.

Maria bent over a weeping Mrs. Culver. "*Cara signora.* I promised I would fix it, but first I had to see if there was any love left between you and Mr. Culver. Was your plan to kill yourself, Mrs. Foley, or your husband? I did not know, so I pretended to believe you. Then I told Mr. Culver, to see what he does. The result is no love at all."

Edwina howled, "Poison!"

"No, signora. What Peppe gave your husband was not poison, but a strong laxative. Forgive me, it was necessary to trick Mr. Culver."

The sound of the gunshot came just as Maria slipped her arms under Mrs. Culver's armpits. Edwina screamed. Peppe ran out of the room. Maria heaved her client to her feet.

"You are a free woman now, signora. Tomorrow you will be fine. Your husband was deep into debt, his law partners wanted him to leave the firm, and he was a man too proud to ask his wife for money. He chose the gentleman's way out. That is all anyone will know."

Maria felt Mrs. Culver shake under her hands. She was in shock, as well she should be. Tomorrow the woman would wail about the scandal, but Maria knew there was a solution to that, too. After a suitable period of mourning, a long trip to *la bella Italia* would restore hope. Judge Ashton had loved Italy. He would approve.

"Now let me help you to the bathroom, signora."

◼

PASTICCIO DI PRIMAVERA

SPRINGTIME PASTA AND VEGETABLE CAKE

1 bunch asparagus, each cut about 4 inches long, then cut into thirds
2 small zucchinis, cut into ¼-inch slices
1 ½ cup string beans, trimmed and cut into 1-inch lengths
1 cup frozen baby peas
3 tablespoons olive oil
1 pound mushrooms, thinly sliced
Salt and freshly grounded pepper

½ teaspoon dried red pepper flakes
4 tablespoons flat-leafed parsley, chopped
1 teaspoon garlic, finely chopped
3 cups ripe tomatoes, cut into ½-inch slices
8 fresh basil leaves torn into small pieces or 1 teaspoon dry
1 pound fresh angel-hair pasta
½ cup heavy cream
1 ½ cups freshly grated Parmesan cheese
1 tablespoon butter

1. Steam green vegetables separately until crisp and tender. Run under cold water (except zucchini) to stop cooking process. Drain and combine in a large mixing bowl. Season well.

2. Heat oven to 400 degrees.

3. Set salted water to boil in a large pot.

4. Heat 1 tablespoon of oil in a large skillet. Add mushrooms. Sauté in two batches if necessary, adding another tablespoon of oil after the first batch. Season and sauté until mushroom liquid has evaporated and slices take on a golden color. Add to vegetables along with parsley and red pepper flakes.

5. Wipe skillet clean and use to heat 1 tablespoon of oil. Add garlic and tomatoes. Sauté for 3–4 minutes. Add basil. Season well and fold into vegetable mixture.

6. Spray a 9 ½-inch springform pan with cooking spray. Cover outside of pan with aluminum foil to prevent leakage. Place pan on an edged cookie sheet.

7. Drop pasta in boiling water. Stir often to prevent strands from sticking together. Cook until al dente (about 3 minutes if using fresh pasta). Drain and mix with vegetables.

8. Add ⅔ cup of Parmesan cheese to pasta and mix well. Pour into springform pan and press down well with the back of a large spoon. Sprinkle rest of Parmesan on top of pasta. Dot with butter.

9. Cook in oven for 25 minutes. For a crusty top, remove from oven after 20 minutes and broil for 5 minutes.

10. Let cool for 2 minutes. Remove tin foil from pan. Place pan on a round serving platter. Release and remove rim. Bring to table and serve by cutting wedges with a sharp knife. Serves 8.

—CTC

EVEN BUTTERFLIES
CAN STING

MIKE RESNICK

If Marlowe could have laughed, he'd have been rolling
on the floor, holding his sides and gasping for breath.
Marlowe's my dog. I don't like him much. He doesn't
like me at all. But we're all each other's got, so I feed him
and he hangs around.

Right at the moment, he was staring intently at me as I
was struggling with the black tie. He'd been watching me
for the better part of half an hour as I cursed my way
through the suspenders, cummerbund, and the cuff links.
He cocked his head to one side and grinned—yeah, I know,
dogs can't grin . . . but no one ever told that to Marlowe—
as if to say that everything that went before was merely
amusing, but my struggle with the tie was hilarious.

It wasn't that I was a stranger to tuxedos. I'd worn one
to my junior prom in high school, and that had only been
twenty-seven years ago. Well, maybe twenty-eight. I could
have sworn that first one was a lot easier to get into.

Maybe it's just that I was out of practice. I only owned
two neckties, and I never untied them. I just slipped them
over my head and slid the knots up, like you do on a noose.

The only cuff links I'd seen in the past decade were the fake gold ones that Benny Fourth Street gave me as collateral for a twenty-dollar loan right before he took off for Gulfstream Park.

I looked at the face in the mirror. It glared back accusingly at me, as if to ask why I was inflicting all this suffering and humiliation on it.

The answer was easy: money.

I can still remember receiving the call from Bill Striker. He and I had been cops at the same time, and we had become private eyes at the same time. And there all resemblance ceased. The Striker Agency was the biggest in Cincinnati. Their clients all knew how to tie black ties, except for the *really* rich ones, who just knew how to hit home runs or throw touchdown passes or sing rock songs. *My* clients—on those occasions I had any clients—paid me with phony gold cuff links.

Striker had heard I'd needed money (so what else was new?) and he thought he'd throw a little work my way. I was just a bit leery, since the last time he'd tossed me a bone it had teeth and damned near bit my ass off in a Mexican slum. But his information about my finances was dead-on, so I figured I would at least listen to his proposition.

It seems that one of his clients was Clara Bigelow, the uncrowned queen of the Cincinnati Opera Society. The organization was having its annual formal dinner, and she was planning on wearing her diamond earrings, which were worth a cool half million an ear, and she wanted a bodyguard. But no one ever gets as rich as Clara by tipping the chauffeur or remembering the maid's birthday, and she told Striker that since she was leaving the matching necklace at home, and it was worth another two million, she would only pay a third of his agency's usual fee.

He spent an hour trying to explain that what she wore

didn't influence the service she would get, and when she refused to budge, he knew it was time to farm the job out to someone who needed the work—and the aggravation— more than he did.

Enter Eli Paxton, cut-rate protector of opera ladies' diamonds.

At least I would be, if I ever figured out the intricacies of the damned tie.

I finally managed to wrestle it into a respectable bow. I checked my watch—six-thirty. Her limo would be pulling up in about five minutes. I decided to go downstairs and wait for it. It was easy to spot. Whiter than a bridal gown and longer than a dinosaur. I opened the back door and bent my head down, preparing to climb in.

"The hired help sits in front," said a wiry silver-haired woman in a brocaded satin pantsuit. She was smoking a cigarette in an exquisite jeweled holder. I didn't even have to check her ears to know it was Clara Bigelow; the manner said it all.

"Yes, ma'am," I said. "I'll be happy to."

"And if you ever work for me again," she added as I closed the door, "learn how to tie a necktie."

If I ever work for you again, I'll know that an ice-skating rink has opened in hell, I thought, but I smiled and assured her I would.

Her driver, a heavyset black guy in a uniform that made him look like a refugee from a halftime marching band, shot me a sympathetic look. He didn't say a word, though. I didn't blame him.

We drove in perfect silence to Nicole's Restaurant. I'd walked past Nicole's a few times, and once in a while I wondered exactly what it was that made its lunches cost a hundred bucks apiece while its dinners ran into *real* money. Now I'd finally get a chance to find out.

The limo pulled up to the front door. I scrambled out, intent on making a good impression by opening the door for the old girl, but a pair of uniformed doormen, dressed like two of the Three Musketeers, beat me to it. She emerged, shot me a contemptuous glare, and walked into the restaurant. I fell into step behind her and got my first good look at the earrings. I decided it was no wonder that she'd left the necklace behind; if its diamonds were anything like the earrings, she'd have to add ten pounds of muscle before she was strong enough to wear them all at the same time.

Suddenly she stopped and turned to me.

"You!" she said imperiously.

I looked around, hoping she was speaking to someone else. No such luck.

"What's your name?" she demanded.

"Eli," I said. "Eli Paxton."

"Of the Boston Paxtons?"

"If I am, they've never told me."

She shook her head. "No, you couldn't be. No touch of elegance at all. And that name! No one is called Eli."

"I am."

"Nonsense," she shot back. "You are Elias, and that is what I shall call you."

Just make sure you pay me $250 and take care of my tux rental and you can call me Jack the Ripper if it makes you happy.

"Then Elias is what I'll answer to, Miss Bigelow."

"I am not a Miss."

"Mrs. Bigelow," I corrected myself.

"*Ms.* Bigelow."

"Whatever you say," I replied pleasantly.

"On second thought, I think you had better call me Clara," she said after a moment's consideration.

"Isn't that a bit familiar?" I said. "After all, I'm just the hired help."

"I'd rather have them think you're my gigolo than my bodyguard," she answered. "Why alert them to the fact that I'm wearing the real earrings?"

It made sense. It also reminded me that when you're as rich as Clara Bigelow, you probably have fakes of all your jewelry. Although "fake" is a little misleading; I know something about jewelry, and her fakes were probably worth more than most women's real McCoys.

We were ushered into a large private dining room, with an elaborate bar set up at one end.

"Keep your eyes open, Elias," she said harshly. "I'm not paying you to enjoy yourself."

"We're on the same page, Clara," I said. *I haven't enjoyed myself since this damned evening began.*

"Good. Now, what are you going to have for dinner?"

"I hadn't given it much thought," I said. "Maybe a hamburger . . ."

She looked like I'd just suggested setting fire to the Opera Palace. "You will most certainly not embarrass me by ordering a hamburger!" she snapped.

"Okay," I said. "A steak, well done, smothered in onions."

"Shut up."

I shut up.

"Do you like seafood?"

I made a face.

"Their shrimp de Jonghe is superb. I will order it for both of us." I was about to ask if Nicole's supplied doggie bags so I could share this treasure with Marlowe, but one look at her face made me change my mind.

She pulled a cigarette out, inserted it into her holder, and waited until I lit it. "Do you smoke, Elias?"

"Not anymore," I said. "Well, maybe a cigar when the Bengals win, but it's been so long since they won that I can't be sure."

"I presume that passes for humor among your friends?"

"It's been known to bring a smile to a face or two," I answered.

"All of them unwashed and unshaven, no doubt," she said, closing the subject.

I looked around, matching faces against their newspaper photos, as the room filled up. There were a couple of bankers, some developers, a handful of local politicians, a pair of professional philanthropists, the owner of a car dealership, and a few faces I was sure I'd never seen before. The average age was somewhere close to sixty, and the average tax bracket was somewhat higher than the summit of Mount Everest.

They milled around for maybe twenty minutes. I spotted three other bodyguards—they all looked as uncomfortable as I did, and they all had bulges under their arms. I also spotted a couple of gigolos; they were too pretty to be bodyguards, too young and unmarked, and they *didn't* have bulges under their arms. There were a few good-looking women, though it was difficult to tell if they were trophy wives or just trophies.

Suddenly an elbow dug into my ribs.

"Stop staring down Maria Delacourt's neckline and pay attention!" hissed Clara.

"Pay attention to what?" I asked, rubbing my rib cage gingerly.

"He's here!"

"Who's here?"

"Do you see that bald man, the one with the thick glasses, who just walked in?"

I looked and saw a man limp into the room, leaning on a silver-handled cane. "Jason Woodford?"

"That's the one. Watch him like a hawk."

"He's the guy who's trying to bring a pro basketball franchise to Cincinnati."

"He's a thief and a liar!"

"It probably goes hand in glove with owning a sports team," I said.

"I will tolerate no more insubordination, Elias!" she snapped. "I want you to keep an eye on him."

"Are you seriously suggesting that he might grab your earrings and run for it?" I said. "I think I read somewhere that he lost a leg in Korea."

"He is a dreadful man," she said adamantly. "Nothing is beyond him."

"All right, Clara," I said. "I'll make him my special project."

"See that you do."

An old gentleman announced that we'd be sitting down to eat at seven-thirty, which was coming up fast, and Clara walked over to the table to stake out a pair of good seats for us.

"Elias," she said, after I'd pulled a chair out for her and she'd sat down, "get me a Purple Butterfly."

I looked around, trying to figure out what the hell she was talking about. "I think it's the wrong time of year for them."

"That's a drink, you fool."

"And if I just walk up to the bar and ask for a Purple Butterfly, someone on the other side of it will know what I'm talking about?"

"They'd better," she said ominously. "I've been ordering them here for forty years."

"Uh . . . Clara," I began. "I hate to bring this up, but it's a cash bar, and . . ." I let the sentence linger and die. She reached into her purse and pulled a bill out without looking at it.

"Here," she said, thrusting it into my hand. "Buy one for yourself, too. And I expect change."

I looked down. It was a fifty. I walked over to the bar

and ordered a pair of Purple Butterflies. I half expected the bartender to laugh in my face. Instead he nodded, muttered, "Mrs. Bigelow, of course," and began mixing up a wildly exotic concoction. When he was done he stuck it in the blender for a moment, then poured the purple drink into two glasses, filling them all the way to the top. All that was missing were the paper umbrellas.

I picked them up, realized that I'd never make it back to the table without spilling something, and took a sip of each. They were a little sweet for my taste, but not bad. Maybe the rich folks knew a little something about how to enjoy themselves after all. Maybe I might even eat a few of my shrimp before poisoning Marlowe with the rest of them. "Here's your drink," I said, handing it to Clara as I reached the table.

"And my change?"

I gave it to her. She counted it to the penny, then dumped it into her purse.

They began bringing out the food just then. There was a lobster soup—they didn't call it soup; they gave it some other name—and a salad with vegetables that I'll swear didn't grow within five thousand miles of Cincinnati, and then came the main course. I wasn't three bites into it before I decided to tell the guys at Luigi's Cut-Rate Pizza that they had to add shrimp de Jonghe to their menu. I mean, hell, shrimp and garlic and breadcrumbs was almost an Italian dish anyway, no matter how fancy they spelled it.

"Don't eat the plate!" whispered Clara disapprovingly as I attacked my meal with increasing enthusiasm.

I finished in two more bites, straightened up, placed my knife and fork on the plate the way I saw a number of other people doing, and waited for dessert. I checked my watch: it was eight-thirty. The Reds were playing the Dodgers on the road; if the speeches weren't too long, I might even get home in time to hear the last few innings.

The waiters bused the plates off the table, and Jason Woodford walked over.

"Good evening, Clara," he said.

"Good evening, Jason," she said coldly.

"Tonight is the night," he said with a smile.

"You're welcome to think so."

"I've got the votes," he said.

"We'll see."

"No hard feelings," he said. "You made a good fight of it."

"Go away, Jason."

His gaze fell on her drink. "You still drinking Purple whatevers?" he said, picking it up. "Every year I try to figure out why." He took a sip.

An instant later he staggered as if he'd been shot. He grabbed at his throat, tried to say something, and collapsed onto the table.

Three or four women screamed. A couple of men jumped to their feet. The bodyguards sprang into action, drawing their weapons, looking fruitlessly for a killer.

The bodyguard who had walked in with Woodford searched for a pulse. Then he laid a hand against the old man's neck, but there was no sign of life.

"He's dead," he announced. And then, so softly that no more than half a dozen of us heard it, he added, "Shit! Striker's gonna have my ass for this!"

"Are you working for Bill Striker?" I asked.

"Yeah." He gestured toward the corpse. "The man had enemies out the wazoo."

"Some bodyguard!" snarled Clara Bigelow. It took me a moment to realize she was speaking to me. "Whatever killed him was meant for me! Now take me home before whoever did it tries again!"

"That's out of the question, Clara," I said.

"Why?" she demanded imperiously.

"A murder's been committed. The police will want to question everyone."

"But it's obvious that the killer is in this room!"

"You have four trained bodyguards in this room, all of us armed," I said. "If everyone can refrain from eating and drinking until the police get here, no one else is going to die." I turned to Striker's man. "Make sure none of the cooks or waiters leave."

He nodded and raced off to the kitchen while I considered what to do next.

"I'd better report this to Homicide," I announced.

"You can use my cellular phone," offered a man.

"Thanks," I lied, "but I have to give a very blunt description of what happened, and I don't want to upset any of the ladies present."

Thankfully no one challenged that, and I walked out of the room to the pay phone by the front door, alone with my problem.

I knew who the killer was, and I had no way of proving it.

It was Clara, of course. I'd taken a sip of her Purple Butterfly as I carried it to the table, and I was fine. Jason Woodford had taken a sip an hour later and he was dead. No one had touched that glass during the interim except Clara.

I didn't know how she'd managed to sneak the poison into the drink, or when, but there was no question that she'd done it. The problem was that it was going to be my word against hers, and if you were a Cincinnatian, you just naturally took Clara Bigelow's word over that of a broken-down private eye who was moonlighting as a cut-rate bodyguard.

My contact at Homicide was Jim Simmons. We'd been drinking buddies for years. He might believe me. But the last time he believed me when I'd gone up against certain powers that be, it almost cost him his job.

Still, I didn't have much choice, so I reached into my pocket for some change—and my fingers came into contact with something that didn't belong there.

I pulled it out and held it up to the light.

Clara's empty cigarette pack.

Now I knew how she'd smuggled in the poison. She'd been playing with her cigarettes all night. At some point she had emptied the poison at the bottom of the pack into her own drink. Or maybe she'd been even more subtle. She could have emptied it onto a spoon and transferred it that way—much less attention getting. It didn't really matter how; the pack itself was enough to convict her.

Except that it was now in my hand, with my fingerprints all over it, and doubtless with enough residue to send me away for a long, long time. I was supposed to use a cellular to report the murder; I wasn't supposed to know what was in my pocket until the police found it.

I knew what I had to do, and I couldn't tell Jim Simmons about it, so I put in an anonymous call to 911 and returned to the room. The corpse still lay on the table, and everyone else milled around aimlessly.

"They'll be here any minute," I said, walking over to Clara.

"They'd better be!" she said.

And indeed they were. I acted startled, accidentally backed into Clara, and made the switch before she even started cursing me for a clumsy fool. She never relinquished her death grip on her little purse; I probably couldn't have opened it without someone noticing anyway. All I kept thinking was: Thank God for pant suits.

The cops were thorough. They questioned each diner, and went through their possessions thoroughly. When they came to Clara, they rummaged through her purse, and then a policewoman gently patted her down—and pulled the empty cigarette pack out of her jacket pocket.

She took a sniff of it, frowned, and handed it to her superior.

I fought back a grin as Clara glared furiously at me. She was hooked—and there wasn't a thing she could do. What could she say: "I planted it on my bodyguard and the dirty bastard sneaked it back into my pocket!"

Everyone knew she smoked. I could produce enough witnesses to prove I gave it up years ago.

QED, as they used to say in some math class or other.

Later it was reported that she and Woodford had fought all year long over who the opera's next musical director would be, and when it became obvious that he was going to win, she decided to kill him. Most murders are committed for love or money, but I suppose when you don't love anyone and you're worth twenty gazillion dollars, you find other reasons to kill people.

Every year Woodford took a sip of her Purple Butterfly and made some deprecating remark about her taste, which I'm sure he hoped would imply she had no taste in other matters, like musical directors. It had almost become a ritual, and she'd counted on the fact that he would do it again this year. I don't know what she'd have done if he *hadn't* taken his annual sip.

I stopped by Bill Striker's office the next morning to pick up my $250.

"I don't have it, Eli."

"I'll take a check," I said.

He shook his head. "Eli, you performed a wonderful public service last night, and I'm grateful—but you don't seriously expect Clara Bigelow to pay us our fee."

I tried Clara's lawyer that afternoon. I think he's still laughing.

I couldn't even claim credit for nailing a killer. There's this annoying little statute that says you can't plant evidence of a crime on someone, even if she's guilty.

The kicker came when I got home. Marlowe must have spotted a bug sometime during the day, and had decided that the best way to kill it was by lifting his leg and drowning the poor little sucker.

I'd just finished scrubbing down the couch and a couple of chair legs when the phone rang.

"Mr. Paxton?" said a precise, high-pitched man's voice.

"Yeah."

"This is Fabulous Formals."

"Look," I said. "If it's about the rental fee, talk to Mrs. Clara Bigelow."

"Mrs. Bigelow paid the fee before you picked it up."

"Then what's the problem?" I asked.

"It seems a dog has chewed one of the pants cuffs past the point of repair. I'm afraid we are going to have to bill you for the purchase price of the tuxedo."

I just hate being a hero.

◆

SHRIMP DE JONGHE

1 cup unsalted butter (no substitute), softened to room
   temperature
2 cloves garlic, peeled and crushed
2 shallots, peeled and minced, or 1 scallion, minced
1 tablespoon minced parsley
1 tablespoon minced chives
¼ teaspoon tarragon
¼ teaspoon marjoram
¼ teaspoon chervil
⅛ teaspoon nutmeg
3 cups soft white breadcrumbs
2 tablespoons lemon juice
⅓ cup dry sherry
3 pounds shelled and deveined boiled small shrimp

Preheat oven to 375 degrees. Cream butter with garlic, shallots, herbs, and nutmeg until well blended. Mix in crumbs, lemon juice, and sherry. Layer shrimp and crumbs into 8 well-buttered individual ramekins, ending with a layer of crumbs. Bake, uncovered, for 20 minutes until topping is lightly browned and mixture heated through. Do not serve with Purple Butterflies.

—MR

GEORGE WASHINGTON
CRASHED HERE

JEAN HAGER

Ellie Hawkins promised herself, when she retired, that she would take time for reading, needlepoint, traveling, and perhaps a little volunteer work—all the things she'd always wanted to do but hadn't had enough time for when she had a full-time job. But somehow things had gotten out of whack; the volunteer work had grown like the mouth of some giant, out-of-control monster, until it gobbled up most of her free time.

The problem was there were so many good causes, all of them shorthanded and desperate for volunteers. As a probation officer for twenty-three years—a job she had taken when her husband died and left her with a daughter to raise—Ellie was well known throughout the county. As soon as she retired and "had so much free time on her hands," her phone rang off the hook with calls from directors of volunteer services.

Finally, as the second year of her retirement ended, she had decided that enough was enough and had cut her volunteer activities to two very worthy organizations. But that was before the woman from the homeless shelter had shown up on her doorstep and issued such an eloquent plea for help that Ellie just couldn't say no—not to her face, anyway. Which was how she came to be in charge of the annual fund-raising drive for the shelter.

She'd gathered an energetic group of volunteers for her committee and their first strategy session—a dinner meeting—was scheduled for 8:00 P.M., less than an hour from now, at the Presidents' Hotel. She had chosen the hotel because her favorite nephew, Rick, was the manager. Fresh out of hotel management training, Rick was eager to make his mark with his first job and Ellie saw no reason why she shouldn't help him out, given all the hours she put in for the shelter. Besides, it was the nicest hotel in town.

As Ellie entered the Presidents', Rick was crossing the lobby. He met her near the registration desk and gave her a hug.

"You look absolutely stunning in that pink dress, Aunt Ellie."

Ellie patted her gray-streaked hair, which had been styled in a new, shorter do that day. "Mauve, Rick, and flattery isn't necessary." Her nephew had learned in his training to be generous with compliments, but sometimes he overdid it.

"Did the caterers get here on time?"

"Five o'clock sharp."

Ellie relaxed a little. The caterers were very dependable, but it was a relief to know they hadn't been unavoidably detained.

"Are you sure you didn't mind contracting with an outside catering service, Aunt Ellie?" Rick had told her when she reserved space for the dinner that he expected three hundred people in the banquet hall that evening and his staff would be fully occupied there.

"Not in the least." The hotel's catering service would have been satisfactory, but the fact that they would be tied up with the banquet freed Ellie to choose the best caterers in town—Gourmet Gatherings, operated by husband and wife Bing and Stella Mayhew.

"I have to go up to five and check out the banquet hall," Rick said. "The girl at the desk can find me if you need me."

"I'll manage, dear. You go on about your business."

From where she stood, Ellie could see the long table assigned to her committee in the space beyond the lobby, a large rectangle surrounded on three sides by the mezzanine, making for a two-floor-high ceiling from which hung a huge, elaborate crystal chandelier. They would be looked down upon by a dozen past U.S. presidents, whose stone busts were stationed on pedestals built into the mezzanine railing.

The table was spread with a burgundy cloth and the hotel's gold-rimmed white china and crystal glassware. A brass ring held a burgundy napkin, spread out like a Victorian lady's fan, beside each plate. Excellent, Ellie thought. The only thing lacking were the place cards, which she had in her purse. But before taking care of that, she went back to the kitchen that served the main floor.

Another kitchen on the second floor was used for the hotel restaurant and events in the banquet hall.

Bing Mayhew, a tall, distinguished-looking man in his early forties, moved about the room, supervising four employees—two men and two women—who were preparing various dishes. Stella, Bing's wife, short, plump, and getting plumper, stood at the end of a counter, chopping salad vegetables. All six of them wore white aprons with GOURMET GATHERINGS stenciled in black on the bibs.

Ellie paused in the doorway. "Can I do anything to help?"

Bing looked up, a smile banishing the furrows in his brow, and Ellie noticed, not for the first time, what lovely even, white teeth he had. "We've got everything well in hand, Mrs. Hawkins."

"Don't even think about it," Stella added. "You might get something on that pretty dress."

"Okay, then I'll go and put out the place cards."

Arranging the cards took some deliberation. As she would be in charge of the meeting, she put herself at the head of the table. John Dickey, CEO of the town's largest hospital, would be at the other end of the table, Ellie decided, with his wife, Dorothy, on his right. She sat Kate Derring on John Dickey's left and Kate's sister-in-law, Meredith Wellton, at the opposite end of the table, on Ellie's left. Kate was in the process of divorcing her husband, Meredith's brother, and Ellie thought the two might find conversation a bit strained. On her right, she placed Reverend Jacobson, a widowed Presbyterian minister who was always an interesting dinner companion. The reverend had recently returned from a month in the British Isles, and Ellie looked forward to hearing all about his trip.

Among the remaining places, she distributed the last four cards, seating sisters, Joan and Deanne Masters, of the wealthy Masters family, side by side. Both women had retained their maiden names when they married. Across from the sisters were Jane Lansing and Betty Vian, whose husbands were among the town's business leaders. Having placed all the cards, Ellie walked slowly around the table, reading names. Satisfied with the arrangement, she took the stairs to the ladies' room on the mezzanine to give her hair and makeup a final inspection. And perhaps she'd rest for a bit on the ladies'-room chaise longue.

When Ellie returned a half hour later, all the members of the committee had arrived and were standing in a cluster at the end of the dining area, having drinks. Ellie greeted them, thanked them for coming, and suggested that they be seated.

As two of the caterer's employees began taking drink orders and serving salads, Ellie turned to her right to speak to the reverend. "How was your trip, Rev—"

Ellie halted, embarrassed, as she realized that Kate Derring was smiling at her expectantly. Was her memory deserting her? She thought she'd placed Reverend Jacobson on her right and Kate at the opposite end of the table. Not that it mattered, as long as Kate and Meredith weren't seated side by side. "Sorry, Kate. I'm a bit scattered tonight. I thought I'd put Reverend Jacobson there."

"You did," the reverend said, "but I asked Kate to change places with me. I don't hear very well in my left ear, and I wanted to enjoy a nice conversation with you, Ellie."

He'd changed places with Kate, not Meredith, who was seated at the other end of the table? Apparently Ellie's memory had mixed up where she'd placed Kate and Meredith. She *was* distracted.

"Little wonder you're scattered," Kate said, "with all you have to do. Honestly, Ellie, I don't know how you cram so much in."

"I'm beginning to wonder that myself. In fact, I've dropped some of my volunteer activities. When I retired, I meant to do some traveling—" She turned to her left. "Like Reverend Jacobson here."

"Tell us about your trip, Reverend," Kate said.

The minister, a small man with a round face and shining bald pate, did so with relish. In fact, he didn't stop talking until the entrée, shrimp and green noodles, was served.

Time enough to call the meeting to order after they had dessert, Ellie thought. Glancing around the table, she saw that several conversations were going on. Everybody seemed to be enjoying the dinner, all except Meredith Wellton, who was unusually quiet. Ellie had seen her cast a covert glance in Kate's direction several times, and then look quickly down at her plate. Kate was unaware of the surveillance by her soon-to-be-former sister-in-law, or she was doing a good job of ignoring it. Kate, in fact, looked years younger than she had the last time Ellie had seen her. She'd lost weight and was sporting a new, curly hairdo that added to the youthful appearance.

Beside Ellie, Kate spoke. "This shrimp dish is delicious. I must get the recipe from the caterer."

"You can ask," Ellie told her, "although the Mayhews are very secretive about their recipes."

Kate gave her a small smile. "I'll turn on the charm." Which, Ellie thought, might just work with Bing—as long as Stella wasn't around.

The next moment Ellie happened to glance toward the ceiling and saw the crystal chandelier sway ever so slightly. She had about decided she'd imagined it, when George Washington's bust fell off its mezzanine pedestal and came crashing down on Reverend Jacobson, then bounced to the stone floor, where it broke into several pieces.

The minister slumped sideways out of his chair. After an instant of shocked silence, Ellie jumped to her feet as gasps and stunned exclamations came from the others at the table. Ellie dropped to her knees beside the minister, whose head was bloody and looked oddly dented on one side.

Kate joined Ellie in kneeling beside Reverend Jacobson. "Somebody call nine-one-one," Ellie said, and heard high heels clicking hurriedly across the stone floor as one of the women went to the telephone.

Kate reached out to touch the reverend. "Don't try to move him," Ellie cautioned.

"I'm feeling for a pulse," Kate said, pressing her fingers just below the minister's jaw. After a moment, she looked up at Ellie, her face gray. "He's dead."

The police and paramedics arrived a few minutes later. By then, Rick had been notified of the accident and, practically wringing his hands, rushed up to the two officers. "I checked every one of those busts myself," he said. "I was sure they were secure."

Ellie joined him. She recognized both of the officers—Gray and Dormer—and they greeted her by name, remembering her from her probation officer days. "Just before the bust fell," she said, "I chanced to look up at the chandelier and I thought it swayed a little."

Gray and Dormer both looked ceilingward. "Looks okay now," Gray, the older of the two, said.

"At first, I thought I may have imagined it," Ellie went on, "but then the bust fell. Could we have had an earthquake tremor?"

"In Oklahoma?" Dormer asked doubtfully.

"It's been known to happen," Kate said. "In fact, it probably happens more often than we realize, because the tremors aren't strong enough to be noticed."

Rick grasped this explanation eagerly. "Could've shaken the bust enough to make it fall."

Gray frowned. "I'll check with the weather bureau."

The medics had loaded Reverend Jacobson on a gurney and now rushed out with him.

At that moment, the caterers—all six of them—led by Bing Mayhew, came out of the kitchen. Mayhew took in the scene and rushed forward as the medics crossed the lobby and went out the door. "Oh, my God. What happened?"

"George Washington fell on Reverend Jacobson," Ellie told him, "or rather his bust did."

Mayhew stared wide-eyed. His wife, who stood beside and a little behind him, had gone pale, and one of the female helpers shrieked and covered her mouth. Gray had taken out a tablet and pen. "Did anybody notice the time when the bust fell?"

When no one responded, Ellie said, "It had to be about eight-thirty. We were well into the main course."

Gray made a note. "I'll need the names and phone numbers of everyone who witnessed the accident." Since none of the caterers had been in the room when the bust fell, he asked them to wait in the kitchen.

As Gray took down names, Ellie began picking up pieces of the broken bust and making a pile against the wall, where nobody would stumble over them until someone came to remove the debris. As she picked up one of the stone chunks, she noticed a piece of Scotch tape about three inches long stuck by one end to what had been the back of George Washington's head. Odd, she thought, and couldn't imagine how it had gotten there.

Ellie called the hospital as soon as she arrived home from the hotel and was told that heroic efforts to revive the minister had failed. She finally went to bed but got very little sleep. She kept seeing George Washington's bust dive off the mezzanine and crush Reverend Jacobson's skull.

When a gray dawn peeked around her window blind, she gave up trying to sleep and got dressed. Her nephew called as soon as he got to the hotel at eight.

"Have you talked to that Officer Gray this morning, Aunt Ellie?"

"No, Rick. Should I have?"

"I'm just wondering what he found out from the weather bureau. I feel terrible about Reverend Jacobson. I'm also worried sick that the hotel will be sued. I don't mean to sound crass, Aunt Ellie, but that could ruin my career."

"The reverend didn't have any close relatives, Rick, so don't worry too much about being sued."

"If there was an earthquake, there would be no grounds for a suit, would there?"

"I don't know. I'll call Officer Gray, if you like."

"Would you, Aunt Ellie?"

Ellie was put through to Gray right away. She identified herself and asked, "Have you had a chance to check with the weather bureau?"

"Yeah. There was no earthquake anywhere in the area last night, Ellie."

Oh, dear. Rick would be beside himself when he heard. She thanked Gray, hung up, and decided to go to the hotel and tell her nephew in person.

Rick's reaction was predictable. "This is going to ruin me!" He paced his office like a caged animal.

"You're worried about something that may never happen," Ellie said in a calm voice.

He raked both hands through his dark hair, leaving tufts standing up on top. "I don't understand how it could have happened. I checked those busts." He suddenly looked alarmed. "My God, what if another one falls? I'd better have them all removed right away."

Ellie followed him out of his office. He found the director of housekeeping and told him to get some men to remove the busts. "Just leave them on the floor beside the pedestals for now," he said.

Ellie and Rick then went up to the mezzanine, where Rick again checked several of the busts and found them solidly placed in the center of the pedestals. Ellie ran her hand down the back of Andrew Jackson's head, then nudged it. It didn't move. "There's no way somebody brushing against one of these could knock it off," she mused. "It would take a good shove."

Rick turned to stare at her. "You mean if somebody fell against it hard? You think that's what happened?"

"I didn't notice anybody on this side of the mezzanine before the bust fell," Ellie said.

"I've got a meeting, Aunt Ellie. If you want to hang around for a while, I'll buy you breakfast."

"Thanks, but I've had my cereal," Ellie said. "You go on."

Left alone on the mezzanine, Ellie walked slowly around the three sides with pedestals, looking at all the busts. That piece of Scotch tape she'd seen on the broken bust had begun to nag at her, but there was no Scotch tape on any of the others. What did it mean? Probably nothing, she told herself. Glancing toward the ceiling, she studied the heavy chandelier. Of course, it didn't move. Had it swayed last night before the bust fell, or had she imagined it?

All right, suppose the chandelier really had swayed. What could have caused it? And did it have anything to do with the bust falling?

Two big men wearing hotel security uniforms arrived and began lifting the busts off their pedestals and sitting them on the carpeted floor. Ellie ignored them and walked around the mezzanine several times. The four-foot-high railing formed the "wall" that overlooked the lobby and dining area where Ellie's committee had met last night. There was a plush-carpeted walking area, about six feet wide, between the railing and a pale gray wall with doors at intervals opening into offices and a storage closet. She didn't know what she was looking for—just anything that seemed odd or out of place.

And she almost missed it. On her fourth trip around the mezzanine, she was studying the gray walls, letting her glance sweep from ceiling to floor as she walked. She saw what looked like a small black dot above the storage closet door near one corner. Ellie stepped closer and stood on tiptoe. It looked like a hole. She glanced across to the other side of the mezzanine. The closet was almost directly opposite the pedestal that had held George Washington's bust. She reached for the doorknob, found it unlocked, and opened the door.

One of the security guards who was nearby, said, "Ma'am, that's just a storage closet."

"I know," Ellie said. "I just want to look around. It'll only take a minute."

He eyed her warily. "I don't know, ma'am . . ."

"Look at this." Ellie pointed toward the top of the door. "Why would there be a hole up there?"

He came closer. "Don't know, but it's hardly noticeable."

"By the way, I'm Ellie Hawkins, Rick Stiles's aunt."

"Oh. Then I guess it's okay if you take a look. Anything in particular you're searching for?"

"No," Ellie told him, "but maybe I'll know it if I see it." Shaking his head, he backed away.

Ellie found the light switch and flipped it on. There was just enough room between shelves on one side and mops, brooms, and a vacuum sweeper on the other, for her to step inside. The hole was high on her left, next to floor-to-ceiling shelves containing cleaning supplies. She scanned the shelf nearest the hole. It held paint cans and two large boxes of plastic trash bags. There was something, a large spool of some sort, tucked in between two of the cans. Ellie reached up, just managed to get her fingers on it, and pulled it forward until she could grasp it.

It was a moment before she realized what she held in her hand. Ellie's husband had been an avid fisherman, and although it had been many years since his death, she remembered seeing something just like this in his tackle box. It was a spool of fishing line, strong, thin, and very nearly transparent.

"Why would this be in here?" she called to the security officer.

He came over. "It's fishing tackle. Can't think why it would be in the cleaning supply closet."

Nor could Ellie. She needed some time to figure it out. "I'll just put it back where I found it." She closed the closet door and walked slowly toward the stairs.

Half an hour later, she was in Rick's office. "I think I know why that bust fell," she told him. "It was no accident or act of God. Somebody did it deliberately."

Rick looked horrified. "But I thought you said you didn't see anybody near that bust right before it fell."

"That's true, but they didn't have to be. They were on the opposite side of the mezzanine in the cleaning supply closet."

"I don't understand, Aunt Ellie."

Ellie explained her theory, then said, "I think it's time to call the police."

When Officer Gray arrived, he, Ellie, and Rick went up to the storage closet on the mezzanine. Ellie opened the door and pointed at the spool of fishing tackle, then showed them the hole in the wall next to the shelf. "Whoever did it," she said, "had to have set it up earlier in the day, or maybe even a day or two before. It had to be a time when nobody was about because he or she had to tape the end of the fishing line to the back of George Washington's bust. They used Scotch tape. I found the tape on a piece of the broken bust."

"But they'd have to string it clear across to this side of the mezzanine," Rick said. "Surely somebody would have noticed a fishing line running across the open space on this side of the mezzanine. They could have run right into it."

"No," Ellie said, "it was too high up." She pointed toward the hole.

Officer Gray was gazing across the mezzanine to the opposite side. "At that height, the line would've run right alongside the chandelier."

"Exactly," Ellie said. "Which explains why it swayed when the killer entered the closet and tugged on the line. The weight of the bust as it fell would've pulled the line free of the tape."

"So," mused Officer Gray, "the killer just stood in the closet and wound the line back on the spool."

"Very quickly, I would imagine," Ellie added. "So it wouldn't fall down on anybody who happened to be passing on this side of the mezzanine."

Rick sighed heavily. "I don't guess you noticed anybody on *this* side of the mezzanine about that time, Aunt Ellie."

She shook her head. "The killer escaped while we were all focused on poor Reverend Jacobson."

"Or just hid out in the closet until later that evening when the coast was clear," said Officer Gray.

"That's a possibility, too," Ellie said. "But we can be sure of one thing. It wasn't one of the members of my committee. They were all downstairs when the bust fell."

"They could've had an accomplice," Officer Gray suggested.

Ellie hadn't thought of that. "Maybe," she admitted grudgingly, "but it's likely that the killer wasn't even in the hotel until fifteen or twenty minutes before the bust fell, and that he sneaked out again during all the confusion."

Rick was staring at Ellie in awe. "I'm amazed at you, Aunt Ellie. How in the world did you ever figure this out?"

"My dear, when you work with criminals for over twenty years, you learn how they think."

Officer Gray nodded in agreement and Rick said, "There's only one thing about all this that doesn't make sense. Who in the world would want to kill Reverend Jacobson?"

"I don't think he was the intended victim," Ellie said.

Both men looked at her closely. "Who, then?" asked Officer Gray.

"Kate Derring," Ellie said, and then she explained how Kate's place card had been switched with Meredith Wellton's after she'd arranged the cards and had gone up to the ladies' room. "There was a space of time when nobody was near the table and someone wanted Kate in that chair."

Rick looked nonplussed. "But she wasn't."

"Only because Reverend Jacobson asked Kate to change places with him so that he could have his good ear on my side." Suddenly Ellie felt faintly ill. "In a way, it's my fault the reverend is dead."

"If it wasn't him, it would've been the Derring woman," Officer Gray told her, "if it went down like you say."

Ellie nodded sadly. "Now all you have to do is figure out who wanted Kate Derring dead."

"What about her husband?" Rick suggested. "Didn't you say they're getting a divorce, Aunt Ellie?"

"That's true."

"I'll talk to him," Gray said. "Can you think of anybody else who's had problems with Kate Derring?"

Ellie and Rick shook their heads. Ellie was remembering how Meredith Wellton kept casting covert glances toward Kate all evening. Could she have known what her brother had planned? Ellie found that hard to believe. Surely Meredith would have done something to get Reverend Jacobson out of that chair, once she realized he'd switched places with Kate.

"Well, I'll have a talk with her," Gray said. "See if she has any idea who wants her dead." He took the spool of fishing line, in case the lab could lift some fingerprints, and left the hotel.

Ellie pondered the situation. Whoever did this seemed to have laid his plans well, but he must have been unaware that somebody besides Kate Derring was sitting in that chair when he pulled the bust off its pedestal. Therefore, she realized, it couldn't have been anybody on her committee—unless, the committee member had been unable to inform an accomplice of the change in seating.

Well, the investigation was in police hands now.

She decided to go by the Mayhews' house on her way home and deliver their check. In all the confusion last night, she'd forgotten to pay them. As it turned out, she didn't have to go that far. Driving down Eighth Street, she saw Bing Mayhew come out of a restaurant, and pulled over to the curb.

"Bing," she called as she got out of her car. She dug the check out of her purse. "I forgot to pay you last night. I was headed to your house when I saw you." She handed him the check.

"Thanks, Ellie. I wasn't worried. I knew you were good for it."

They parted and returned to their cars. Bing drove off and Ellie was about to back out of the parking space when she saw Kate Derring come out of the restaurant. She rolled down her window.

"Kate! I think Officer Gray wants to talk to you."

Kate came over to the car. "Why?"

"I'd better let him tell you. Call him."

"I will." Kate tilted her head quizzically. "What are you doing here?"

"I saw Bing Mayhew and pulled over to give him the check I neglected to deliver last night."

"Oh. I ran into Bing in the restaurant. I have breakfast here often, you know." She grinned impishly. "And I got that recipe."

"Good for you," Ellie said, but as she drove away, she felt a little hurt. She'd tried to get one of the Mayhews' recipes several times, but had never been successful. Kate must *really* have turned on the charm. She was an attractive woman, and Ellie supposed Bing was as susceptible to that as any man.

It wasn't until she was reading the paper the next morning that she began to wonder if Kate's encounter with Bing Mayhew had been more than a mere accident. Listed under *Divorces Asked* was "Mayhew, Bing vs. Stella."

Now, Ellie, she told herself, don't jump to any conclusions. She put in a call to Officer Gray. "Did you find any fingerprints on that spool of fishing line?"

"A nice, clear thumbprint," Gray said. "Which won't do us much good unless we can find out who left it there. It doesn't match anything in our computer."

Ellie hesitated, then took a deep breath, and suggested, "Try taking the prints from the people who catered our dinner. It's Gourmet Gatherings." She gave him the phone number.

"They were all in the kitchen when the bust fell."

"So they said," Ellie told him. "But it would have only taken a couple of minutes for somebody to slip out of the kitchen, dash up to the mezzanine, pull on that fishing line, wind it up, and return to the kitchen."

"Do you know something I don't know?"

"No, it's just a hunch."

"If it were anybody else, Ellie, I'd blow it off."

That evening, Gray called Ellie. "Good hunch you had. We got a match."

"From Stella Mayhew?"

"How'd you know?"

"Bing is suing her for divorce. I saw it in this morning's paper. And yesterday, I saw Bing and Kate Derring coming out of a restaurant on Eighth Street. Kate told me she'd run into Bing by chance and had gotten a recipe from him."

"Hmmph! I'd say she's been getting more than recipes from Mayhew. When I confronted Stella Mayhew about the fingerprint, she broke down and confessed everything, said Bing and Kate Derring have been having an affair for months, and when he asked for a divorce, she thought if Kate was out of the picture, he'd stay in the marriage. Of course, she didn't realize Kate had changed seats with the reverend until it was too late. She's devastated about that."

"Poor woman," Ellie murmured.

"She's still a murderer, Ellie."

But in the grainy photograph on the front page of the next morning's paper, Stella looked like anything but a murderer. She looked like an ordinary, plump, middle-aged housewife who might be headed for the supermarket instead of jail. And she looked very sad.

"Poor woman," Ellie said again, and she wondered how Bing and Kate were feeling about their affair, which had resulted in the death of Reverend Jacobson. No doubt they were sad, too. In fact, there was only one person she could think of who had anything to be happy about in the way things had turned out—her nephew, Rick.

There would seem to be no grounds for a lawsuit against the hotel.

▪

SHRIMP AND GREEN NOODLES

½ 8–ounce package of spinach noodles
2 pounds shrimp, peeled and deveined
1 can cream of mushroom soup
1 cup dairy sour cream
1 cup mayonnaise

½ teaspoon Dijon-style mustard
2 tablespoons chopped chives
5 tablespoons dry sherry
½ cup Cheddar cheese, grated

Cook noodles as directed on package. Line a casserole with noodles. In a large skillet, sauté the shrimp in ½ cup butter until pink and tender, about 5 minutes. Cover noodles with shrimp. Combine soup, sour cream, mayonnaise, and chives; add mustard and sherry. Pour sauce over shrimp and sprinkle Cheddar cheese over all. Bake at 350 degrees for 30 minutes, until cheese has melted and is bubbly.

—JH

THE BOXING
DAY BOTHER

PATRICIA GUIVER

Later, when it was all over, everyone swore they'd seen the whole thing, though at the time no one possibly could have, least of all Great-uncle Jasper. Oh, there was one other person, of course. But I'm getting ahead of myself.

It was several years since I'd been in England for Christmas, but this particular December, I gave in to the wave of nostalgia that usually affected me during the holidays. I locked the front door of my Surf City, California, cottage, boarded Watson, my dog, at the vet's, left a message on the answering machine to the effect that the Delilah Doolittle Pet Detective Agency would be closed until January 15, and headed home for the annual family Boxing Day dinner at The Feathers in Buddington, the Surrey village where I was born.

This year the event promised to be more interesting than usual. Great-uncle Jasper, the family patriarch, had finally decided to make a will, and had chosen the occasion to announce his heir.

"And not before time," exclaimed Jasper's daughter, my

aunt Millicent, with a toss of her gray mane, when she picked me up at Gatwick. "The old boy's in his eighties. He's refused that fence a couple of times before. But this time he swears he's going to go the distance. Made an appointment with his solicitor for the first week in January."

So expectations were running high as the family gathered in the private dining room of the seventeenth-century coaching inn.

The grandfather clock in the saloon bar chimed the quarter hour and most of the company was already seated around the long refectory table, tradition dictating that dinner begin promptly at eight-thirty.

"It's just like Jasper to be late," sniffed Aunt Maud, the plump little woman seated on my left, her silver curls bouncing with indignation. "He's doing it on purpose, keeping us all in suspense. He knows we can't start without him."

"He's probably still trying to make up his mind," put in her husband, Major Tom, robust and ruddy-faced. "Wouldn't have stood for it in the regiment, late for mess. Lets the side down."

I recalled my mother saying that the Major had never been the same since the war. Whether from shell shock or delusions of grandeur was never made clear.

His loud tone caused the little Yorkshire terrier sitting in Maud's lap to wake up and growl. "There, there, Precious," Maud murmured, patting the dog's head.

"About time you had that runt put down," said Millicent, with a disapproving stare at the Yorkie. "Jasper, too," she continued with a dry laugh. "He's been getting more and more senile recently. He'll probably leave everything to the RSPCA, or the Society for Indigent Dartmoor Ponies, or some such nonsense."

"He could do worse," I said with a smile, attempting to lighten the mood. I thought fondly of my dear Watson, and felt a pang of guilt for leaving her at the vet's.

"Easy enough for you to say," Uncle Alfred tossed at me from across the table. "You don't stand to inherit anything since you're not in direct line." My grandmother had been Jasper's youngest sister.

The centerpiece candle flames flickered in the draft as the door suddenly opened.

"Here he is at last," muttered Alfred.

Jasper, tall and straight, walked into the room unaided by anything but his stout walking stick with the ivory carved horse's-head handle. That horse, wild-eyed, nostrils flaring, had struck terror into my heart years ago, whenever some childish transgression caused it to be waved in my direction.

Reaching his place at the head of the table, Jasper glared at the empty chair at the opposite end. "Justin not here yet? Where is the young scamp?"

Justin, Maud and the Major's only child, was Jasper's favorite, and we all fully expected, despite any secret hopes anyone might be harboring, that he would be the one to inherit.

"Up to no good, I'll be bound," muttered Millicent audibly, with a piercing look at Maud. "That young man needs to get a job. Gallivanting around on his motorbike, scaring the locals. Going to come a cropper one of these days."

"Had the cheek to touch me for a tenner yesterday," added Alfred.

"Did you give it to him?" I asked.

"Of course not," he replied, obviously surprised that I needed to ask. "Set a bad example for little Tim here." He nodded at the child seated between me and Jasper.

"He'll be here if he knows which side his bread's buttered on," put in the Major, looking impatiently toward the door for his son.

Boxing Day dinner was a ritual in our family, something not to be missed short of being bedridden or out of the

country, and I'm not sure that even those were considered
good enough excuses. As in many English families, Christmas Day is for the children, but Boxing Day, December
26—a national holiday originating from the time when the
lady of the manor would visit the deserving poor to distribute Christmas gift boxes—is for the adults to enjoy at their
leisure, snacking on leftovers while the children play with
the not yet discarded toys. Or, as in our case, visiting with
family.

Most of my generation, in a burst of pent-up postwar
restlessness, had scattered to the four corners of what used
to be the British Empire. Four-year-old Timmy, myself,
and the visiting Australian cousins were the only represen-
tatives of the younger set on this particular evening. And
Justin, of course, if he ever arrived.

The festive table was set with fine crystal goblets, silverware, and crisp white napery. Aunt Maud and Miss Lydia had been there earlier in the day to arrange the place
settings and decorations. Garlands of fir and red velvet ribbon swooped around the edges of the tablecloth. Holly and
red candles filled brass bowl centerpieces, and red or green
Christmas-cracker favors decorated the place settings. Not
the kind of crackers you eat, but tubes of crepe paper with
snappers, paper hats, and mottoes inside.

A perfect English Christmas-card picture. "Can I look
at those later?" I asked Cousin Betty, who, with husband
Cyril, had shown up unannounced two days earlier on their
first visit from Australia. Now, seated opposite each other
at the far end of the table, they took turns jumping up to
snap Polaroid pictures of this special occasion.

Little Timmy started to whimper. I picked up his cracker
and shook it. "I wonder what prize is in here for you," I
said. The tears didn't surprise me. Eight-thirty was no time
for a toddler to be eating dinner.

"We're not going to leave him at home with Nanny," declared Millicent, Timmy's adoptive mother, when I protested that we ought not to drag him out on a cold winter's evening. "This is a family occasion. It's not too soon for him to learn what he's a part of."

Perhaps it also had something to do with Timmy's expectations, I thought.

I regarded her from across the table. A large-boned woman, she was head and shoulders above her husband, Alfred, seated next to her. A tapestry bag hung on the back of her chair, feeding a string of yarn to the shapeless garment in her lap. I hoped it wasn't a present for me. At one time or another we had all been hapless recipients of her garish tea cozies or afghans. Millicent had three hobbies. The knitting was harmless enough, but the others—hunting and riding to hounds—were neither one of them likely to endear her to me. I tend to see things from the fox's point of view.

But she was right about one thing. Protest as we might, family traditions are worth suffering for. Boxing Day dinner had been an annual ritual for as long as any of those present, including Jasper, could remember. My mother and father had brought me here as a child, and I'm sure I had done my share of sniveling then, just as Timmy was doing now.

"Now then, Sheriff Tim," I whispered, "don't let Grampa Jasper see you crying." Jasper's stern countenance had been enough to stem my tears as a child—and he'd been a half century younger then!

Timmy was wearing the cowboy outfit I'd brought him from America. *Cowboy crazy, the lad is,* Millicent had written in the letter she'd sent me announcing that she and Alfred had formally adopted the boy after his parents, my cousin Elaine and her husband, had been killed on a climbing expedition in the Himalayas a year earlier. "Bad business that," Major Tom had explained. "Their Sherpa let them down."

It seemed no one in my family ever died of natural causes. Great-aunt Ada had been hit by a stray bullet while an ambulance driver during the Spanish Civil War. My own grandfather had died in India during the British Raj—trampled to death by a rogue elephant. I sometimes wondered what gramps had done to provoke the poor beast.

I noticed that mud still clung to Timmy's boots, dangling over the high-chair footrest. Alfred should have wiped them clean when he helped me lift him in, I thought with annoyance. The child's jeans were held up by an overlarge gun belt, a silver toy pistol in one of the holsters. Surely he hadn't lost the other gun already? I could have sworn he'd had them both when we left the house. His cowboy hat, held in place by a leather thong, lay on the back of his neck. A red flannel shirt and black leather vest bearing a tin star completed the outfit. All day long he'd insisted we call him "Sheriff Tim."

Everyone else was in formal wear: the men in black tie, the women in evening gowns, though as a concession to the drafty old inn, most of the ladies had covered their shoulders with mohair or cashmere shawls, or, in the case of Great-aunt Nell, a tattered brown cardigan which, with mismatched buttons and ragged cuffs covered a rusty black frock of uncertain vintage. An octogenarian, she, like young Timmy at the other end of life's span, was allowed to wear exactly what she pleased.

My own dress, a knitted tube of bright orange with matching cardigan, had been plucked from my wardrobe at the last minute without proper consideration for whether it might perhaps be a little too flashy for this occasion, the dress code at which could best be described as shabby genteel.

Great-aunt Nell's companion—Miss Lydia was the only name anyone knew her by—was trying to keep her employer in the table talk by shouting into the ear trumpet, which, disdaining that modern marvel the hearing aid, the old lady flourished, first on her right side, then her left, much to the consternation of the young waitress who was trying to set out the vegetable dishes.

"What's Delilah saying," Great-aunt Nell demanded.

"She got the cowboy suit in California," bellowed Miss Lydia.

The old lady looked puzzled. "California? Why go all that way? Surely they have them at Harrods?"

Across the table Millicent blushed as Alfred whispered in her ear. Their devotion to each other was something of a puzzle; they seemed so incredibly ill-suited. Childless, they'd always said that having each other was enough, that children would spoil things, and I had been surprised to learn they had taken on Timmy's care.

To the day she died—drowned while attempting to break the English Channel swim record—Mother had never approved of Millicent's choice of a husband. "Alfred's an outsider. We know nothing about him, except he claims kinship with some obscure baronet and has a modest private income." She'd married him to spite Jasper, Mother said. He'd always neglected her in favor of his sons, William (Timmy's grandfather) and the Major. But as I had pointed out at the time, Millicent was happier than we'd ever seen her, and it wasn't as if, with her unfortunate looks and horsey mannerisms, she was besieged by beaux.

Nevertheless, I was somewhat surprised at how fond Alfred appeared to be of Timmy. As we all squeezed into the small Morris Minor on the way to dinner, for example, he insisted that the child sit on his lap, even though Maud and I both offered.

The grandfather clock had just started striking the half

hour when a "ho-ho-ho" came from the doorway, and a blond, good-looking young man in a Father Christmas hat entered. Justin had grown so tall in the past few years, I scarcely recognized him. He had his arm around a young woman dressed in a short leather skirt and jacket, her long dark hair tossed back over her shoulders.

"Hi, everyone. This is Debbie."

"What's that on her face?" asked Great-aunt Nell loudly.

"A nose ring," shouted Miss Lydia.

"A what?"

"A nose ring, Aunt," said Justin, going over to kiss her. "You'd look great in one, too. Oh . . ." He turned and noticed me. "Hi, Delilah. How's the pet-detective business going. Still chasing those surfer dudes?"

"Oh, no, they're chasing me, luv."

"Well said, old girl." The Major chuckled.

There was much laughter as Justin continued to make his way around the table, kissing the ladies, not ignoring Miss Lydia, who blushed at the attention. He shook Jasper's hand, hugged the cousins, greeted his parents, scratched Precious's head, and said, "Stick 'em up, cowboy," to Timmy, much to the delight of the child, who instantly recognized a soul mate.

Meanwhile the waiter hastily set another place for Debbie.

"Thirteen at dinner," sniffed Millicent. "That's unlucky."

"Thirteen's always been my lucky number," I said. Justin shot me a grateful glance.

His arrival lightened the mood, as if a conscious collective decision had been made to put aside mutual animosities in the name of Christmas goodwill and family unity.

The meal started with the traditional toasts. Jasper, leaning on his cane, stood and called on us to raise our champagne glasses first "to absent friends," reading from notes the names of those who either through death or distance were unable to join us, and finishing with "to the Queen, God bless her," a toast without which no self-respecting English dinner party would have been complete.

"Did you hear the Queen's speech yesterday?" asked Lydia of no one in particular. "I thought it was one of her best, especially the bit about—" Flustered at having spoken up and getting no response, she dropped her napkin and fell silent.

The Feathers boasted an excellent chef who knew from experience just what was required: a traditional Christmas dinner, never mind that it was a repeat performance of the turkey blowout of the previous day.

"No more of that heathen yam-and-marshmallow rubbish," Jasper had decreed after one unfortunate occasion when some American cousins had tried to introduce their own favorites. "What we want is plain food and plenty of it."

And that's what we got: after the oxtail soup had been served, platters of turkey and chestnut stuffing, dishes of mashed and roast potatoes, onions in white sauce, and brussels sprouts were handed around the table in quick succession.

"I think I'd like to try a little giblet gravy," said Miss Lydia, looking longingly at the gravy boat, which had come to a halt in front of Cousin Cyril, who, busy taking pictures, had neglected to pass it along.

"Now for my favorite," said Maud, when the mince pies and brandy sauce were brought in. Though most of us, including Jasper, expressed a preference for the sherry trifle as being a little lighter.

Finally, while the waiter filled our demitasse cups with steaming coffee and milk, the lights were dimmed, and to a chorus of "ahs" the Christmas pudding—that's plum pudding across the pond—was brought in and with great ceremony the brandy-soaked sugar cube in its center set aflame. Heavy with suet, raisins, sultanas, and currants, it was dark brown with half a glass of stout—or as much as the cook thought she could part with. A must at every Christmas dinner, though I didn't know a soul who really liked it.

"Jolly fine!" pronounced the Major.

"Quite the nicest I've ever tasted," agreed Miss Lydia.

Last came the Christmas crackers. Amid much noise and laughter each guest turned to assist his neighbor in pulling them until, with a sound like a cap gun, they fell apart. Then the party hats were unfolded, the prizes exclaimed over, and the mottoes read aloud.

"A tall, dark, and handsome stranger is about to enter your life," I read.

"Do you reckon he'll be waiting for you when you get back to California, Delilah?" called Justin from the far end of the table.

Cousin Betty was on her feet snapping pictures, and I had to lean forward around her to catch Justin's eye.

"I'm sure of it." I laughed.

Timmy's prize was a loud tin whistle, which he proceeded to blow in my ear every few seconds.

"Here. Let's read your motto," I said, gently removing the whistle from his mouth just as he was about to let go with another ear-piercing toot.

"Come on, Jasper," called someone. "We haven't heard yours yet."

We all turned toward the head of the table in anticipation of hearing our patriarch rumble out his motto.

But facedown in his pudding plate, Jasper clearly was not in the mood. More to the point, he never would be, I thought, noting the trickle of blood running from his temple into the yellow trifle custard.

Others saw it, too. Major Tom and Justin rushed to the

old man's side. As they raised his head from the trifle, I shielded little Timmy from the sight of the ugly wound in his grandfather's temple.

Cries of "He's been shot!" and "Good God!" replaced the previously happy conversation.

"Is he—?" cried Aunt Maud.

Justin looked up, nodding his head sadly.

"Let's get the child out of here, Delilah," said Millicent, coming around from the other side of the table. I recall a waft of lavender sachet as Miss Lydia picked up the fallen cowboy hat and smoothed Timmy's yellow hair while Alfred lifted him out of the high chair and into my arms.

Justin took over with surprising efficiency. The waiter was dispatched to call the police. "The rest of us must remain until they get here," said Justin, holding the door open for me to carry Timmy out and effectively barring anyone else from following.

Children were not allowed in the saloon bar, but it was the only warm place for us to wait. I felt sure that given the exceptional circumstances, our transgression would be forgiven.

We sat on a padded oak bench, Timmy solemnly munching on the mince pie I'd had the presence of mind to grab on my way out of the dining room. I wondered how the family was coping while they waited for the police. Aunt Maud would no doubt be having an attack of the vapors while poor Miss Lydia would be at her wit's end shouting the news into Great-aunt Nell's ear-trumpet.

"Look at the pretty Christmas tree," I said to Timmy, pointing to the elaborately decorated tree in the lobby. It was hard to keep my voice from trembling. In my career as a pet detective I had seen my share of dead bodies, but this was the first time the victim had been a member of my own family.

Once more I relived the scene: the lights dimming for the Christmas pudding ceremony, the popping of the crackers, the flash of Cousin Betty's Polaroid.

But that meant that the gun must have gone off at precisely the moment the crackers were being pulled! Whoever had fired the gun must be familiar with our ritual, which led me to the reluctant but certain conclusion that the culprit was one of the family, not some hidden interloper. I must tell the police as soon as they arrived. I looked anxiously toward the entrance.

In the chimney nook of the huge stone fireplace, adorned with gleaming horse brasses, a couple of elderly patrons sipped mild and bitter through heads of thick foam, the firelight reflected in their glistening pewter tankards. An Old English sheepdog, his shaggy black-and-gray coat damp from the rain, steamed in front of the crackling log fire, sending up a pungent odor of wet dog.

The two old codgers, obviously unaware of the tragedy being played out in the private dining room, looked at Timmy with interest. "'E'll come into a tidy sum when t' old gaffer kicks the bucket," I overheard one of them say.

"You reckon?"

His friend wiped the foam from his gray mustache and lowered his voice. "Old Jasper ain't got much longer, what with 'is dicey ticker, an' all. It'd be worth baby-sitting the young'un for a few years, if they end up holding the purse strings for him."

I realized they were talking about Alfred and Millicent, and it was then I remembered that Timmy would inherit a considerable fortune through his mother—the direct line—if Jasper died intestate. As he just had.

Sleep overtaking him, the young heir slumped against me. I tried to make him more comfortable, easing off first the cowboy hat, then the boots, and unbuckling the belt. To my surprise I saw that both guns were now in their holsters. Not a very good match, I thought, holding one in either hand. In fact, one of them felt oddly warm to the touch. Slowly the realization dawned that the gun I held in my right hand was not a toy.

I felt a prickle of fear run from the back of my neck and down my arms.

From the distance came the sound of approaching sirens. Thank God—the police!

Led by the waiter, the police and the paramedics rushed past me into the dining room.

After twenty minutes or so Detective Inspector Derek Booker of the Surrey Constabulary, a longtime family friend, returned to the saloon bar. He posted a constable at the dining-room door, then walked over to where I was sitting.

If I hadn't been so preoccupied with Jasper's death, I might have made more of the fact that here, indeed, was a tall, dark, and handsome man.

"Nasty business for you to come home to, Delilah," he said. "Sorry about your uncle."

I spoke in a whisper, not wanting to wake Timmy. "Which one? The one who's dead, or the one who killed him?"

Derek's puzzled look slowly changed to one of comprehension as I explained.

"Well, either Major Tom or Uncle Alfred must have replaced one of the toy guns with the real thing," I said, indicating the two guns in Timmy's holster. "I'm sure he thought that way he'd be able to get the gun out of the pub without arousing suspicion. No one would suspect the child, even if everyone else in the dining room was searched.

"My money's on Alfred," I continued, going on to tell

Derek how he had insisted on holding Timmy in his lap in the car. "I think if you search the car, you'll find the toy gun."

Gingerly I handed him the real gun. "Sorry, it's got my fingerprints on it. But my guess is that you'll find Alfred's there, too."

Looping a pencil through the handle, Derek took the nasty little gun and dropped it into a plastic bag. "It's a derringer," he said, regarding it with interest. "One of those two-shot affairs. Haven't seen one in years. Not too accurate at a distance. Must have been very close range."

It wasn't until after Derek had left for the parking lot that I remembered the cousins and their picture-taking. He was gone for what seemed like an hour, but actually the grandfather clock had chimed only one more quarter when he returned.

"I've made a quick search of the car but there's no sign of the toy gun," Derek said. "And short of tearing it apart, for which I'd need a search warrant—"

"I jumped to the wrong conclusion, then," I interrupted. "I'm sorry. I thought Alfred must have slipped it behind the upholstery while Timmy was on his lap. There wasn't time to stash it in the boot, or under the bonnet."

Derek gave a rueful smile. "Well, don't look so downcast. You've already been a great help by discovering the derringer." He thought for a moment or two. "Who else was in the car?"

"The Major was driving, Aunt Maud was in the passenger seat. They picked us up. Alfred, Millicent, and I were in the back."

By now it was 10:00 P.M. "Time gentlemen, please," called the barkeep, a signal that no more drinks would be served. People began to leave—even more reluctantly than usual, it seemed. By then all were aware of what had occurred, and lingered in the entryway, no doubt hoping to glean some information they could later contribute to the village gossip mill.

Signaling to the barmaid that I was returning to the dining room, I left Timmy stretched out asleep on the bench seat.

"Okay, love. I'll keep me eye on the poor little mite," she said cheerfully.

Such a different picture greeted me in the dining room compared with the merriment of an hour or so earlier. The coroner had been and gone, and Great-uncle Jasper had been taken away by a side door. Millicent sat solemnly knitting; Maud was complaining to the constable that Precious really needed to go outside to do his business.

Great-aunt Nell was asleep in her chair. Miss Lydia, temporarily relieved of her duties, and looking more distraught than one might have expected, stood by Jasper's chair staring at where he had breathed his last.

Millicent paused in her knitting to look at me. "I told you thirteen was unlucky."

Debbie started to cry. Justin put his arm around her and gave her a quick hug. "Soon be over," he reassured her. I was surprised, but nonetheless pleased, at his kindness.

"Well, Detective Inspector, are you going to make an arrest?" demanded the Major.

The DI took out his notebook. "Just a few more questions."

He looked directly at Miss Lydia, who, flustered at suddenly being the center of attention, said nervously, "I'm afraid I can't tell you much. I was helping my employer with her paper hat and didn't see a thing."

Derek nodded. "What was your relationship with Jasper?"

"Relationship? We weren't related." Then, realizing the import of the question: "Why, whatever do you mean?"

"It's common knowledge in the village that some years

ago, soon after Jasper's wife died, you had an affair with him, but that it never came to anything because he turned his attentions elsewhere. Correct?"

Flushed, Miss Lydia put a hand to her throat.

"But I'd never—kill—him . . ." she stammered.

There were mumbles of "I say, old chap," and "Have a care there," from Alfred and the Major.

"Stuff and nonsense," said Millicent, looking up from her knitting.

Derek turned to her. "I understand you and your husband recently adopted young Timmy?"

Millicent stiffened but continued to knit, pulling the tapestry bag into her lap. "That's right. What's that got to do with anything?"

Silently I motioned to Cousin Betty, standing nearby, to hand me the photos. I quickly shuffled through them, placing one in particular on top.

Derek continued talking to Millicent. "If your father died without a will, then young Timmy, being in direct line, would inherit. And, since he wouldn't come into his inheritance until age twenty-one, you and your husband would have control of the estate for the next seventeen years. Am I right?"

Millicent put down her knitting and nodded nervously.

The room had gone deathly quiet. Derek continued, "Tonight Jasper planned to announce his heir, which might well have been anyone in this room."

Millicent stood up as if about to argue. As she did so the contents of her knitting bag spilled out onto the floor. There, among the needles and balls of yarn, was the toy gun. Derek picked it up.

"Alfred!" Millicent appealed to her husband.

But Alfred, ghostly white, had collapsed in a chair. Speechless with horror, he watched as Derek compared the toy gun with the derringer in the plastic bag. Then, as he grasped the enormity of what his wife had done, he buried his face in his hands.

I handed the photos to Derek. "I think you'll find some corroborating evidence here."

When taking the top photo Cousin Betty had obviously been intent on capturing Alfred, his back to his wife, pulling crackers with Miss Lydia. But behind him, though partially hidden by the centerpiece, it was clearly Millicent's hand pointing the gun at Jasper.

Before leaving the inn that night, curiosity led me to sort through the discarded wrappings of Jasper's cracker for his unread motto. Instead, I found his notes for the evening. First, the list of absent friends to be toasted, followed by a few words on the disposition of his estate. After several bequests, including one for Justin, *provided he found a job within thirty days,* the bulk of the estate was to go *to Millicent and Alfred in appreciation of their kindness in adopting my great-grandson Timothy.*

With a shiver at life's ironies, and grimly contemplating that yet another member of my family had died a sudden and unnatural death, I turned and left the scene of what I was sure had been our last family Boxing Day dinner at The Feathers.

❖

UNCLE JASPER'S BLOODY DELICIOUS SHERRY TRIFLE

Sherry trifle originated as a way of using up stale cake. It is a dessert that allows for creativity, depending on the size of the bowl and what's on hand. Jelly roll can be substituted for ladyfingers; any jam, canned fruit, or dessert gelatin will

*serve. Everything's optional except the cake, the sherry,
and the custard. Best made the previous day. Directions are
for an 8 x 3½–inch deep, 2–quart glass bowl.*

2 3–ounce packages of lady fingers (12 in package)
½ cup raspberry jam
3–4 ounces cream sherry (not cooking sherry)
10 ounces sweetened frozen raspberries, thawed and drained
    (save juice)
3–ounce package of raspberry gelatin dessert
1 pint Bird's custard (a British import available at most major
    supermarkets and English specialty stores)
1 pint milk for custard
2 tablespoons sugar for custard
1 cup heavy cream
Glacé cherries, chopped nuts, and angelica to decorate, as
    desired

Prepare gelatin dessert, substituting raspberry juice for
part of the water. Fold in raspberries. Cool to a soft set. Prepare custard according to package directions. Let cool.
Cover with wax paper to prevent skin forming.

ASSEMBLY:

Split ladyfingers, spread with jam, reassemble.

Arrange half ladyfingers upright around the sides of
bowl, layer remainder at the bottom.

Sprinkle sherry over the bottom cake layer and halfway
up sides.

Spread the raspberry gelatin over the bottom cake layer.

Pour cooled custard over gelatin.

Chill.

AN HOUR BEFORE SERVING:

Spread whipped cream over custard, and decorate with nuts, glacé cherries, and angelica, as desired. Yield: 6 to 8 servings.

—PG

PLANT ENGINEERING

NANCY KRESS

"In Europe," Judy said innocently, "they call it 'Frankenfood.'"

Robert Cavanaugh, off-duty FBI agent, looked at his wife with some irritation. She was a science writer; she was supposed to know things like that. It was still irritating. Or maybe it was just irritating because Cavanaugh did not want to be at the Glentree Mall on a Friday night, at Judy's cousin's book signing.

"In America I call it boring," Cavanaugh said just as flames shot up from Marilyn's skillet onstage and the crowd went "Ooooooooohhhhhhhh" as if they'd never before seen cherries flambé.

The stage was actually a makeshift platform in the middle of the mall, between The Gap and Weismann Jewelers, set under a sign suspended from the ceiling by chains. The sign said:

MEET MARILYN BAKER!
AUTHOR OF
COOKING WITH GENETICALLY ENHANCED FOODS!

The first, fourth, and fifth words were burned into the sign in elaborate curlicues; the rest were assembled from plastic letters inserted into slotted trays. Under this reusable endorsement, Judy's cousin demonstrated how to prepare dinner using the increased-flavor, increased-shelf-life, decreased-waste, disease-resistant miracles of genetic engineering. Her ingredients were prominently displayed with the brand names facing outward: Sheffield Orchard Cherries, Konig Currant Jelly. Plus, to Cavanaugh's surprise, bottles of Bacardi rum and Courvoisier. His surprise was not as strong as his irritation.

Cavanaugh was not interested in cooking, which was the first irritant. The second was that Marilyn had started her demonstration half an hour late, while various curious passersby climbed on the stage to inspect the microphone and "kitchen counters" and two-burner portable stove. The third irritant was that Judy hadn't actually seen Marilyn, only a second cousin, in years. Moreover, Judy had told Cavanaugh she hadn't ever liked Marilyn, who was "loud and unpleasant." Yet here they were, wasting a perfectly good evening, partly because of Judy's guilt over neglected family (Cavanaugh's own family lived two thousand blessed miles away) and partly because Judy had just happened to be planning a major freelance article on genetic enhancements to tomatoes.

"Who wants a taste of cherries flambé?" Marilyn shrilled from the stage. "You, sir? Climb right on up here! No? What, you don't like cherries flambé? Oh, come on, everybody likes cherries, it's positively un-American to not like cherries! George Washington and his little tree, 'Can you bake a cherry pie, Billy Boy?'—you don't want to be un-American, do you? What are you, a foreign terrorist?"

The crowd laughed. The un-American cherry-hater, a burly man in his forties, flushed and scowled. Smoke from the portable stove curled upward. Quite a lot of smoke,

Cavanaugh noted; Marilyn must have sloshed food on the burners. Judy's cousin was a sloppy cook. The thought filled him with obscure satisfaction.

"No cherries for the un-American wimp!" Marilyn said, pouring the flaming fruit over scoops of hard vanilla ice cream set out in Styrofoam cups. The flames went out. With exaggerated grimaces of enjoyment, she put a heaping spoonful into her own mouth.

Everything happened at once.

Two dozen people streamed toward the stage from a side entrance to the mall. Dressed in bright green overalls and T-shirts, they all shouted unintelligibly, waving signs that said NO FRANKENFOOD HERE and NO MUTANT CROPS! and STOP THIS TERRIFYING TAMPERING. Onlookers laughed and pointed. All of the protesters stayed well back from the stage, behind the crowd. Onstage, Marilyn went wide-eyed and spat out her mouthful of cherries and ice cream, which spattered the heads and shoulders of those in the front rows. These people yelled out and wiped themselves in disgust. Marilyn lurched sideways and fell over. Someone screamed.

Judy gasped and pushed her way through the crowd. Cavanaugh pulled out his cell phone and dialed 911. By the time he caught up with Judy, Marilyn lay gasping vainly for breath, fumbling at her clothing. She tried to speak and failed. Her face had broken out in huge red splotches. Then her eyes rolled in her head and she went still.

Judy started CPR. Cavanaugh seized Marilyn's mike and shouted, "Is there a doctor here? Medical emergency . . . we need a doctor here!"

No doctor appeared. Judy continued CPR. Most of the crowd, either fleeing involvement or wiping off spat-out cherries, fled the area. The medtechs were prompt, but by the time they whisked Marilyn away in an ambulance, Cavanaugh doubted that there was much point.

From force of habit he looked at his watch. It said eight-thirty.

"Your cousin died of severe anaphylactic shock," the ER doctor said to Judy, after a long wait in a hospital lounge more dismal than some police interrogation rooms Cavanaugh had seen. "We found this in her pocket."

She handed Judy a small object that Cavanaugh didn't recognize. Judy drew in a sharp breath.

"It's EpiPen, a spring-loaded injector of epinephrine," the doctor said. "Commonly used for the most severe allergic attacks. Did your cousin have, say, a food allergy?"

"I don't know," Cavanaugh said. He looked at his wife. Her face was ash gray. Marilyn had been fumbling in her pocket when Judy had reached her, fumbling to reach her injector. If Judy had only known . . .

"It's not your fault," Cavanaugh said quietly into his wife's ear. To the doctor he said, "Marilyn was a cooking expert in genetically altered food. She was very knowledgeable about it—she wouldn't have been using anything she was severely allergic to. It had to be something else entirely."

"Genetically altered foods?" the doctor said doubtfully. "I'm afraid I don't know very much about them yet."

"Nobody really does," Judy said. "They're so new. In Europe they call them Frankenfoods."

"I'm sure they're safe," Cavanaugh said. "Something else is going on here." Something else, anything else that would take that ashy look off Judy's face.

The doctor shook her head. "Anaphylactic shock is pretty unmistakable. I don't know what Ms. Baker was allergic to, but it was to something. I'm sorry."

Judy said nothing. Her face did not change.

"It wasn't your fault," Cavanaugh said. He said it on the way home from the hospital. He said it as they got into bed. He said it at dinner, on their front porch, as they sat watching TV. It didn't seem to make any difference. Judy's replies all seemed to be non sequiturs, although of course they were not.

At dinner Judy said, "I called Marilyn's sister, my cousin Pam. Pam said Marilyn was allergic to peanuts. Fatally allergic. Everyone in the family knew that, Pam said. *Everyone.*"

"You didn't know it, honey."

"Ignorance does not wipe out culpability," Judy answered, and Cavanaugh had no reply. He was FBI. Culpability was his job.

Sitting on the front porch, Judy said, "The shock reaction is caused by a specific protein in peanuts. Protein DNA can be transferred between species when the scientists do the genetic engineering. They tried splicing Brazil-nut genes into soybeans to make them more nutritious, and you know what happened? The soybeans triggered reactions in people allergic to Brazil nuts. You don't know anymore what foreign genes you're getting in your food."

"Well, that just means Marilyn caused her own death. Inadvertently, I mean."

"Not if I had recognized EpiPen."

As they watched TV Judy said, "All kinds of groups have launched public education programs about peanut allergies. Schools, government, medical groups. Everybody knows about it, that is, everybody with the awareness of a head of cabbage."

Genetically altered cabbage, no doubt, Cavanaugh thought but didn't say. Judy had lost weight. Her hair hadn't been washed. Worse, his wife had lost her argumentative sass. Judy was wallowing in unearned guilt, and

Cavanaugh thought she should stop it. Still, if it had been his cousin, and he who *hadn't* found the epinephrine . . .

"Judy, honey, you don't even know for sure that it was a peanut allergy. There's no proof."

Her only answer was to read more news articles on genetic engineering. These were everywhere, all featuring Marilyn's picture as she crumpled under the cheery sign advertising her book. The press hadn't shown up at Marilyn's signing—she wasn't important enough—but the damn amateur photographers were always in the wrong places at the right times.

"Judy, honey—"

"Did you know," Judy said, "that forty percent of the U.S. soybean crop is genetically engineered?"

"Vic, I need a favor."

Victor Spelling, FBI DNA lab, paused beside his Toyota in the Hoover Building underground parking lot and eyed Cavanaugh. "A favor? What kind of favor? What's all that stuff?"

Cavanaugh tilted his two brown paper shopping bags so that Vic could see inside.

"Rum, brandy, ice cream—you giving a party? Am I invited?"

"No. I mean, if I were giving a party, you'd be invited. Sure. But I'm not. I need samples of all these things analyzed, Vic, down to the DNA level. To see if any of it has any DNA from peanut genes spliced in. Specifically, the DNA that makes the proteins that cause peanut allergies."

Vic's eyebrows, already generous, seemed to grow bushier. "Peanut DNA? In Bacardi Gold?"

"No, huh? Well, good. One less thing to analyze. How about the brandy?"

"Not in this world. Courvoisier would die first. You got a case number for this analysis?"

"It's off-the-record."

The two men locked eyes. They had been at college together, fifteen years ago. Cavanaugh tried to get into his eyes powerful reminders of frat parties and study sessions. Once he had actually rewritten an English paper for Vic, who had been too hung over to realize that Wordsworth was not a novelist. "Robert . . ."

"Please, Vic. It's a personal matter, and really important." Judy's hair was still greasy, and she looked as if she'd lost as much as ten pounds, which she could ill afford. The Unhealthy Obsession Diet.

Vic sighed. "Give it here. Oh, God, the ice cream's melting."

"It's genetically engineered," Cavanaugh said, which may or may not have been a non sequitur.

The DNA analysis took a week. Cavanaugh was astonished at what went into genetically altered food. The sugarcane used in the currant jelly had a gene splice to make its own insecticide. The currants had been engineered for shorter growth time. The cherries were enhanced for sugar production and hence greater sweetness. The soy in the ice cream had been modified for greater yield. The lab report was complete, detailed, fascinating. Nowhere did it mention anything connected to peanuts.

Whatever had killed Marilyn Baker, it hadn't been her cherries flambé.

So what had?

The ER doctor was not happy to see Cavanaugh a second time. She stood in bloodstained scrubs, scowling at him. But she answered his questions without his having to pull out FBI credentials. This was good because Cavanaugh hadn't the faintest claim to jurisdiction, nor any plausible grounds for claiming a crime had been committed, nor any real idea what he was doing.

"I already told you, Mr. Cavanaugh, that the evidence for an allergic reaction in your wife's cousin was as close to certain as we come, but that we didn't identify the specific causal agent. You'd need an autopsy to do that, and of course we had no reason to perform an autopsy. Did Ms. Baker have multiple severe allergies?"

"No," Cavanaugh said. He'd already questioned Judy's aunt. Subtly, he hoped.

"Then that's your cause of death. Why do you doubt it?"

"Because there were no peanuts around."

The doctor moved away. Over her shoulder she said, "If Ms. Baker's allergy was the most severe kind, a whiff of peanuts from someone in the crowd might have set off a reaction. Sometimes that's all it takes—the odor."

"To kill her?"

"Well, no, probably not. Not unless it were very concentrated. She would have had time to get to her EpiPen under normal circumstances. I'm sorry, I must go."

Under normal circumstances. So, as a working assumption, these were not. What about them had been abnormal? Carefully, Cavanaugh reviewed every detail he could remember about Marilyn's book signing.

Someone had happened to have a camera all ready to take a media-grabbing shot of Marilyn collapsing . . . a shot that just happened to include clear focus on the sign advertising her book: *COOKING WITH GENETICALLY ENHANCED FOODS!*

None of the protesters against genetically modified foods had come anywhere near the mall stage. Not usual demonstration behavior. Usually protesters against anything tried to intimidate, getting as close to the target as possible, waving their signs aggressively.

Marilyn's onstage stove had smoked. A lot, although Cavanaugh had not seen any cherries flambé slopping onto the burner.

"Can I help you, sir?" a nurse said pointedly. It took Cavanaugh a moment to focus on her, and on where he was. "Are you looking for someone?"

"No," Cavanaugh said. "Yes. I don't know yet." She watched him all the way through the ER glass doors and halfway across the parking lot to his car.

At home, Judy said, "Did you know that two percent of the population has some form of peanut allergy? And that it's on the increase?"

Cavanaugh bit back his answer. Instead—he had been married awhile now—he carefully took her in his arms and, just as carefully, withheld all explanations, solutions, and logic. He just held her.

It didn't seem to help.

From his office, Cavanaugh called *The Washington Post.* A chatty secretary who sounded about fifteen was glad to give him the credit on the photograph of Marilyn collapsing. It was offered gratis, the girl said helpfully, by a Mr. Colin Wilson of Bethesda.

Cavanaugh ran the name through NCIC: nothing. But a search on the Internet led him to a home page jammed with anti-genetic-engineering messages. He spent an hour following the links from the home page. This netted him a list of seventeen names, all members of an organization called FOFFGEN: Free Our Food From Genetic Engineering Now. Members dressed in green overalls and T-shirts and spent their weekends protesting at supermarkets around Washington.

FOFFGEN. It sounded like an alien race invented by George Lucas or Steven Spielberg. Sometimes Cavanaugh suspected that protesters formed their groups solely for the weird names.

In the next half hour, he revised this opinion.

One of the seventeen FOFFGEN members, "Harold Keller," turned up only once on the welter of linked sites. Every other name was featured over and over, with many pictures, on the slightest of pretexts: people screaming for attention. There was no picture of Harold Keller.

On impulse, he entered Marilyn's name into the search engine. The Internet gave him her home page. Biography, book promotion, career in food preparation, lifelong fascination with cooking, childhood memories . . . why did people assume others were interested in all this personal trivia? But, yes, there it was, a whole section of the home page: *My Deadly Battle with Mr. Peanut.* Illustrated with tiny hopping peanuts dressed like pirates and wielding scimitars.

Cavanaugh went downstairs to the information analysts.

"Jim, I need a name check. Whatever you can find for me."

"Yo," Jim Nedermeier said. Tall, weedy, he spent his days navigating seas of bits and bytes, a captain on invisible oceans. Like all explorers, he harbored a secret scorn for the landlocked. "Case number?"

"Well, there isn't one. It's by way of a favor."

"I can't—"

"It's really for my wife," Cavanaugh said. "She's in a bad way over her cousin's death, this Marilyn Baker thing."

Nedermeier gazed at Cavanaugh. Steadily Cavanaugh gazed back. Nedermeier had married a year ago, a girl he'd met on-line, who had moved to Washington for him and had hated the place ever since. Awkward and shy, Sandra Nedermeier languished for Montana. Judy had gone out of her way to be kind to Sandra. Cavanaugh refused to feel ashamed of himself.

Nedermeier finally said, "What's the name?"

"Harold Keller. H-A-R-O-L-D K-E-L-L-E-R. I have a hunch he may be European, possibly British."

"Yo," Nedermeier said unhappily, and retreated to the bounding electronic deep.

At the end of the day he dropped a report on Cavanaugh's desk. Harold Keller was indeed British, having legally entered the United States on a U.K. passport two months ago, on June 6. He was thirty-six years old, until recently employed as an equipment engineer in a fish-packing plant in Hull, Yorkshire, England. On June 8, a warrant for his arrest had been issued by the constabulary of Hull. On June 5, Harold Keller had allegedly participated in a crop trashing, in which, during cover of night, twenty people had destroyed an experimental farm raising canola plants genetically engineered by a German biotech company. To his brief report Nedermeier had attached two documents. The first was an article from the London *Daily Telegraph,* discussing the large number of upcoming trials of crop-destroying food protesters in the U.K. The other was from Scotland Yard, summarizing a telephone transcript that linked Harold Keller, albeit inconclusively, to two counts of first-degree murder of Canadian fishermen caught harpooning whales. At the bottom of this Nedermeier had scrawled, in the awkward handwriting of someone who habitually typed: *But maybe the whales were growing GM canola.*

Cavanaugh smiled, even though it really wasn't all that funny. But you took what you could get.

"Karen, it's Robert Cavanaugh."

"Oh, hello, Robert," Marilyn's sister said, without enthusiasm. Robert *didn't* take this personally. Nor did he take it as a sign of mourning. Karen Baker, a perpetual complainer, never had enthusiasm for anything, and she had disliked her deceased sister, along with almost everyone else she encountered. Cavanaugh didn't have to worry about offending Karen's sensibilities. Only about beating down his own.

"Listen, I'm doing some follow-up for Judy on Marilyn's death, and I wondered—"

"For Judy? She feeling guilty? Well, maybe she should."

"And I—"

"I mean, the whole world knew Marilyn had a peanut allergy. If Judy ever paid any attention to our branch of the family, she'd have known, too, and poor Marilyn might be alive."

Cavanaugh held on to his temper. "I wondered what happened to the equipment Marilyn was using onstage the night she died. The stove and pans and stuff."

"Why do you want to know?"

"Like I said, it's follow-up for Judy." This uninformative phrase had cost Cavanaugh some thought, as had his next. "For emotional clarity."

"Well, Judy certainly always needed more of that. I suppose Marilyn's equipment is still in her apartment. The police delivered it there, and Mama just hasn't had the heart to go through the apartment yet. Marilyn was always her favorite, you know, even when we were kids."

Heroically, Cavanaugh refused the bait. "Could you let me in? Do you have a key?"

"I don't have time for Judy's emotional crises, Robert. But there's a key above the door frame in the hallway. Marilyn wasn't very bright, you know."

"Thanks," Cavanaugh said, hung up, and considered disinfecting the phone. Instead, he drove to Marilyn's apartment before Karen decided to remove the key, from sheer cousinly spite.

Too bad it was illegal to genetically enhance a family for greater sweetness. On the other hand, you might get increased shelf life. Not worth the risk.

Marilyn Baker had lived in a nondescript apartment building in Silver Spring. As far as Cavanaugh could see, no one had disturbed anything since her death, except to leave a pile of cardboard boxes in the tiny foyer. These contained the ingredients for cherry flambé, her cooking equipment, and forty-two unsold copies of *Cooking with Genetically Enhanced Foods!* Cavanaugh was glad he wasn't an author.

He lifted the portable stove from its box and sniffed the burners. With his fingernail he scraped cautiously. Both burners were indeed crusted with spilled food. Peanut oil?

If Harold Keller, or someone else in the anti-genetically-engineered-food camp, had wanted a high-profile death to bring attention to their cause, they might easily have engineered this one. No one had monitored Marilyn's equipment after it was set up for the cooking demonstration and before she showed up, late. Pour peanut oil on the burners, and when they smoke, the fumes deliver peanut essence to Marilyn in the concentrated form necessary for a possibly fatal attack. Even if it's not fatal, the resulting photo would look like a horrible seizure from eating genetically engineered cherries flambé. By the time the newspapers printed a modification to the story, after the doctor's report went public, the photo would already be burned into people's brains. Meanwhile, keep your protesters well away from the stage during the actual demonstration, to make crystal clear that they never touched Marilyn.

Cavanaugh carried the portable stove to his car. He'd have to go to the cops, of course. Out of his jurisdiction. But they'd listen to him, and probably appreciate the legwork. First, however, there was a stronger priority. He drove home to tell Judy that her cousin had indeed been killed, but not by her.

I t didn't go exactly as he'd planned.

Judy sat on the sofa, legs curled under her, hollow-cheeked and big-eyed. She listened to Cavanaugh in silence. The only sign that his theory touched her was her left hand, which played with a strand of lank hair. When he'd finished explaining—the explanation that was supposed to release his wife from her guilty melancholy—Judy leaned forward and kissed him.

"I'm glad I married you, Robert," she said, and he heard the sadness in her voice.

"Judy, don't you understand? Somebody, most likely the GM protesters, set it up for Marilyn to have that attack. It was planned. Of course, I still have to have the burners analyzed, but they smell like some kind of oil was put on them, and Marilyn with her allergy would never have used peanut oil herself. If it *is* peanut oil, then that's where the peanut fumes came from, not from the engineered foods that Marilyn was—"

"Robert, you don't understand," Judy said, but without her old argumentative spirit. "Even if you're right—and you're not—it doesn't matter where the peanut fumes came from, or if they were deliberate. I still could have saved Marilyn if I'd known about her allergy and gotten to the EpiPen in time."

This view of the crime hadn't occurred to Cavanaugh. He'd been so intent on proving that it *was* a crime, an attempted murder, that he hadn't seen how Judy would view it. She was looking not at the first cause, as he was, but at the immediate result, and her failure to stop it.

"You went to a lot of trouble," Judy said. "And you did

it for me, I know. Thank you. But, honey, apart from me, there's another problem with your theory. Even if it is peanut oil on the burners, that wouldn't have killed Marilyn. I've been researching on the Net. The refining process to turn peanuts into oil removes the allergenic proteins. Peanut oil doesn't trigger anaphylactic shock."

Cavanaugh got up and paced around the sofa. "So it has to be peanut solids?"

"Pretty much. But, honey, listen . . . I'm glad to know it wasn't in the genetically engineered foods. I'm really glad to know that. I believe in genetic engineering, you know."

Cavanaugh nodded, although at the moment Judy didn't look as if she believed in much of anything. Cavanaugh pictured again the scene at the mall. Marilyn saying, *No cherries for the un-American wimp!* and then pouring the flaming fruit over hard vanilla ice cream set out in Styrofoam cups. Putting a heaping spoonful into her own mouth . . .

The ice cream had melted. From the heat, of course. But the heat had also risen upward, traced by those plumes of smoke from the burners. Upward, to wreath that tacky reusable sign: MEET MARILYN BAKER! AUTHOR OF *COOKING WITH GENETICALLY ENHANCED FOODS!* That sign, with slots to hold different letters. Or anything else.

"Wait right here," Cavanaugh said.

The manager of the Greentree Mall, Allen Sussman, required that Cavanaugh produce FBI identification. Cavanaugh did, hoping no one at the Bureau would ever find out. Immediately Sussman became cooperative.

"Glad to help, Agent Cavanaugh, although I have to say I'm sorry to hear this isn't about the break-in we had at our own security office. Happened the day after Ms. Baker's death. Embarrassing, when it's the security office broken into, although nothing was really taken, they just trashed the place . . . The sign? The mall maintenance crew puts the letters into the sign and then hangs it up the afternoon of each event. Usually before they leave for the day at five-thirty. We let it hang there overnight—it doesn't bother anybody—until the crew removes it in the morning. However, the night Ms. Baker died, we took it down right away. To keep down rubbernecking, disruption of mall traffic, that sort of thing."

"Who took the sign down? Where did it get put?"

"Well, usually, as I say, it would be put back with regular equipment, but that night the maintenance crew had gone home, so . . . I don't think I know where it got put!"

"Who took it down? Were you here?"

"Oh, yes. I'm always in on Friday nights. Let's see—I remember I asked Brian, he's our security chief, to get it taken down. Brian Selenski. Just a minute, I'll page him."

While they waited for Brian Selenski, Cavanaugh said, "Who was on maintenance duty that afternoon? Who hung the sign up?"

The manager pulled a duty roster from his drawer. "I don't know who did the actual work. We'd have to ask. But we usually have a four-person crew on maintenance at any given time . . . Here we are. Sally Lieber, Bill Reese, Jeff Handerman, Harold Keller. Keller's new, just been on the job a few months. English. They're good workers, you know."

Cavanaugh sat quietly until the mall security chief showed up. Brian Selenski was a big man, balding, dressed in a uniform a little too tight across the chest. Cavanaugh knew the type: a square badge who enjoyed playing cop but would resent the real thing on his turf. Selenski listened sullenly while the manager explained what Cavanaugh wanted.

"That sign? Took it down myself. Trivial detail. Until

this very minute, I forgot about it; we have bigger things to deal with here, Mr. Cavanaugh. Security break-in at my office. Not that the cops were any help with that."

"Where is the sign now?"

Selenski shrugged. "Still where I stowed it. In with the day rentals, the kid strollers, and wheelchairs. You want it, Mr. Sussman? I'll get it."

"I'll go with you," Cavanaugh said. "And, Mr. Selenski, I think you need a better background-check system."

"Yeah? Why is that?"

"I'll show you. Let's go get that sign."

"So it was heat-activated," Judy repeated, "and it was Harold Keller after all. He's gone underground, of course, but you'll get him eventually." Judy put down her fork. Her eyes hadn't left Cavanaugh's face since he started explaining. Around them in the Georgetown restaurant waiters served drinks and diners clattered silverware.

"Smoke-activated, actually. Like a smoke alarm. The smoke opened a spring door and a tiny fan drove the peanut fumes directly downward into Marilyn's face. A simple piece of engineering."

"And the whole thing fit behind one of the movable letters on the sign?"

Cavanaugh held up a thumb and forefinger to show the size of the device. "Plenty of room to plant it. The letters are just painted on thin blocks that slide into a tray. Cheesy."

"Ingenious."

"Deadly."

"Unfortunately."

Cavanaugh reached across the restaurant table to take his wife's hand. "You seem better, honey."

"I am." Judy pushed her clean hair back off her face.

"I realized that I did what I could, even if it was the wrong thing. And if I hadn't done it, there's no evidence Marilyn would have got the EpiPen out in time, anyway. Her eyes were already rolling when I grabbed her. She might have gotten the injector out of her pocket, but she might not."

Silently Cavanaugh thanked Providence for his wife's good sense. It disappeared under cover occasionally—actually, quite often—but eventually it reappeared.

"You know what, Robert," Judy said, "Everything's dangerous. Genetically engineered food, genetically natural food, treated water, untreated water, food additives, nonpreserved food that's been sitting around too long . . . Nobody should ever eat anything."

"Not very practical."

"No. So let's order."

They opened their menus. Cavanaugh studied the entrées. Battered cod with skewered vegetables. Blackened trout with beaten biscuits. Spitted pork . . . He glanced ahead at the desserts. Blitz tort. Whipped cream pie. Death by Chocolate . . . even dessert was a violent risk.

Cherries flambé.

He ordered the pasta primavera.

❖

CHERRIES FLAMBÉ

(genetically enhanced ingredients are optional)

Vanilla ice cream
¼ cup rum
2 cups pitted dark sweet cherries, fresh or canned and drained
¾ cup currant jelly
1 teaspoon grated orange peel
¼ cup brandy

Scoop the ice cream in serving-sized portions into dessert dishes; refreeze. Pour rum over cherries. Refrigerate four hours. Just before serving, heat jelly over low heat until melted. Stir in cherry mixture and orange peel. Heat to simmering, stirring constantly. Heat brandy just until warm. Ignite and pour flaming over cherries. Serve hot over the ice cream.

—*NK*

THE BAGEL MURDERS

DAVID A. KAUFELT

We finished the last scene—a multiple torture-
murder, don't spare the ketchup, take five—by
midnight.

The assistant director, a top-heavy gal named Whinny,
who lived on Fountain, said it would be no trouble whatso-
ever to drive me to the airport. She was ready to be obliging to the fourth leading man. She said you never know
who you meet on the way up. Or down.

I told her thanks for the offer but I was catching the
L.A.–Miami red-eye and anyway, I had a serious squeeze.
I slow-talked myself into first class and kibitzed over a
penny-ante gin rummy game between two stars of yester-
year. We drank nostalgic highballs—your Seven and Sev-
ens, and your old-fashioneds, your Cuba libres—for five
and a half hours. Miami International, through my blood-
shot eyes, looked like the third-world country that it is, tiny
women wearing babushkas trying to smuggle live chickens
aboard planes headed for such garden spots as Tegucigalpa.

The beautiful Cubans who used to haunt the exclusive
clubs of MIA, their noses rimmed in pricey white powder,

have moved their venue to the private airports. Now they can afford Gulfstreams.

I got into a taxi jockeyed by a seriously bald fellow named Dave Wallowitz, who took me to South Beach via Camarsie. Dave regaled me all the way up and down A1A with tales of his sexual conquests. "The babes love bald men."

"Who doesn't?" I asked. Dave looked at me funny, decided I wasn't gay, and chuckled in time to the *click-click* of the meter. He figured he had a live one.

The warm breeze off the Atlantic was sultry November Miami at its most seductive, the beaches wide and warm and welcoming. By the time we crossed over into Miami Beach, I was nearly ready for Thanksgiving dinner with my mother, her friend Rose Nozick, and, for my sins, my brother-in-law, Leonard.

First I had to take care of a little misunderstanding. As we drove through the concrete condo canyons blocking the ocean and Indian Creek—this is the ritzy section, Dave informed me—I broke it to him that he was going to have to eat half the fifty dollars showing on the meter.

In the rearview mirror I could see his brow furrow like an Indiana cornfield. He was weighing the pros and cons of taking a swing at me.

At a stoplight on Twenty-first and Collins, Dave swiveled in his cramped seat, eyeballed me up and down and sideways. He stayed in his seat, evidently thinking again. "What are you, a private eye?"

What I am is a movie gangster; my most recent role is the fourth and craziest of the Diane brothers in the soon-to-be-released remake of *Murder Inc.* I have big shoulders, hooded black eyes, and, my pièce de résistance, a fortuitously broken nose (Rollerblade pileup on Santa Monica Boulevard). My agent tells me if I ever get my schnoz fixed my career is kaput.

I look like a dangerous citizen from Little Italy via Sicily. In reality, I'm a first-generation Jew from Jersey with a BA in physical therapy from Tufts who got lucky when I was hired to be a stunt double on a Warners flick the summer after I graduated. I did a few stunt gigs after that and eventually I was discovered for what I'm doing now.

Ophelia, my mom, buys the whole tough act. She wanted me to come out to Miami Beach to celebrate Thanksgiving and "teach that *bastardo* what for. If you want, you can liquor him up first to make it easy."

I told her that unless he was an agreeable actor and I was getting paid scale, I couldn't teach him what for.

She said it would be easy. "Don't forget it's Leonard we're talking about. *I* could take him."

Leonard, my brother-in-law, is a short, wide-hipped, receding redhead with licorice-stick arms. "Why don't you, then?"

"It's not my place. Leonard is coming for Thanksgiving dinner, too," Mother informed me. "I'm making it late in deference to your plane and filming schedule. We're going to sit down at eight-thirty sharp."

I got out at Meridien and Eleventh in the dark heart of South Beach at the residence hotel known as the Monte Excelsior Apartments and Leisure Club. I left Dave sitting in his cab, twenty-five bucks in his disconsolate mitt.

"No tip?" he asked, outraged. I gave him an extra five for chutzpah and winning ways.

The Monte is a Spanish Med structure, built with substandard concrete in 1928, when, thanks to a big-time hurricane, Miami Beach was in the depths of an early depression.

Like the women who have inhabited it over the years, the Monte's been interfered with many a time. Towers added, cupolas taken away. Painted pink, sand, blue, sienna, pink again. It's the last big apartment house on

Meridien. All the others have been condominiumized and sold to flash New Yorkers who like to spend weekends in SoBe, downing designer drugs, raving the night away to techno crap.

A square, tarnished brass sign, affixed to the Monte, caught my eye: APRIL POLLACK, PROP. it read in elaborate art deco type.

April—the unlovely Leonard's proud mom—and my mother, coincidentally, shared a childhood on Avenue A in Brooklyn. April's family owned the original brick house that had been split down the middle. April and hers lived in the right half; Ophelia's family in the left. The Pollacks and the Meyers hated one another bitterly from day one.

"Such a wonderful instance of life's parallelisms," April, an Ayn Rand fan, enthused. This was in the fall of 1987, when the widow Ophelia signed the long, wonderfully cheap lease on the grander of the Monte's two penthouses. "Not only are our children in love"—Ophelia's daughter and April's son had met during early deliberations—"but we're going to be neighbors again. How do you like that?"

"I'm not wild about life's parallelisms, April," Mother said. "And you can stop smiling and coming on all sweetie-do. I'm bailing you out by taking this dump at a time when only half a dozen people will rent on Meridien Avenue in South Beach and all of them are dead or certifiable."

This was during the period when Miami Beach's South Beach was in the painful process of becoming cool; when SoBe, as it has come to be known, once peopled by little old Jewish ladies in black rolled-down stockings speaking guttural Yiddish to strictly kosher butchers on Washington Avenue, were literally dying out.

Their place was taken by Spanish gents in unwashed shirts who were juggling at least five scams in the air and were looking for a ticket to ride.

Both the ladies and the low rollers were squeezed by high rents off of Ocean Avenue and then Collins Avenue; they had made their last stand on such lesser streets as Meridien.

Now they had been replaced by buff Rollerbladers in leopardskin thongs and flamboyant movie stars in retro cars. The remaining Hispanics were now better dressed thanks to the proliferation of Armani and Gap-like boutiques, hanging out in oceanfront bistros with both cell phones going twenty-five hours a day.

Now buildings that once sold for fifteen thou (if they sold) were going for one-point-five mil. Ophelia's skin crawled, she said, whenever she sighted a pack of developers in their sharkskin suits swarming up the streets of South Beach, their two-hundred-dollar ties afloat, their Dolce & Gabbana loafers pinching their toes, their long yellow teeth itching to sink into such ripe properties as the Monte Excelsior. In the case of the Monte, Ophelia, her best friend, Rose Nozick, and their guru, the ancient Felicia Feinswog, stood firmly in the way.

Their leases were the last, old-time leases, unbreakable and unbeatable, signed by April Pollack herself.

What's more, the ladies were invincible against the lure of money and the enticements of Fort Lauderdale, West Palm Beach, and other less hip, more respectable places where cheaper Floridian condos bloomed.

My brother-in-law—my sister's husband, Ophelia's daughter's scummy spouse—Leonard Shumsky, was one of the Johnny-come-lately developers, the leader of the Monte's would-be takeover pack.

Leonard had it all together, he said on any number of occasions. "Architects' final drawings are in. Contractors' and subcontractors' bids are in. Articles of condominium-ization are in . . ."

"But you're not in," Ophelia told him.

Leonard was relentless. "Mother Meyer," Leonard said to Ophelia. "Do you think I want you living here in this godforsaken place when you can reside in sumptuous Azalea Gardens, minutes away from Fort Lauderdale's lovely New River, surrounded by your people . . . people of your social class and income?"

"You're just waiting for me to drop dead, Leonard, so you can knock down the joint and put up one of your cookie-cutter condos. It's not going to happen for years, Leonard. Felicia, Rose, and I are all, knock wood, from long-lived families."

"We'll bury you," Rose chimed in. Leonard resorted to time-tested methods to break the three women's leases: sporadic garbage pickup; mostly out-of-order elevator service; local thugs let loose in the basement laundry room, pilfering quarters and unmentionables; a/c turned way up or way down; yellow stains in the pool waters attributed to poor Rose Nozick's infirmity in the urination department.

While these outrages were in progress, April Pollack stood by in the penthouse opposite Ophelia's, dusting her television-purchased atomic cuckoo clock, which was programmed to chime at eight-thirty every evening and eight-thirty every morning for eternity. It's cuckoo could be heard throughout the Monte Excelsior. It was, needless to say, a matter of some little and venomous discussion.

April spent her days spying on those coming and going to Ophelia's through the peephole in her door; she was waiting for the undertakers. April would get the lion's share of any deal her son managed to bring off.

Leonard filed a lawsuit, arguing it was an unconscionable burden on the corporation to force continued operation of the Monte Excelsior for just three tenants.

The unsympathetic judge, Her Honor Ruth Weinstein, threw the case out of court. She called Leonard a new carpetbagger; she told Leonard the hardship would disappear if he rented the other fifty-nine apartments; not a difficult thing to do considering the demand for, and lack of, suitable middle-income housing in South Miami Beach.

Furthermore, she let Leonard know that future shenanigans at the Monte would negate any possibility of his ever getting his hands on said property. The Monte would go into receivership.

This struck terror in Leonard's dried little apricot of a heart, as Judge Ruth knew it would. Properties in state receivership could be tied up for decades. I was supposed to be the coup de grâce, in town to talk tough to Leonard and send him back to Fort Lauderdale to his unspeakable wife (my sister) and to leave Ophelia, Rose, Felicia, and the Monte alone. Or I would break his head and knees with a baseball bat.

All in all, Ophelia figured out, there had been a dozen murders. The victims were all lease owners and were killed in ways that agreed with what she called the modus operandi.

Audrey Lustig bid adieu on the Friday before I arrived and it happened thusly. The still sexually active Audrey, 6A, was treated by an anonymous admirer to a poolside lunch provided by the Bagel Chateau, which leased space in the southwest corner of the Monte.

The Shah of Iran (reputedly once a guest at the Monte) Special was a full half pound of curried chicken salad on an extra-large toasted onion bagel accompanied by a whole kosher pickle, a side of creamy coleslaw, and a bottle of Dr. Brown's Diet Cel-Ray Tonic.

After she made short work of the Shah of Iran Special, Audrey announced to the girls around the pool that she was retiring for her midday nap. She hoped—she expected—that her admirer would duly follow.

Mother found her at exactly eight-thirty; the cuckoo clock was cuckoo-ing its head off. Ophelia had gone down to the sixth floor to alert Audrey that the *Seinfeld* episode she prized above all—"The Soup Nazi"—was being rerun on Channel 27. "I knew Audrey wouldn't want to miss it."

The front door was ajar. Ophelia thought Audrey might still be waiting for her secret admirer. Ophelia knocked and yoo-hooed to no avail; could they be, she wondered, in flagrante delicto? Ophelia pushed the door open.

Audrey's once all-white studio was the yellow color of curried chicken salad, the walls a victim of projectile vomiting.

Putting the scented handkerchief she always carries to her nose, Ophelia found Audrey in the bathroom, astride the commode, dead as the proverbial doornail.

"It was the curried chicken salad," Ophelia told me. "That's what the autopsy determined. It had been laced with cilantro and everyone knew Audrey was highly, dangerously allergic to this year's designer herb, cilantro."

"Surely not *everyone*," I objected.

"That schlemiel Leonard knew. He and April had to take Audrey to Mount Zion after she accidentally ingested a cilantro-and-mortadella sandwich."

The autopsy had decided this latest cilantro mishap was a tragic accident. "A tragic murder, more likely," opined Ophelia.

"I'm telling you, Nick, your brother-in-law is trying to kill us. I want you to come right out here and protect us."

"I'm to be your taster?"

"They're dying like flies, Nick. Are you coming?"

"You know I am."

Thus I found myself in South Beach again. I like SoBe as well as the next sex/drug maniac but not as a steady diet. There's a miasma that hangs over South Beach that would do you if you gave it half a chance.

Nor do I mind living on the thin edge of danger. But it's the Miami Beach version—young minds and buff bodies going to the dogs—that excludes me. At thirty-two, I hide out in West Hollywood, way old for the SoBe game.

So on Thanksgiving night, I was at my destination. I took the iffy claustrophobic elevator up to the penthouse floor and stood in the bleak corridor for a minute, halfway between the two towers (a penthouse in each), getting that old creepy feeling. Like someone was behind the door to Penthouse B, scoping me out.

Ignoring this, I rang my mother's melodious bell. I was looking forward to seeing her.

Ophelia herself, in a cloud of roast turkey aroma, answered the door. "Happy Thanksgiving," I said, pleased she had finally located a good colorist, that she still looked pretty good for a sixty-eight-year-old silver blue-haired siren, that I still loved her; always had.

"My boy." She put her arms up and around me and held on tight. I heard Rose Nozick calling from the kitchen to make it snappy, that the turkey was coming out of the oven no matter who had or had not arrived.

Still, Mother held on. She's always there for me, and if I needed her last dime, she'd hand it right over. Yeah, I know all the clichéd jokes about Jewish mothers, but bottom line is she's the first woman I ever loved and I still do. People who have tried to psychoanalyze me say it's a wonder I'm not sharing a studio in the East Village, begging Curtis to go easy on the celery salt. But I had a pretty good dad. Many's a time he straightened both Ophelia and me out.

The apartment—one of two designated penthouses facing one another on the top floor like elderly tontine survivors—is a huge L-shape. Two bedrooms and two baths in the short bar; a long living-room-cum-kitchen in the long bar, with a narrow terrace running between the two apartments.

April's is done in the French Provisional style that characterized her Brooklyn homes, while mother has gone the new beige, minimalist route.

"The smell of turkey is driving me nuts," I said to no one in particular, studying my reflection in the mirror over the strictly ornamental fireplace.

Rose came in and reached up and pinched my cheek, hard. When I was a kid she was a relatively tall lady, but now she's a walking caution, ladies, to take your calcium.

"Oy," she said, looking me over, shaking her head. "Oy." She went back into the kitchen to help Ophelia pry the big bird out of the tiny oven.

"I said eight-thirty and we're going to eat at eight-thirty. You sit down," Ophelia ordered. "Rose and I will get the rest."

"Where is the fair Leonard Shumsky?" I asked. "Isn't he coming?"

"In a nutshell, no," Rose said, entering the dining area of the living room, holding the turkey high over her head, which means it came to about table level.

"He canceled maybe a half hour ago. Felicia Feinswog said she hated turkey anyway and had no desire to sit across from those murderers. So here we are. Good. More for us."

Rose carved the turkey expertly in thirty seconds. She gave me one leg and herself the other. "Ophelia, are you going to sit down or what?"

Ophelia was standing at the open front door, peering into the hallway. "I thought I heard something."

"She's always hearing something."

"Shush." Ophelia stepped into the hall, saying as she went, "Listen, you two go right ahead. I'll be back in a jiff."

"Where you going, Ma?"

"Just to the service stairway. I want to see how Felicia is doing."

The ninety-year-old Felicia Feinswog jogged every night up and down the service stairs for a half hour, plugged into her earphones, listening to the recorded music of Sigmund Romberg.

Felicia, who even at her age had a wild-eyed intensity, was determined not only to reach her centennial but to stay healthy while doing so.

"'I'm going to live till I die,'" she sang at full vibrato, the last time I visited, scaring the hell out of me as I hiked up the slick, white service stairs. "'I'm going to fill my cup/till my number's up/I'm going to live live live until I die.'"

Felicia wasn't singing that night. "I don't like the silence," Ophelia said, and disappeared, headed for the service stairs.

"I'm coming with you," I told her, through a mouth filled with moist, tasty turkey.

"Sit still," Ophelia called. "I'll be right back."

"Leave the service door open," practical Rose yelled. "So we can hear what's going on."

"Nothing's going on," Ophelia reassured us. "I'm just checking."

Two sounds occurred almost simultaneously. April's damn clock went off, indicating it was eight-thirty, and then Ophelia's lyrical scream echoed around the hard surfaces of the service stairwell. It was a scream filled with sadness and disbelief. Rose and I ran to and down the shiny white service stairs.

Felicia Feinswog, in her blue-green high-school gym bloomers and state-of-the-art taxicab-yellow Nikes, was sprawled halfway down the blindingly white stairs, her silver hair streaked red with blood, a gaping wedge chopped out of her head. Ophelia, who is not an easy tear shedder, sat on the step beside her, holding Felicia's hand, sobbing.

I developed a lump in my chest the size of Charlton

Heston's ego. I hate to see my mother's heart break. I hated to see the courageous Felicia lying there like a rejected lox under the full neon light of the service stairwell, so completely discarded. She had lived too long and brave a life for this ignominious end.

Little Rose had plopped down on the nearest stair and put her head in her pretty hands. "I don't think I can take any more of this," she said, as usual making herself the focus.

"Felicia can't take any more of this either," Ophelia retorted.

Standing just above her was April Pollack, doing a Lady Macbeth with her hands. Her wrinkled, unhealthy, and tanned face set in an unnatural, caring expression. We hadn't heard her descend the stairs.

"She fell and she tripped," April pronounced in that hoarse wisdom-of-the-ages voice. She lit a Lucky Strike and inhaled deeply. "I told her a million times not to run up this stairwell like a madwoman, and did she listen? No. This is what happens when people of a certain age don't listen."

Leonard appeared just above April, looking like an alien angel in his white suit. "What's going on?" he wanted to know. "I was just going up to Ophelia's to see if there were any leftovers when I heard the commotion on the stairwell."

I told Leonard what was going on.

"Poor woman," Leonard said in his most unctuous voice. "She shouldn't have been jogging at her age and in her condition."

Whereupon I moved up to the step he was standing on and capped him a good one in the ear. He looked astounded.

He and his mother told the police it was obviously an

accident. Ophelia and Rose said it was murder, plain and simple. The police declared it an accident unless someone could prove otherwise, and that's the way we left it.

Rose Nozick, equipped with her pillow and her nightgown, moved in with Ophelia in her king-size bed.

I was under orders to sleep with one eye and my bedroom door open in case "that bastard comes in to choke us to death."

I woke in the morning, wrapped a towel around my nether regions, checked on the sleeping girls, and went into the living room and stared out the terrace. The Miami sun was shining, as it usually does; the woman in the apartment opposite closed her blinds with a sassy movement; I thought of the woman I left behind and called her and even said I missed her. "Ditto," she said.

Then I saw Leonard, wearing ill-advised plaid shorts, strolling across the terrace. He rapped on Ophelia's terrace door. I opened it and he jumped back.

"You're not going to hit me, are you, Nick?"

"No. I'm sorry about last night. In the heat of the moment, I got carried away."

"My ear still hurts." He slithered past me into the room and sat on the beige sofa, and I sat opposite him in the beige club chair.

"Nick, trust me. I only want what's best for Ophelia. She shouldn't be living here; the Monte is falling down around her.

"More importantly, Nick, I want you to know I didn't kill those women. Do you really think I'm capable of killing them? I'm your brother-in-law, for God's sake."

Leonard is pathetically greedy; second-rate from his morals to his intellect to his convenient religious beliefs; he's capable of stealing from his mother-in-law, having done a number on his own brother; but he's not capable of killing either Audrey or Felicia or a wee mouse in a trap. He hasn't got the guts.

"I'm here to make a peace offering."

"Yeah?"

"Mother—April—wants you all to come for a snecken tonight at eight-thirty. She wants the war to be over. We've talked it over and we're prepared to wait until Rose and Ophelia die of natural causes."

Not much to say to that bit of magnanimity. I told him we'd be there for the snecken. He slithered out the terrace door and I went to talk to Rose Nozick and Ophelia. They agreed with me without even an arm twist.

"You're right, Nick. What are we staying in this broken-down apartment house with little or no a/c and that eerie Leonard calling the shots?

"No, we've had our eye on a smaller but lovely pair of condos, side by side, on the nine-hundred block of Collins Avenue. Actually, to tell the truth, we've already bought them."

"Then my schlepping out here was for naught?"

"I wanted to see you, Nick. And we wanted to give Leonard a little of his own. And we're frightened. Look what happened to Felicia."

"The cops are pretty sure she tripped, Ma."

"Let's put that away for the moment, Nick. We're moving *mañana*. All we have to do is get through the night."

"After we have a little dessert with April Pollack and son," I announced.

Ophelia opened her killer green eyes wide. "Whatever for?"

I sat down on one of the bar stools. "I've come round to your way of thinking. I don't believe Felicia tripped. I talked to the cops today. They said they'd take further action if I could provide the weapon that knocked her down. I think I can.

"I went to the Bagel Chateau today, also. There was no way Audrey or anyone who knew her would have ordered the curried chicken salad sprinkled with heavy cilantro for her. She was very vocal about her allergy.

"Listen, I want to catch the killer before you rip up your leases and depart."

"Then you'll have to do it tonight. No way," Rose said, "am I going to dicker with that sleazeball moving man again."

"You won't have to, Rose. We're spending the early evening with Pollack and Son, over a peace offering April herself is putting together."

"Fine," Ophelia said. "I wouldn't let one item from that filthy kitchen pass my lips. But I'll make an appearance."

"Ditto," Rose allowed.

The three of us ate a light dinner and then, a little after eight, Ophelia and Rose Nozick, dressed to the eyeballs in their jet-black embroidered cocktail dresses, made their way to the opposite penthouse for the last time. I told them I would join them in a very few moments.

I stepped out onto the terrace into Miami's velvet painting of a night and walked as softly as my huaraches allowed over to April's side of the building.

In her kitchen, April was standing in front of her side by side Kelvinator, looking at a cache of frozen bagels. She was swinging one in a plastic Ziploc against her tough little thigh, with some vigor.

I let myself in through the glass sliding door. April showed no surprise. She just went on banging that frozen bagel against her thigh. She was going to have a bad hematoma in the morning, I thought and said.

She ignored this and cut right to the quick. "I thought you indicated, Nick, that my Leonard was the killer."

"I never did."

April came toward me with that tiny grin and that

swinging pendulum of a bagel and I was admittedly scared. Scared of a little old lady with sad, thinning hair, weighing in at maybe ninety pounds.

"The Monte Excelsior belongs to me, Nick. That worm Leonard is not going to profit from me. Two old farts like your mother and Miss Rose Nozick are not going to keep me from my millions. This building is my nest egg, Nick."

"So you killed Audrey Lustig by doctoring her curried chicken-salad-cum-cilantro on a toasted onion bagel, and you killed Felicia Feinswog by braining her with a frozen bagel . . ."

"And I killed Morty Appleroth with an out-of-service elevator sign and made him walk five flights to pick up a free dozen bagels that never existed. He had the heart attack right there on the landing.

"Listen, Nick, I'd kill a hundred just like them. This is my one and only shot. I've got what, five years left? I never had anything. Now I'm going to have something."

Her little yellow teeth suddenly appeared and—in an amazing non sequitur—she said, "What time is it, Nick?"

I was turning to check the damned clock when it struck eight-thirty. I looked back to tell April what she must have already known thanks to the cuckoo and caught her winding up like the president at the first day of the baseball season, giving her all as she swung at my head.

I was not once a Hollywood stuntman for nothing. I managed to block the frozen bagel, an action that took a nice slice out of my forearm but saved my scalp.

April hadn't noticed that the open Kelvinator door had started the defrosting cycle. There was a small pool of water on the slippery linoleum and April, off balance, fell backward, her soft head striking the open Kelvinator door, splitting her soft skull, depriving her of her triumph.

N o surprise, after a suitable mourning period (three days), Leonard signed the papers that would raze the Monte. In time, a new ugly building reminiscent of 1950s Soviet architecture took its place. Leonard, that sentimental sap, is calling it the New Monte Excelsior.

Mother and Rose Nozick are divinely happy in their condos and expect me and mine (I haven't told her we were married yet, but I think she's guessed) for the Easter holidays.

"We have plenty of room," Ophelia told me. "Why spring for a hotel? You stay with me . . . and your girlfriend can stay with Rose."

We're springing for a hotel.

Meanwhile, I've been cast as the third mean guy in a new gangster flick, and this time I'm telling the caterers no bagels on the set.

❖

The Basic Bagel Recipe

If you want a bagel and you live in New York, all you have to do is go to the corner bodega and ask for a bagel with a schmear (cream cheese for the uninitiated).

If you live in L.A., Chicago, Miami, and virtually any other large American city, you may or may not get a bagel according to Kaufelt's definition of a bagel: large, crusty, chewy, firm, just this side of stale with a definite hint of the backbreaking old world where labor was not a party but that indefinable ingredient you put into what you ate. Now, when you ask for a bagel, all you get is a roll with a hole in the middle and the soft, mushy taste of what passes for bread stuff in this age of unreality.

Don't talk to me about Lenders. Bagel shops with their

array of flavors, from basic to novelty green for St. Patrick's Day, have proliferated across the land, and if you think you're going to be biting into a nice, hard, chewy bagel when you order an everything with Nova (lox) and onions and a slice of tomato, you're not; and I wouldn't be too sure about the Nova or the onion or the pale tomato.

Sad to say, nowadays bagels are produced in a commercial, cost-cutting way: today's chain "bagels" are machine-mixed and steamed in a rack rather than boiled according to the old-fashioned labor-intensive method.

If your teeth are sound and you want a real bagel, one you have to grapple with a bit, here's a recipe for you.

Hand-mix high-gluten balancer flour, salt, brown sugar, malt, and water (some say only New York water will do but to me that's a grandmother's tale) until the dough is strong and resilient and a touch stiff. Working by hand, this should take not a second less than 30 minutes.

After the dough is mixed, place it on a bare wood table, form it into what looks like bagels (I like mine on the large side), cover them, and allow to proof. Then place the bagels in a kettle of boiling water that will produce a shine and maintain the center hole of the bagel. Afterward, you can cool them with cold running water so they won't be too hot to handle.

This recipe takes a little of this and a little of that and a certain amount of experimentation, but if you stick with it, you'll end up with a real bagel.

—DAK

DEATH BEFORE
COMPLINE

SHARAN NEWMAN

Spring 1146; the convent of the Paraclete, Champagne

Catherine sat on a stone step, a basket of grain between her knees. She tossed it lazily in the direction of a flock of chickens who seemed more
interested in pecking at her bare toes than in eating their
dinner.

Behind her were the walls of the convent of the Paraclete. Once Catherine had thought she would spend all her
days behind those walls, but her life had flowed in channels
she hadn't expected and now she was able to make only an
occasional visit.

The calm of the place refreshed her, as did the fact that
many of the nuns and lay sisters were happy to relieve her
of her duties to her two small children, James and Edana.

Catherine scattered a last handful of the seeds before
she stood, shook out her skirts, and went back into the
cloister to be sure that her active progeny weren't wearing
out their welcome.

Inside she found not the peace she'd come to expect, but

commotion. The nuns and lay sisters were hurrying toward the guest house with bundles of linen, pitchers, and washing bowls.

"What's happening?" she asked.

Sister Cecile paused only a moment. "Company coming," she panted. "Count Thibault, Lord Henry, Lord Milo, their families, retainers. Wherever shall we put them all?"

She dashed on.

Catherine looked around for someone who could give her more information.

Outside the chapter house stood the abbess of the Paraclete, Heloise. Despite the activity around her, the abbess was calm, briefly answering and directing the women who fluttered by her like bees seeking nectar. As each of the sisters received her orders, she sped away.

Catherine hovered on the edge of the group, not sure if she should offer to help, now that she was only a visitor to the convent. Heloise noticed her and beckoned her closer.

"You might see to Sister Genevieve," she said. "She's in the chapter now, drawing up our copy of the sale."

"Yes, Mother," Catherine said.

Heloise nodded approval and turned to the next problem.

What sale? Catherine thought as she edged around the others and went into the chapter, the room next to the chapel where the nuns met each week for lectures and work assignments. At a table under a window sat Sister Genevieve, sharpening her reed pen.

Catherine didn't know Genevieve well; she had arrived at the convent after Catherine had left to be married. She was in her mid-twenties, with fair skin and amber eyes. Without speaking to her, Catherine had formed the impression that she was both competent and devout, if a bit skittish. She tended to start like a frightened colt when caught unawares. As Catherine entered, Genevieve looked up. There was ink at the corner of her mouth. She started to speak but coughed instead. Her cheeks were flushed, as with fever.

"Mother Heloise thought you might be able to use me," Catherine told her.

Genevieve's forehead wrinkled. "I can't imagine why," she said, her voice hoarse. "I'm simply making a list of the land Lord Milo is selling us the use of to pay for his pilgrimage to the Holy Land. I'm not too ill to do this."

"Lord Milo's going on the expedition as well?" Catherine said. She supposed it shouldn't surprise her. It seemed that everyone from King Louis down to the beggars in the road was taking the cross.

"But why are we buying the tithe from him?" she asked. "With what? It was Lord Milo who gave the land for the Paraclete in the first place. Have we become rich since I was here?"

Genevieve shrugged. "That's Mother Heloise's affair. My job is to itemize the various properties so that we have our own record, as well as the charter drawn up by Lord Milo's clerk."

Catherine came around her to see what had already been written. One glance told her why the abbess had wanted someone else to assist the nun. Genevieve wrote a good clear hand and her Latin was excellent, but she appeared to have no sense of geography.

"You can't mean this," Catherine said tactlessly, pointing to a line. "These boundaries would give us a field three miles long and only a handbreadth wide. Why would we want the verge of a road?"

Genevieve coughed repeatedly as she looked at the words. "That's what is written on the tablet that Lord Milo's clerk gave me."

She handed it to Catherine, who studied the abbreviated words scrawled in the warm wax. Genevieve was right.

"Then the clerk must have made a mistake," she said. "I'll ask Mother Heloise about it."

Genevieve jerked the tablet back. "I can ask her myself, thank you," she snapped. "You might remember, Catherine, that you're but a guest here. You had your chance to stay, but you rejected God for the life of the flesh. So don't try to wiggle back in, especially with the evidence of your lust so obvious."

Catherine was taken aback. It was a moment before she realized that Genevieve was talking about James and Edana. She supposed that her children might be considered proof that her marriage had been consummated and she couldn't deny that she was more than happy to do her wifely duty, but . . .

"What has that to do with an error in computation?" she asked.

Genevieve didn't answer. She bent to her work once again, blunting the reed tip with the pressure she put on the parchment. Her coughing was strong enough to cause her to blot the page.

"Could I get you a posset to ease your cough?" Catherine asked.

"Sister Melisande gave me a syrup, thank you," Genevieve didn't look up.

Catherine was dismissed.

She wished that her husband, Edgar, were here so that she could relieve her indignation by telling him. But Edgar had gone to see about arranging for the care of some horses that they were buying from a Spanish merchant and selling at the fair in Troyes. He wouldn't be back until the end of the week.

Checking to see that Sister Jehanne wasn't being worn out by her children, Catherine found the nun, the baby, and Edgar's sister, Margaret, washing clothes. The room was steamy, but Catherine made out the strong arms of Sister Jehanne as she lifted the soaking cloth from the hot water and into the cold to rinse. Margaret had a long paddle to push the cloth under the water. Out of the way in a corner, baby Edana was sitting naked on a pile of what Catherine devoutly hoped were soiled robes. James was trotting back and forth, handing the nun new pieces to push into the cauldron.

"You could help Margaret," Sister Jehanne told her, "but the other paddle seems to have disappeared. Don't worry. We're almost finished, anyway."

Since they all seemed quite happy without her, Catherine went to the guest house to see if she could help there.

"No, no, dear," the portress, Sister Thecla, said. "Only Lady Isabel and her maid will be staying here. We can handle that. Count Thibault and Lord Milo are bringing tents for the men. But we'll have to give them at least one good meal and I have no idea how that will be managed."

Cooking wasn't one of Catherine's accomplishments. In Paris they had either had their own cook or had bought from the bakeshops. She decided not to offer her services in the kitchen.

Without the children or the running of a household to occupy her, Catherine realized that she didn't know what to do with herself. The only thing that appealed was to go back to the chapter house to read, but having to pass Sister Genevieve was more than she could face.

She made her way to the abbess's room, where Heloise sat alone, having finally given the last of the lay sisters her assignment.

"Mother?" Catherine instantly regretted interrupting. Heloise sat at her table, her head bowed in prayer.

At once the head came up. Heloise smiled and rubbed her eyes.

"Forgive me!" she exclaimed. "I must have dozed a moment. Yes, Catherine? Did you finish helping Sister Genevieve?"

Catherine told the abbess of Genevieve's reception of her offer.

"Oh, dear." Heloise shook her head. "It's not anything you've done, my dear. Genevieve is upset by our visitors. She's related to Count Milo, you know. There was some fuss about her entering the Paraclete and I fear she's always resented the members of her family who made it difficult for her. I pray that someday she'll be able to forgive them and be at peace."

Catherine's feelings were somewhat assuaged by Heloise's explanation. Perhaps Genevieve felt that the rights Count Milo was selling the nuns should have been donated freely.

Since she was not needed anywhere, Catherine wandered out the gates of the convent to watch for the visitors. She was standing outside the guest house when she spotted the procession coming north up the dusty road.

"Sister Thecla!" she called. "Count Thibault's party is coming!"

Shading her eyes with her hand, she watched the riders approach, first Count Thibault and his son, Henry, on fine destriers, and the others behind riding palfreys or leading pack mules. They carried banners with the standard of Champagne and the pilgrim's cross, to proclaim the vow Henry had made to fight in the Holy Land.

Catherine was so caught up in watching them that she didn't notice the smaller group that came from the opposite direction until she was startled by the hot breath of a horse on her neck and a rough voice shouting.

"You! Girl! What do you think you're doing, standing gaping in the road?"

Catherine looked up. She didn't know the man who

spoke. He was about her own age, with light eyes and hair the color of unpolished brass. She was about to answer angrily when Sister Thecla came out of the gate, followed by several of the lay brothers of the convent.

"Welcome!" she cried to them all. "Welcome to the Paraclete. My lord count, Lord Milo, we're honored to have you here. The brothers will show you the best places for your tents. Be careful, the land is marshy near the river."

Count Thibault rode up to her and dismounted.

"Sister Thecla." He beamed. "Always good to see you." He looked past Catherine, then looked at her again.

"By the Magdalene's tangled hair!" he exclaimed. "It's Hubert's girl! Catherine, isn't it?"

Catherine was scarlet with mortification. She had hoped no one would spot her until she could return to the guesthouse and change into proper clothes. She bowed to the count, trying to stoop a bit to hide her naked feet.

"My father will be sorry he missed you," she murmured.

"Not at all," Thibault said. "I saw him in Troyes. He sent some casks of wine on ahead. Have they arrived?"

Sister Thecla nodded. "Yesterday morning," she said. "We thank you for providing them."

"We'll open one tonight for dinner." The count laughed. "See that the ladies in the cloister get a cup as well."

As the visitors were led either into the guest house or out to the field, Catherine slipped away as unobtrusively as possible. She prayed that her husband and father would never learn that she'd been taken for a kitchen maid, but knew that prayer would not likely be granted. The best she could do was to bedeck herself so elegantly that evening that no one would remember her earlier state.

In her room, Catherine rummaged through the packs to find a pair of clean hose and a head scarf. She put these on and laced up her shoes. From the guesthouse window she could see men loading a huge barrel cask onto a platform

next to the area where tables were being set up for the banquet. She frowned. With that much wine on hand, perhaps
it would be better if the children slept somewhere else. The
singing alone would keep them awake, and while Count
Thibault and Lord Milo were good, pious men, there were
a number of young bachelors in the company. The sort of
antics they enjoyed after an evening of wine was not something she wanted James imitating.

Four of these young men had gathered under the window. She didn't recognize any of them but there was a
slight family resemblance to Lord Milo in all. Their heads
moved closer together as they spoke; Catherine could hear
nothing of their conversation, although from the waving
arms, the discussion appeared to be intense. As she
watched, the voices rose so that she could make them out.

"Roric knows there's nothing he can do," said the man
who had yelled at her. "He's been excommunicated. That's
why he didn't even bother to come."

"What, again?" One of them laughed. "I knew he was in
for trouble when he started sleeping with the bishop's con-
cubine."

"What of it?" the third man said. "He's never let excom-
munication bother him before. He'll repent for Easter, as
always. Earlier if he tires of her."

"Stephan is right; Roric will be here," another grum-
bled. "He'll show up at the worst possible moment, wait
and see."

The others nodded glum agreement. Then the men wandered off toward the tents.

As Catherine looked in her hand mirror to check for
stray curls escaping from her scarf, she wondered idly who
this Roric was who put the desires of the flesh above the
safety of his soul. But then her primary concern returned
and she headed for the infirmary to ask Sister Melisande to

keep the children safe there for the night. She only hoped there would be no unexpected patients.

Much later, properly attired, wearing her best pearl earrings, Catherine was presented to Lord Milo; his daughter, Isabel; her husband, Girard; and then the line of men she had seen from the window—Freer, Joiffroy, Gaucher, and Stephan, Milo's nephews. Gaucher, it turned out, was the copper-haired man who had yelled at her in the road.

He bowed over her hand with an amused expression.

"I beg your forgiveness, kind lady, for not seeing your true station beneath the dust."

"Perhaps the sun was in your eyes," Catherine answered, then bit her tongue at the warning glance from Abbess Heloise.

Gaucher stepped back with a polite grimace and they all made their way to the chapel for vespers.

From behind the screen the voices of the nuns rose clear and pure. Catherine forgot her petty irritation in the beauty of the music. The others, too, seemed entranced by the singing of the psalms and stood quietly until the end.

Or did they? From the corner of her eye, Catherine thought she saw a movement as if someone had opened the door. She tried to look without turning, but could see no one. Was it someone arriving late or a music hater trying to slip out? She couldn't tell.

The meal that night was fish, caught in the trap set in the Ardusson River and made into a thick stew with dried fruit and herbs. There was bread and egg soup with fresh greens. Later there would be more fruit, dipped in honey and walnuts. Catherine knew that such a feast was as much as the nuns ate in a week but abstinence indeed for the nobles, who gorged on meat every night if they could, and complained of deprivation on fast days.

A cheer went up as Count Thibault's pincerna drove a spout into the wine cask and held a pitcher beneath. The wine flowed for several seconds and then stopped. The servant shook the spout, then signaled to one of the men to tip the cask.

"It's full, I'm sure," one man said. "It was so heavy when we put it up here that I thought we'd drop and spill it."

They gave the cask a turn and the wine flowed once more.

When the pitcher was full, the wine steward offered the first cup to Abbess Heloise. She let him pour a small amount and then filled the cup with water. Next, the count and his son were served. When all the cups were full, Thibault lifted his to drink to the safety of those about to leave for the Holy Land. He then took a huge gulp and choked, spraying wine across the table and down his tunic.

"Saint Vincent's rusty pruning hook!" he exclaimed. "This can't be my wine! It tastes like it's been strained through a sheep!"

Catherine had done no more than smell the wine before quickly setting the cup down. Thibault ordered his men to pry open the top of the cask. Lord Milo made a joke about the possible contents. His son-in-law and nephews all laughed. As the lid came up, Catherine saw that there was wine enough. It splashed over the men. Then one of them pulled out something floating on the top.

"Well, that explains it," Count Thibault said. "One of the vintners dropped his hood in the cask. I thought I tasted raw wool. Disgusting."

But the servant was still poking in the wine. Suddenly he gave a cry of terror and leaped from the platform. He crossed himself repeatedly and then began frantically wiping his hands on his tunic.

"Holy Mother!" he said over and over. "Blessed Virgin protect me!"

"What's wrong with the man?" Count Thibault had risen and was striding to the platform, Heloise and Lord Milo close behind him.

"My lord count, my lady abbess," the servant babbled. "You mustn't look!"

By now everyone was gathered around the platform as the count climbed up to the cask. He took one look and blanched. He motioned for Abbess Heloise to stay back, but she ignored him. Gazing down into the wine, Heloise saw a face looking back at her, the eyes wide with shock. Then she realized that the head floated so easily on the surface because it was no longer attached to a body. Beside it, an arm bobbed up, fingers splayed.

Catherine saw the abbess's expression and pushed through the throng to reach her.

"Mother Heloise," she said. "Let me help you."

"I'm fine," Heloise told her although she was still pale. "Much better than this poor soul. Does anyone know who he is?"

Lord Milo had climbed up as well. He nodded with more sorrow than shock. "Indeed. This is Roric, my eldest nephew. I should have known that only death would keep him from disputing my decision."

In the pandemonium that followed, Catherine was able to help the abbess down and lead her away. It was a sign of her shock that Catherine could think only of platitudes.

"How dreadful!" she said. "Who would do such a thing? And why put the body in a wine cask? Think of the mess in having to cut it up to fit like that."

Her mind began to work again. "There are a hundred places in the woods where the poor man could have been hidden and never found at all. Someone must have wanted the body to be found like that! How wicked! Mother? What should we do?"

Heloise took a deep breath.

"First, Catherine," she said, "we pray for his soul."

"Yes, Mother." Catherine crossed herself and started a Pater Noster. Then she stopped. "Mother, if this was Roric, I don't think our prayers will help him. I overheard his brothers saying that Roric was an excommunicant."

For the first time, Heloise's face showed true horror.

"Then whoever has committed this awful act has robbed him not only of his life here, but eternally as well," she stated. "Catherine, you're right; we must discover this murderer at once."

"But, Mother Heloise," Catherine said, "the man may have been killed anywhere and shipped here in the cask."

"No, Catherine," Heloise said firmly, "you didn't see the face. He couldn't have been in the wine for above a few hours. His skin wasn't stained at all. Wherever he was killed, he was put into the cask after it arrived here. This is an insult to God and to our order. I intend to get to the bottom of it."

Catherine shuddered, thinking of what else might be submerged in the wine.

"But, if the man is a nephew of Lord Milo, then he'll be the one to investigate," she suggested hesitantly. "Neither he nor Count Thibault may want our advice."

They had entered the cloister now, and were almost at Heloise's room. The abbess stopped and gave Catherine a look of surprise, her eyebrows raised.

"My dear, of course they will," she said firmly.

Count Thibault had also realized that the body of Lord Milo's nephew had to have been put in the wine cask after it arrived at the convent. Furthermore, there had only been a few hours between the delivery of the wine and the time the cask had been set on the platform.

"It makes no sense," Milo told the count in his tent that evening. "Putting the body in the wine was a direct attack on you, or me. It's as if Roric was only killed to provide an insult to us."

Thibault didn't want to agree. It would be much simpler if Lord Milo's nephew had been waylaid by bandits on the road. But once they had drained the cask and laid out the body, they could find no sign of a death wound. Robbers couldn't have managed to dismember him so neatly. Nor would they have been so foolish as to have wasted time doing so.

With a sigh, Thibault stood up from his cot.

"We're forced to assume that this hideous deed was committed by someone we know, Milo," He frowned. "And, that it was done either shortly before our arrival here or almost immediately afterward."

Milo didn't look up at the count but fixed his eyes on the ground, strewn with hay. His hands rested limply on his knees.

"I know that, Thibault," he said. "And I fear that the finger points to someone of my own household, even of my blood."

"It had been said that Roric opposed the sale of the tithes to the nuns," Thibault continued. "By what right did he claim them?"

"Roric believed that the land at Charmes up to the mill was part of his mother's, my sister's, dower," Milo answered. "It was. But before she died, she told all of us that the nuns were eventually to be given the use of it to help feed and clothe her daughter, Genevieve, who is now a member of their order."

He went and opened the tent flap. "The land is so close that it's possible to see the mill from here, even in twilight."

Thibault followed him out.

"Hardly worth killing a man for," he commented.

"Only Roric wanted it," Milo added. "I can't imagine the abbess wielding an ax on a man for a bit of land. No, I believe we should look for someone with a grudge against us. I fear poor Roric was nothing more than a convenient victim."

The next morning Catherine consulted with the abbess as soon as the morning office was over.

"Someone has started a rumor that it was our lay brothers who murdered this man to keep him from contesting his mother's gift," Heloise told her.

"That's nonsense!" Catherine exclaimed. "Even if any of the brothers were capable of such evil, why arrange for the body to be so publicly found?"

"I didn't say it was logical, Catherine," Heloise answered. "Rumor hardly ever is. But that won't keep people from believing it."

"Would Roric have demanded more money from the convent for the land?" Catherine asked.

Heloise smiled. "You fear we couldn't have paid? Don't worry, my child, Lord Henry gave us five hundred livres to pray for his soul while he's in the Holy Land. There would have been enough to give something more to Roric."

Catherine was ashamed of herself for feeling even a shred of doubt. But if she could have suspected someone from the convent, however briefly, then how much more easily would strangers?

"We need to examine the area around where the casks were first stored," Catherine said. "There may be some evidence to tell us how the body got there."

Heloise shook her head. "Count Thibault was out there

at first light," she said. "The ground is muddy with dozens of footprints. But there is no sign of spilled blood, or wine for that matter."

"But, there must be—" Catherine started.

She was rudely interrupted by a small body wrapping itself around her knees.

"Mama." James's hands reached up and tugged at her braid. "Sister Emily said I could come with her to hunt for mushrooms, but you have to say yes. Do you?"

"I thought you were supposed to be watching your little sister," she said.

"Sister Genevieve and Aunt Margaret are playing with her," James told her. "Edana isn't any fun. She chews my wooden soldiers. Please let me go with Sister Emily."

"Do you think it's safe?" Catherine asked the abbess.

"Emily knows the paths," Heloise assured her. "They won't go out of hearing distance."

Catherine gave her permission. James loped away in delight at the possibility of adventure in the woods. He was a child who could go hunting for mushrooms and come home with tales of dragons and tree sprites. Sometimes Catherine wondered if he didn't really see marvels everywhere he looked.

Assured that the children were taken care of, she turned her attention back to the problem.

"I told you what I overheard from Lord Milo's other nephews," she said. "They seemed not to know where Roric was, but one of them could have been lying. And they certainly didn't sound fond of him."

"Disliking someone is far from the kind of hatred that would allow a person to hack a body into pieces," Heloise reminded her.

"But it was done, Mother," Catherine said. "And it's no less preposterous than the idea that he would be murdered for nothing more than a strip of road and a mill."

She stopped. "A strip of road . . . Mother Heloise, did Sister Genevieve come to you about an error in the measuring of Lord Milo's land? I read it to say that we only had rights to the verge along the road. Genevieve showed me the tablet and it agreed, but that makes no sense."

Heloise rubbed her forehead. "I don't remember the details of the transaction, not with all that has happened. Genevieve didn't come to me, but she probably forgot all about it once she heard her brother had been murdered."

"Brother!" Catherine hadn't known that. "Oh, poor Genevieve. Well, all I can think is that one of Lord Milo's nephews must have arrived here before the others and killed his cousin. But why? And why put him in the wine?"

They were interrupted again by the voice of Sister Emily.

"James!" she was calling. "James, bring that to me at once!"

"What's he done now?" Catherine ran out to find her son.

James was dashing through the open gate, carrying a long piece of wood. He waved it around his head and made as if to tilt it at an imaginary foe. Instead he ran headlong into his mother.

"Naughty boy!" She held him and took away the board. "Didn't you hear Emily? What have you found?"

She looked at it more closely. She knew what it was, one of the paddles used in the laundry. Had James taken it with him? The wood, normally pale from hot water and soap, was stained a dark purple. James, too, was covered in a mixture of mud and what smelled like wine.

Emily hurried to them. "I'm sorry, Catherine. He wandered off from me, hunting for the mushrooms. I don't know how it came to be so wet under the tree. We were well away from the river."

"Did you let him bring the paddle?" Catherine asked.

"No, he found it there."

Catherine lifted James to her hip and rushed back to the abbess. She showed Heloise the paddle and told her where it had been found.

Heloise understood at once.

"It cannot be!" she exclaimed. "And yet, here is the proof."

"It could have been left outside the convent," Catherine ventured.

"For what reason would it even be outside the laundry?" Heloise said. "We must face the fact that it was taken by someone of our order."

Catherine had no answer. Fear was burrowing into her heart.

"Mother," she asked, "Sister Genevieve wasn't well yesterday, a bad cough. Did she attend vespers?"

"No, she asked to be allowed to rest, and with all the guests we thought the coughing would be . . . Oh, Catherine," the abbess exclaimed. "It can't be. Her own brother?"

"And she has my baby!"

Catherine raced to the cloister garden, where she found Margaret alone with Edana. Clutching the child to her in relief, Catherine asked where Sister Genevieve had gone.

"She left a few moments ago," Margaret told her. "She said she had something to clean up."

"Where?" Catherine asked sharply.

Margaret pointed toward the woods.

Catherine gave Edana back and ran for Abbess Heloise.

"She's gone toward the river!"

Both women hurried that way. Heloise sent one of the brothers to fetch Lord Milo and Count Thibault to follow them.

They found Genevieve up to her knees in the water, trying to push a bundle down among the reeds.

"Sister!" Heloise cried. "My dear, whatever are you doing? You're ill; you'll catch your death in that cold water."

Genevieve looked up in panic, but didn't move.

Behind them, Lord Milo came running up.

"Genevieve!" he shouted. "Oh, no, not again!"

Heloise spun to face him, eyes blazing.

"What do you mean 'again'?" she demanded.

Milo jerked back from her anger. "She never killed any-one before!" he protested.

Heloise grew icily calm. "But she did other things? She was unbalanced when she came here and no one of her family bothered to tell us?"

Milo looked over the abbess's shoulder to where Gene-vieve had returned to her task, oblivious of the gathering crowd.

"We thought the calm of the cloister would heal her spirit," Milo said. "She was eager to come. Only Roric op-posed it. But we convinced him it was best for her to be put away."

"Put away!" Heloise exclaimed. "Milo, this is a convent, not a prison!"

In the meantime, Catherine was trying to reach Gene-vieve. She waded into the water, speaking softly as she came.

"Let me help you," she said. "I see the problem. The ax is tangled in your robes. If I take it, you can get them free of the reeds."

Genevieve stared at her, then down at the ax handle, sticking out from the bundle of cloth.

"You gave him a drink of your medicine, didn't you?" Catherine continued. "Sister Melisande told you the dos-age to bring about sleep. It still must have been hard to cut him up."

"Oh, no," Genevieve said proudly. "At home I used to practice on deer and sheep."

Catherine shivered and tried to force her breathing to steady. She had to reach the ax.

"But how did you get him into the cask?" she asked.

"I took the wine out in buckets during vespers." Genevieve smiled. "I said the psalms as I went so I'd know the time. Then I wrapped him up and took him bit by bit to the cask. But he wouldn't sink, so I had to use the laundry paddle."

"But why, Genevieve?" Slowly Catherine reached for the ax.

The nun seemed bewildered. She had finally noticed the men on the bank just behind Catherine; her uncle, cousins, the count and his son.

"To save him, of course," she told them all. "He lived in mortal sin. I had to immerse him in the Blood of Christ to make him change his ways. It's too bad he wouldn't fit in one piece. But I saved them all so that he'd be resurrected whole."

She smiled at them.

Catherine grabbed the ax and backed quickly from the river. As she did, Genevieve's family took hold of her and led her back to the convent.

Catherine was panting with delayed terror as she handed the ax to a lay brother and leaned weakly against Heloise.

"Mother, please don't ever tell my husband what I just did," she said.

Heloise patted her shoulders in reassurance.

"I'll see he never learns of your foolishness, my dear," she said. "But now I must decide what's to be done with Genevieve. Lord Milo, a word with you."

Catherine never heard that word, but when Milo set off for the Holy Land, he had less for provisions than he had anticipated and the Paraclete had the resources to see that Genevieve was never left alone again.

Hoc autem factum est anno ab Incarnatione Domini MCXLVI. Eugenio papa, Ludovico regnante in Francia.

❖

FEAST DAY FISH STEW

About a pound of fish, any kind, whatever swims into your net,
　filleted and cut into chunks

Fresh green herbs, whatever you have: parsley, basil, tarragon,
　watercress, etc., chopped and mixed, about a cup

2 cups white wine

Vegetables: carrots, turnips, celery (no potatoes or corn), about
　2 cups, sliced

Salt and pepper to taste (remember pepper isn't cheap)

Round loaves of whole-grain bread, tops sliced off and a hole
　dug out to serve as a dish

Save breadcrumbs from the scooped-out part

Bring wine to a simmer in a large pot; add vegetables
and cook on low heat 20 minutes or until tender, add herbs
and cook another 10 minutes. Add fish chunks and heat until fish is done to your taste. Thicken with bread crumbs, if
necessary. Season with salt and pepper.

Ladle stew into bread. Cover with the upper crust to
keep it warm during the long walk from the kitchen to the
dining room. Large loaves can be shared by two people.
Eat with a spoon. When done, you may tear the bread and
eat that, too. This recipe should serve about four, although
a hardworking person of the Middle Ages could eat the
whole thing with no problem. They would also have simply
cleaned the fish, maybe chopped off the head and tail, and
thrown it in the pot. The head and tail would be used for
broth or charity. You can give the leftover bread, soaked in
the stew sauce, to the poor at your gate, as well.

—SN

COLD TURKEY

DIANE MOTT DAVIDSON

I did not expect to find Edith Blanton's body in my walk-in refrigerator. The day had been bad enough already. My first thought after the shock was, I'm going to have to throw all this food away.

My mind reeled. I couldn't get a dial tone to call for help. Reconstruct, I ordered myself as I ran to a neighbor's. The police are going to want to know everything. My neighbor pressed 911. I talked. Hung up. I immediately worried about my eleven-year-old son, Arch. Where was he? I looked at my watch: ten past eight. He was spending the night somewhere. Oh, yes: Dungeons and Dragons weekend party at a friend's house. I made a discreet phone call to make sure he was okay. I did not mention the body. If I had, he and his friends would have wanted to troop over to see it.

Then I flopped down in a wingback chair and tried to think.

I had talked to Edith Blanton that morning. She had called with a batch of demanding questions. Was I ready to cater the Episcopal Church Women's Luncheon, to be held the next day? Irritation had blossomed like a headache. Butterball Blanton, as she was known everywhere but to her face, was a busybody. I'd given the shortest possible answers. The menu was set, the food prepared. Chicken-and-artichoke-heart potpie. Molded strawberry salad. Tossed greens with vinaigrette. Parkerhouse rolls. Lemon sponge cake. Not on your diet, I had wanted to add, but did not.

Now, Goldy, she'd gone on, *you have that petition we're circulating around the church, don't you?* I checked for raisins for a Waldorf salad and said, Which petition is that? Edith made an impatient noise in her throat. *The one outlawing guitar music.* Sigh. I said I had it around somewhere . . . Actually, I kind of liked ecclesiastical folk music, as long as I personally did not have to sing it. *And Goldy, you're not serving that Japanese raw fish, are you?* To the churchwomen? Never. *And you didn't use anything from the local farm where they found salmonella, did you?* Oh, enough. Absolutely not, Butt—er . . . Mrs. Blanton, I promised before hanging up.

The phone had rung again immediately: our priest, Father Olson. I said, Surely you're not calling about the luncheon. He said, *Don't call me Shirley.* A comic in a clerical collar. After pleasantries we had gotten around to the real stuff: How's Marla? I said that Marla Korman, my best friend, was fine. As far as I knew. Why? Oh, just checking, hadn't seen her in a while. Ha-ha, sure. I involuntarily glanced at my appointments calendar. After the churchwomen's luncheon, I was doing a dinner party for Marla. I didn't mention this to the uninvited Father Olson. You see, Episcopal priests can marry. Father Olson was *unmarried,* which made him interested in Marla. The reverse was not the case, however, which was why he had to call me to find out how she was. But none of this did I mention to Father O, as we called him. Didn't want to hurt his feelings.

My neighbor handed me a cup of tea. I thought again of Edith Blanton's pale calves, of the visible side of her pallid face, of the blood on the refrigerator door. I pushed the image out of my mind and tried to think again about the day. The police were going to ask a lot of questions. Had I heard from anyone in the church again? Had anyone mentioned a current crisis? What had happened after Father Olson called?

Oh, yes. Next had come a frantic knock at the door: something else to do with Marla. This time it was her soon-to-be ex-boyfriend—lanky, strawberry-blond David McAllister. He had desperation in his voice. *What can I do to show Marla I love her?* Sheesh! Did I look like Ann Landers? I ushered him out to the kitchen, where I started to chop pecans, *also* for the Waldorf salad, *also* for Marla's dinner party, to which the wealthy-but-boring David McAllister *also* had not been invited. Not only that, but he was driving me crazy cracking his knuckles. When he took a breath while talking about how much he adored Marla, I said I was in the middle of a crisis involving petitions, raw eggs, and the churchwomen and ushered him out.

About an hour later I'd left the house. I lifted my head from my neighbor's chair and looked at my watch: quarter after eight. When had I left the house? Around one, only to return seven hours later. The entire afternoon and early evening had been taken up with the second unsuccessful meeting between me, my lawyer, and the people suing me to change the name of my catering business. George Pettigrew and his wife own Three Bears Catering down in Denver. In June it came to their attention that my real, actual name is Goldy (a nickname that has stuck like epoxy glue

since childhood) Bear (Germanic in origin, but lamentable
nonetheless). What was worse in the Pettigrews' eyes was
that my business in the mountain town of Aspen Meadow
was called Goldilocks' Catering, Where Everything Is Just
Right! We began negotiating three weeks ago, at the beginning of September. The Pettigrews screamed copyright in-
fringement. I tried to convince them that all of us could
successfully capitalize on, if not inhabit, the same fairy
tale. The meeting this afternoon was another failure, except
from the viewpoint of my lawyer, who gets his porridge no
matter what.

I nestled my head against one of the wings of my neighbor's chair. Just thinking about the day again was exhaust-
ing. For as if all this had not been enough, when I got home
I heard a dog in my outdoor trash barrels. At least I thought
it was a dog. When I went around the side of the house to
check, a *real* bear, large and black, shuffled away from the
back of the house and up toward the woods. This is not an
uncommon sight in the Colorado high country when fall
weather sets in. But combined with the nagging from Edith
and the fight with the Pettigrews, it was enough to send me
in search of a parfait left over from an elementary-school
faculty party.

Not on your diet, I thought with a measure of guilt, the
diet you just undertook with all sorts of good intentions.
Oh, well. Diets aren't good for you. Too much deprivation.
But on this plan I didn't have to give up sweets; I could
have one dessert a day. Of course the brownie I'd had after
the lawyer's office fiasco was only a memory. Besides, I was
under so much stress, I could just imagine that tall chilled
crystal glass, those thick layers of chocolate and vanilla
pudding. I opened the refrigerator door full of anticipation.
And there in the dark recesses of the closetlike space was
Edith, fully clothed, lying limp, sandwiched between the
congealed strawberry salad and marinating T-bones.

I'd screamed. Rushed over to the neighbor's, where I now sat, staring into a cup of lukewarm tea. I looked at my watch again. Eight-thirty.

My neighbor was scurrying around looking for a blanket in case I went into shock. I was not going into shock; I just needed to *talk* to somebody. So I phoned Marla. That's what best friends are for, right? To get you through crises? Besides, Marla and I went way back. We had both made the mistake of marrying the same man, not simultaneously. We had survived the divorces from The Jerk and become best friends. I had even coached her in figuring her monetary settlement, sort of like when an NFL team in the playoffs gets films from another team's archenemy.

When Marla finally picked up the phone, I told her Edith Blanton was dead and in my refrigerator. I must have still been incoherent because I added the bit about the bear.

There was a pause while Marla tried to apply logic. Finally she said, "Goldy. I'm on my way over."

"Okay, okay! I'll meet you at my front door. Just be careful."

"Of what? Is this homicide or is it a frigging John Irving novel?"

Before I could say anything she hung up.

My neighbor and I walked slowly back to my house. The police arrived first: two men in uniforms. They took my name and Edith Blanton's. They asked how and when I'd found the body. When they tried to call for an investigative team, they discovered that the reason I hadn't been able to get a dial tone was that my phone was dead. The wires outside had been cut. This would explain why my brand-new, horrendously expensive security system had not worked when Edith and . . . whoever . . . had broken in. The police used their radio. While I was bemoaning my fate, Marla arrived. She was dressed in a sweatsuit sewn with gold spangles; I think they were supposed to represent aspen leaves.

The team arrived and took pictures. The coroner, gray-haired and grim-faced, signaled the removal company to cart out the body bag holding Edith. Marla murmured, "The Butterball bagged."

I said, "Stop."

Marla closed her eyes and fluttered her plump hands. "I know. I'm sorry. But she *was* a bitch. Everybody in the church disliked her."

I harrumphed. The two uniformed policemen told us to quit talking. They told me to go into the living room so the team leader, a female homicide investigator I did not know, could ask some questions. Marla flounced out. She said she was going home to make up the guest bed for me; no way was she allowing me to stay in that house.

The team leader and I settled ourselves on the two chairs in my living room. Out in the kitchen the lab technicians and other investigators were having a field day spreading black graphite fingerprint powder over the food for the churchwomen's luncheon.

The investigator was a burly woman with curly blond hair held back with black barrettes. Her eyes were light brown and impassive, her voice even. She wanted to know my name, if I knew the victim and for how long, was I having problems with her and where I'd been all day. I told her about my activities, about the following day's luncheon and Edith's questions. At their leader's direction, the team took samples of all the food. They also took what they'd found on the refrigerator floor: an anti-guitar-music petition. Through the blobs of congealed strawberry salad and raw egg yolk, you could see there were no names on it. Edith was still clutching the paper after she'd been hit on the head and dragged into the refrigerator.

I said, "Dragged . . . ?"

The investigator bit the inside of her cheek. Then she said, "Please tell me every single thing about your conversation with Edith Blanton."

So we went through it all again, including the bit about the petition. I added that I had not been due to see Edith, er, the deceased until the next day. Moreover, I was not having more problems with her than anybody else in town, especially Father Olson, who, unlike Edith, thought every liturgy should sound like a hootenanny.

The investigator's next question confused me. Did I have a pet? Yes, I had a cat that I had inherited from former employers. However, I added, strangers spooked him. Poor Scout would be cowering under a bed for at least the next three days.

She said, "And the color of the cat is . . . ?"

"Light brown, dark brown, and white," I said. "Sort of a Burmese-Siamese mix, I think."

The investigator held out a few strands of hair. "Does this look familiar? Look like your cat's hair?" It was dark brown and did not look like anything that grew on Scout. In fact, it looked fake.

"'Fraid not," I said.

"Synthetic, anyway, we think. You got any of this kind of material around?"

I shook my head no. "Oh gosh," I said, "the bear." I started to tell her about what I'd seen around the back of the house, but she was looking at her clipboard. She shifted in her chair.

She said, "Wait. Is this a *relative* of yours? *Er,* Ms. Bear?"

"No, no, no. Have you heard of Three Bears Catering?"

The investigator looked more confused. "Is that you, too? I wouldn't know. They did the policemen's banquet down in Denver last year, and they all wore bear . . . suits . . ."

She eyed me, the corners of her mouth turned down. She said, "Any chance this bear-person might have been waiting to attack you in your refrigerator? Over the name-change problem? And attacked Edith instead? Do they know what you look like?"

"I told you. I spent the afternoon with the Pettigrews," I said through clenched teeth. "They're suing me; why would they want to kill me?"

"You tell me."

At that moment, Marla poked her head into the living room. "I'm back. Can we leave? Or do you have to stay until the kitchen demolition team finishes?"

I looked at the investigator, who shook her head. She said, "We have a lot to do. Should be finished by midnight. At the latest. Also, we gotta take the cut wires from out back and, uh, your back door."

I said, "My back door? Great." I gave Marla a pained look. "I have to stay until they go. Just do me a favor and call somebody to come put in a piece of plywood for the door hole. Also, see if you can find my cat cage. I'm bringing Scout to your house."

Marla nodded and disappeared. The investigator then asked me to go through the whole thing backward, beginning with my discovery of Edith. This I did meticulously, as I know the backward-story bit is one way investigators check for lies.

Finally she said, "Haven't I seen you around? Aren't you a friend of Tom Schultz's?"

I smiled. "Homicide Investigator Schultz is a good friend of mine. Unfortunately, he's up snagging inland salmon at Green Lake Reservoir. Now, tell me. Am I a suspect in this or not?"

The investigator's flat brown eyes revealed nothing. After a moment, she said, "At this time we don't have enough information to tell about any suspects. But this hair we found in the victim's hand isn't yours. You didn't know your phone lines were cut. And you probably didn't break down your own back door."

Well. I guess that was police talk for *No, you're not a suspect*.

The investigator wrote a few last things on her clipboard, then got up to finish with her cohorts in the kitchen. I didn't see her for the next three hours. Marla appeared with the cat cage, and I found Scout crouched under Arch's bed. I coaxed him out while Marla welcomed the emergency fix-it people at the stroke of midnight. The panel on their truck said: *FELONY FIX-UP—THEY TRASH IT, WE PATCH IT.* How comforting: especially the twenty-four-hour service part.

An hour after the police and Felony Fix-up had left my kitchen looking like a relic of the scorched-earth policy, I sat in Marla's kitchen staring down one of Marla's favorite treats—imported baba au rhum. There's something about being awake at 1:00 A.M. that makes you think you need something to eat. Still, guilt reared its hideous head.

"What's the matter?" Marla asked. "I thought you loved those. Eat up. It'll help you stop thinking about Edith Blanton."

"Not likely, but I'll try." I inhaled the deep buttered-rum scent. "I shouldn't. I ate Lindt Lindors all summer and I'm supposed to be on a diet."

"One dessert won't hurt you."

"I've already had one dessert."

"So? *Two* won't hurt you." She shook her peaches-and-cream cheeks. "If I'd had to go through what you just did, I'd have six." So saying, she delicately loaded two babas onto a Wedgwood dessert plate. "Tomorrow's going to be even worse," she warned. "You'll have to phone the presi-

dent of the churchwomen first thing and cancel the luncheon. You'll have to call Father Olson. No, never mind, I'll
make both calls."

"Why?"

"Because, my dear, I am still hopeful that you'll be able
to do my dinner party tomorrow night." Marla pushed away
from the table to sashay over to her refrigerator for an
aerosol can of whipped cream. "I know it's crass," she said
as she shook the can vigorously, "but I still have three
people, one of whom is a male I am very interested in, expecting dinner. Shrimp cocktail, steaks, potato soufflé,
green beans, Waldorf salad, and chocolate cake. Remember? Beginning at six o'clock. I can't exactly call them up
and say, 'Well, *my* caterer found this body in her refrigerator—'"

"All right! If I can finish cleaning up the mess tomorrow,
we're on." I took a bite of the baba and said, "The cops ruined the salad and the cake. You'll have to give me some
more of your Jonathan apples. Gee, I don't feel so hot—"

"Don't worry. Sleep in. I have lots of apples. And—I'll
send a maid over to help you."

"Just not in a bear suit."

"Hey! Speaking of which! Should we give the Pettigrews a call in the morning? Just to hassle them?" She giggled. "Should we give them a call right now?"

"No, no, no," I said loudly over the sound of Marla hos-
ing her babas with cream. "The police are bound to talk to
them. If they're blameless, I can't afford to have them any
angrier at me than they already are. I'm so tired, I don't
even want to think about it."

Marla gave me a sympathetic look, got up, and made me
a cup of espresso laced with rum.

I said, "So who's this guy tomorrow night?"

"Fellow named Tony Kaplan. Just moved here from
L.A., where he sold his house for over a million dollars.

And it was a small house, too. He's cute. Wants to open a bookstore."

"Not another newcomer who's fantasized about running a bookstore in a mountain town," I said as I took the whipped cream can and pressed out a blob on top of my coffee. Immigrants from either coast always felt they had a mission to bring culture to us cowpokes. "Gee," I said. "Almost forgot. Regarding your busy social life, Father Olson called and asked me how you were."

"I hope you told him I was living in sin with a chocolate bar."

"Well, I didn't have time because then David McAllister showed up at my front door. Wanted to know if there was anything he could do to show you he loved you."

Marla tsked. "He asked me the same thing, and I said, 'Well, you can start with a nice bushel of apples.'"

"You are cruel." I sipped the coffee. With the rum and the whipped cream, it was sort of like hot ice cream. "You shouldn't play with his feelings."

"Excuse me, but jealousy is for seventh-graders."

"Too cruel," I said as we got up and placed the dishes in the sink. She escorted me with Scout the cat up to her guest room, then gave me towels; I handed over a key to my front door for her maid. Then I said, "Tell me about Edith Blanton."

Marla plunked down a pair of matching washcloths. She said, "Edith knew everything about everybody. Who in the church had had affairs with whom . . ."

"Oh, that's nice."

Marla pulled up her shoulders in an exaggerated gesture of nonchalance. The sweatsuit spangles shook. "Well, it was," she said. "I mean, everybody was nice to her because they were afraid of what she had on them. They didn't want her to talk. And she got what she wanted, until she took up arms against Father Olson over the guitar music."

"Too bad she couldn't get anything on him."

"Oh, honey," Marla said with an elaborate swirl of her eyes before she turned away and swaggered down the hall to her room. "Don't think she wasn't trying."

The next day Scout and I trekked to the church before going back to my house. Scout meowed morosely the whole way. I told him I had to leave a big sign on the church door saying that the luncheon had been canceled. He only howled louder when I said it was just in case someone hadn't gotten the word. If I hadn't been concentrating so hard on trying to comfort him, I would have noticed George Pettigrew's truck in the church parking lot. Then I would have been prepared for Pettigrew's smug grin, his hands clutched under his armpits. His foot tapping as I vaulted out of my van. As it was, I nearly had a fit.

"Were you around my house in a bear suit last night?" I demanded. He opened his eyes wide, as if I were crazy. "And *what* are you doing here? Haven't you got enough catering jobs down in Denver?"

"We don't use the bear suits anymore," he replied in a superior tone. "We had a hygiene problem with the hair getting into the food. And as a matter of fact I am doing lunches for two Skyboxes at Mile High Stadium tomorrow. But I can still offer to help out the churchwomen, since their local caterer canceled." His eyes bugged out as he raised his eyebrows. "Bad news travels fast."

Well, the luncheon was not going to happen. To tell him this, I was tempted to use some very unchurchlike language. But at that moment Father Olson pulled up in his 300E Mercedes 4matic. Father O had told the vestry that a priest needed a four-wheel-drive vehicle to visit parishioners in the mountains; he'd also petitioned for folk-music tapes to give to shut-ins. The vestry had refused to purchase the tapes, but they'd sprung fifty thou for the car.

Father O came up and put his hands on my shoulders. He gave me his Serious Pastoral Look. "Goldy," he said, "I've been so concerned for you."

"So have I," I said ruefully, with a sideways glance at George Pettigrew, who shrank back in the presence of clerical authority.

I turned my attention back to Father Olson. Marla might want to reconsider. An ecclesiastical career suited Father O, who had come of age in the sixties. He had sincere brown eyes, dark skin, and a beard, a cross between Moses and Ravi Shankar.

". . . feel terrible about what's happened to Edith," he was saying, "of course. How can this possibly . . . Oh, you probably don't want to talk about it . . ."

I said, "You're right."

Fancy cars were pulling into the church parking lot. George Pettigrew unobtrusively withdrew just as a group of women disentangled themselves from their Cadillacs and Mercedes.

"Listen," I said, "I have to split. Can you take care of these women who haven't gotten the bad news? I have a dinner party tonight that I simply can't cancel."

I almost didn't make it. Cries of *Oh, here she is; I wonder what she's fixed* erupted like birdcalls. Father Olson gave me the Pastoral Nod. I sidled past the women, hopped back in the van, and managed to drive out of the church parking lot without getting into a single conversation.

To my surprise, the maid Marla had sent over had done a superb job cleaning my kitchen. It positively sparkled. Unfortunately, right around the corner was the plywood nailed over the backdoor opening: a grim reminder of last night's events.

I set about thawing and marinating more steaks, then got out two dozen frozen Scout's brownies, my patented contribution to the chocoholics of the world. I had first developed the recipe under the watchful eye of the cat, so I'd named them after him. Marla adored them.

Edith Blanton came to mind as I again got out my recipe for Waldorf salad. Someone, dressed presumably as a bear, had taken the time to cut the phone wires and break in. Why? Had that person been following Edith, meaning to kill her at his first opportunity? Or had Edith surprised a robber? Had he killed her intentionally or accidentally?

I knew one thing for sure. Homicide Investigator Tom Schultz was my friend—well, more than a friend—and he often talked to me about cases up in Aspen Meadow. This would not be true with the current investigator working the Edith Blanton case, no question about it. If I was going to find out what happened, I was on my own.

While washing and cutting celery into julienne sticks, I conjured up a picture of Edith Blanton with her immaculately coiffed head of silver hair, dark green skirt, and loden jacket. Despite being an energetic busybody, Edith had been a lady. She never would have broken into my house.

I held my breath and opened my refrigerator door. All clean. I reached for a bag of nuts. Although classic Waldorfs called for walnuts, I was partial to fresh, sweet pecans that I mail-ordered from Texas. I chopped a cupful and then softened some raisins in hot water. The bearperson had been in my refrigerator. Why? If you're going to steal food, why wear a disguise?

Because if I had caught him, stealing food or attacking Edith Blanton, I would have recognized him.

So it was someone I knew? Probably.

I went back into the refrigerator. Although only a quarter cup of mayonnaise was required for the Waldorf, it was imperative to use *homemade* mayonnaise, which I would make with a nice fresh raw egg. I would mix the mayonnaise with a little lemon juice, sugar, and heavy cream . . . Wait a minute.

Two days ago my supplier had brought me eggs from a salmonella-free source in eastern Colorado. I was sure they were brown. So why was I staring at a half-dozen nice white eggs?

I picked one up and looked at it. It was an egg, all right. I brought it out into the kitchen and called Alicia, my supplier. The answering service said she was out on a delivery. "Well, do you happen to know what color eggs she delivered on her run two days ago?"

There was a long pause. The operator finally said, "Is this some kind of *yolk*?"

Oh, hilarious. I hung up. So funny I forgot to laugh.

I would have called a neighbor and borrowed an egg, but I didn't have any guarantees about hers, either. Many locals bought their eggs from a farm outside of town where they *had* found salmonella, and hers might be tainted, too.

I felt so frustrated I thawed a brownie in the microwave. This would be my one dessert of the day. Oh, and was it wonderful—thick and dark and chewy. Fireworks of good feeling sparked through my veins.

Okay, I said firmly to my inner self, yesterday when you came into this refrigerator you found a body. There is no way you could possibly remember the color of eggs or anything else that Alicia delivered two days ago. So make the mayo and quit bellyaching. With this happy thought, I started the food processor whirring and filched another brownie. Mm, mm. When the mayonnaise was done, I finished the Waldorf salad, put it in the refrigerator, and then concentrated on shelling and cooking fat prawns for the shrimp cocktail. When I put the shrimp in to chill, I stared at the refrigerator floor. I still had not answered the first question. Why had Edith been at my house in the first place?

She had been carrying a petition. A *blank* petition. So?

My copy had had a few names on it. Edith was carrying a blank petition because I had said I didn't know where my copy was. She came over with a new one.

So? That still didn't explain how she got in.

When she got here, she didn't get any answer at the front door. But she saw the light filtering in from the kitchen, and being the busybody she was, she went around back. The door was open, and she surprised the bear in mid-heist . . .

Well. Go figure. I packed up all the food and hustled off to Marla's.

"Oh, darling, *enfin*!" Marla cried when she swung open her heavy front door. She was wearing a multi-layered yellow-and-red chiffon dress that looked like sewn-together scarves. Marla always dressed to match the season, and I was pretty sure I was looking at the designer version of autumn.

"You don't need to be so dramatic," I said as I trudged past her with the first box.

"Oh! I thought you were Tony." She giggled. "Just kidding."

To my relief she had already set her cherry dining-room table with her latest haul from Europe: Limoges china and Baccarat crystal. I started boiling potatoes for the soufflé and washed the beans.

"I want to taste!" Marla cried as she got out a spoon to attack the Waldorf.

"Not on your life!" I said as I snatched the covered bowl away from her. "If we get started eating and chatting, there'll be nothing left for your guests."

To my relief the front doorbell rang. Disconsolate, Marla slapped the silver spoon down on the counter and left. From the front hall came the cry "Oh, darling, *enfin!*" Tony Kaplan, would-be bookstore proprietor.

The evening was warm, which was a good thing, as Marla and I had decided to risk an outdoor fire on her small barbecue. There were six T-bones—one for each guest and two extra for big appetites. I looked at my watch: six o'clock. Marla had said to serve at seven. The coals would take a bit longer after the sun went down, but since we were near the solstice, that wouldn't be until half-past six. The things a caterer has to know.

Tony Kaplan meandered out to the kitchen. Marla was welcoming the other couple. He needed ice for his drink, he said with a laugh. He was a tall, sharp-featured man who hunched his shoulders over when he walked, as if his height bothered him. I introduced myself. He laughed. "Is that your real name?" I told him there was a silver ice bucket in the living room. He just might not have recognized it, as it was in the shape of a sundae. You had to lift up the ice cream part to get to the ice. "Oh, I get it!" There was another explosive laugh, his third. He may have been rich, but his personality left a lot to be desired.

When the coals were going and I had put the soufflé in the oven, my mind turned again to Edith. Who could have possibly wanted to break into my refrigerator? Why not steal the computer I had right there on the counter to keep track of menus?

"We're ready for the shrimp cocktail," Marla stage-whispered into the kitchen.

"Already? But I thought you said—"

"Tony's driving me crazy. If I give him some shrimp, maybe he'll stop chuckling at everything I have to say."

While Marla and her guests were bathing their shrimp with cocktail sauce, I hustled out to check on the coals. To my surprise, a nice coat of white ash had developed. Sometimes things do work. The steaks sizzled enticingly when I placed them on the grill. I ran back inside and got out the salad and started the beans. When I came back out to turn the T-bones, the sun had slid behind the mountains and the air had turned cool.

"Come on, let's go," I ordered the steaks. After a long five minutes the first four were done. I slapped them down on the platter, put the last two on the grill, and came in. In a crystal bowl, I made a basket of lettuce and then spooned the Waldorf salad on top. This I put on a tray along with the butter and rolls. The soufflé had puffed and browned; I whisked it out to the dining room. While I was putting the beans in a china casserole dish, I remembered that I had neglected to get the last two steaks off the fire.

Cancel the "things working" idea, I thought. I ferried the rest of the dishes out to Marla's sideboard, invited the guests to serve themselves buffet-style, and made a beeline back to the kitchen.

I looked out the window: around the steaks the charcoal fire was merrily sending up foot-high flames and clouds of smoke. Bad news. At this dry time of year, sparks were anathema. There was no fire extinguisher in Marla's kitchen. Why should there be? She never cooked. I grabbed a crystal pitcher, started water spurting into it, looked back out the window to check the fire again.

Judas priest. A bear was lurching from one bush in Marla's backyard to the next. In the darkening twilight, I could not tell if it was the same one that had been in my backyard. All I could see was him stopping and then holding his hands as if he were cheering.

I sidestepped to get beside one of Marla's cabinets, then peeked outside. I knew bravery was in order, I just didn't know what that was going to look like. Too bad Scout had never made it as an attack cat.

The bear-person shows up at my house. The bear-person shows up at Marla's. Why?

Oh, damn. The eggs.

"Marla!" I shrieked. I ran out to the dining room. "Don't eat the Waldorf salad! There's a bear in your backyard ... but I just know it's not a real one ... Somebody needs to call the cops! Quick! Tony, could you please go grab this person? It's not a real bear, just somebody in a bear suit. I'm sure he killed Edith Blanton."

For once, Tony did not laugh. He said, "You've got a killer dressed as a bear in the backyard. You want me to go grab him with my bare hands?"

"Yes," I said, "of course! Hurry up!"

"This is a weird dinner party," said Tony.

"Oh, I'll do it!" I shrieked.

I sprinted to the kitchen and vaulted full tilt out Marla's back door. Maybe it was a real bear. Then I'd be in trouble for sure. I started running down through the tall grass toward the bush where the bear was hidden. The bear stood up. He made his cheering motion again. But ...

Ordinary black bears have bad eyesight.

Ordinary black bears don't grow over five feet tall.

This guy was six feet if he was an inch, and his eyes told him I was coming after him.

He turned and trundled off in the opposite direction. I sped up, hampered only by tab grass and occasional rocks. Behind me I could hear shouts—Marla, Tony, whoever. I was not going to turn around. I was bent on my prey.

The bear howled: a gargled human howl. Soon he was at the end of Marla's property, where an enormous rock formation was the only thing between us and the road. The bear ran up on the rocks. Then, unsure of what to do, he jumped down the other side. Within a few seconds I had scrambled up to where he had stood. The bear had landed in the center of the road.

I launched myself. When I landed on his right shoulder, he crumpled. Amazing. The last time I'd seen a bear successfully tackled was when Randy Gradishar had thrown Walter Payton for a six-yard loss in the Chicago backfield.

I leaped up. "You son of a bitch!" I screamed. Then I kicked him in the stomach for good measure.

I reached down to pull off his bear mask. Of course, I was fully expecting to see the no-longer-smug face of George Pettigrew.

But it wasn't George.

Looking up at me was the tormented face of David McAllister. I was stunned. But of course. The hand-paw motion. David McAllister had been doing what he always did when he was nervous: cracking his knuckles.

"David? David? What's going on?"

"I'm sorry, I'm sorry," he blubbered, "I didn't mean to hurt that old woman in your house. I just needed Marla . . . I thought I was going to lose my mind . . . I wanted to hurt her . . . and whoever she was seeing . . . I wanted to make them pay . . . I'm just so sorry. . . ."

Marla and Tony Kaplan appeared at the top of the rocks.

"Goldy!" Marla shrieked. "Are you okay? The police are on their way. What's that, a person?"

Later, much later, Marla and I sat in her kitchen and started in on the untouched platter of brownies. David McAllister had said he figured Marla had asked for the apples for Waldorf salad because she was having somebody else over. (*He knew you better than you thought,* I told her.) He was crazy with jealousy, and I had been no help. Worse, when he was in my kitchen, he had seen "Marla—dinner party" on my appointments calendar. And here I'd thought all he'd been doing was cracking his knuckles. He cut my wires and broke through my back door. He knew I made everything from scratch. (*He knew us all better than we thought*, Marla said.) So he substituted salmonella-tainted eggs for the mayonnaise, to make Marla and her dinner guests sick. When Edith Blanton surprised him, they struggled, and she fell back on the corner of the marble slab I used for kneading. It was an accident. But because David McAllister had broken into my house before his struggle with Edith, the charge was going to be murder in the first degree.

Marla sank her teeth into her first brownie. "Ooo-ooo," she said. "Yum. I feel better already. Have one."

"I shouldn't. I can't." In fact, I couldn't even look at the brownies; my knees were scraped and my chest hurt where I'd fallen on David McAllister.

"Well, you're probably right. If you hadn't gone after that parfait, you never would have found Butterball, I mean Mrs. Blanton. Which just goes to show, if you're going to give up desserts, you have to do it cold—"

"Don't say it. Don't even think it. And no matter how you cajole, I'm not going to join you in this chocolate indulgence."

Her eyes twinkled like the rings on her fingers. "But that's what I wanted all along!" she protested. "Leave more for me that way! Dark, fudgy, soothing . . ."

"Oh, all right," I said. "Just one."

TENNESSEE CHESS PIE

It's not mentioned in "Cold Turkey," but desserts are more fun than turkey! In the period B.C. (Before Children), I taught at the Ashley Hall School in Charleston, South Carolina. The chess pie recipe, in a somewhat different form, was given to me by one of the housemothers there. It has been an enduring family and church favorite!

1 homemade 8-inch pie shell, or 1 store-bought frozen 9-inch
    pie shell (not deep-dish), slightly thawed
¼ pound (1 stick) unsalted butter
1 ¼ cups granulated sugar
1 tablespoon apple cider vinegar
3 large eggs
1 teaspoon vanilla extract

Preheat oven to 325 degrees. Using a fork, prick the bottom of the shell in about 8 places. If you are using a frozen pastry shell, flute the rim when it is malleable. Bake the shell for 7 to 10 minutes, or until the crust is just beginning to crisp. Set it aside to cool while you prepare the filling.

In a heavy-duty saucepan, melt the butter over medium-low heat. Add the sugar and vinegar and cook, stirring constantly with a heavy wooden spoon, until the mixture comes to a slow boil. Remove from the heat and set aside to cool slightly. In a large bowl, beat the eggs well, until they are frothy and completely combined. Stirring constantly, pour the butter mixture over the beaten eggs. Add the vanilla and stir well. Immediately pour the egg mixture into the prepared shell. Bake for 30 to 35 minutes, or until the center is set and no longer wobbles when gently shaken.

Cool completely on a rack, then cut into wedges and serve with best quality vanilla ice cream or whipped cream flavored with vanilla extract.

Makes 8 large or 12 small servings.

—DMD

ABOUT OUR AUTHORS

Claudia Bishop published her first Hemlock Falls Mystery, *A Taste for Murder,* in 1994. Its immediate popularity surprised her, and the novel is still in print, along with the eight others she has written to date. *Marinade for Murder,* Claudia's most recent, was published in spring 2000 by Berkley Books. *Death Dines at 8:30* is Claudia's first editorial effort, and she has offered up for us the very first Meg and Quill short story she's ever written.

What's the trouble with **Camilla T. Crespi**? It's probably got something to do with her Simona Griffo mysteries, *The Trouble with Going Home, The Trouble with a Bad Fit, The Trouble with a Hot Summer,* and many other "troublesome" novels. Camilla spent much of her youth traveling in Europe and living in Rome. She worked for a number of years dubbing films and working with Italian icons like Fellini, Mastroianni, and Sophia Loren. Fortunately for us, she's a fabulous cook living in America now, flexing her MFA from Columbia University and writing terrific stories. (Camilla also wins our Most Complicated Recipe award.)

Bill Crider is the author of *A Dangerous Thing* and *Death by Accident,* a Sheriff Dan Rhodes Mystery. We were delighted when Bill asked if he could collaborate on a Dan Rhodes story with his wife, **Judy Crider.** The happy couple adds some Texas flare to our already spicy menu. Don't let the title of their story, "Chocolate Moose," fool your delicate palate. Their chicken-fried steak recipe is not for the dainty eater. I wonder which of them is the real cook in the family?

Barbara D'Amato is the author of the Cat Marsala Mystery Series and other novels, including *Hard Evidence, Good Cop Bad Cop,* and *Help Me Please*. In addition, Barb is the past president of the Mystery Writers of America. As you might imagine, sitting at the helm of MWA was a time-consuming affair. We were thrilled when she agreed to take time out of her busy schedule to contribute a story to our anthology. She also helped us make some important contacts during the piecing together of this book. All this, and we get a great story and spectacular recipe, too.

Who is **Nick Danger**? Relatively new to the mystery field, Nick has been knocking around for quite some time as a freelance writer, the editor of a small literary magazine in a small literary town, a creative-writing professor, and short-story author. We're glad to have a bit of Nick's unique work for *Death Dines at 8:30*. "8-3-Oh" is his first culinary short, and we hope everyone gets a chance to see more of his work in the future.

Wow, what can we say about **Diane Mott Davidson** that mystery readers all over the planet don't already know? Her marvelous Goldy Bear is a staple in every culinary mystery fan's diet. Diane has been nominated for a number of awards, including an Agatha, Anthony, and Macavity.

She has written such entertaining works as *Dying for Chocolate, Cereal Murders, Killer Pancake, Tough Cookie,* and *The Grilling Season*. "Cold Turkey" is an Anthony award-winning Best Short Story, we're lucky to have it, and we're thrilled to be able to present it to you here, along with a fine new recipe from Diane.

Patrica Guiver is the author of the Delilah Doolittle Pet Detective Mystery Series. The series has been a favorite among Berkley readers since its inception in 1997. Her most recent book, *Delilah Doolittle and the Canine Chorus,* is just as delightfully entertaining as the other four books in the series. I'm glad Patricia has added a Delilah short story to her repertoire, just for the sake of our anthology.

Jean Hager is the author of the Iris House B&B Mystery Series. She has also written a number of other mystery titles, including *The Grandfather Medicine* and *The Spirit Caller*. In addition, Jean has penned a popular how-to book for budding mystery writers. She's pretty darn good at short fiction, too, as I'm sure you'll agree after reading "George Washington Crashed Here."

We can't begin to tell you how thrilled we are to have a Nick Velvet story in this anthology, from one of our all-time favorite writers and a giant in the mystery genre, **Edward D. Hoch**. Although Ed has written a handful of novels and done a good bit of editing, he is one of the few writers of our time known primarily for his short fiction. If you'd like to read some of his work, just pick up any *Ellery Queen's Mystery Magazine* from the past thirty years or so, and you'll find one of Ed's stories within its pages. "The Theft of the Sandwich Board" is typical Velvet and everything we had hoped for when Ed promised to write us a story. Ed admits that he's no great cook, but you couldn't prove that by his recipe.

David A. Kaufelt writes the Wyn Lewis Mystery Series that includes such intriguing titles as *The Fat Boy Murders, The Winter Women Murders,* and, most recently, *The Ruthless Realtor Murders*. I'm glad he took time out to write a bagel murder for the pages of *Death Dines at 8:30*. Although David lives in Florida, he seems to have a fondness for New York City bagels. Can't say as we blame him.

Since her first novel appeared in 1981, **Nancy Kress** has seen eighteen of her books published, including short-story collections and writing instruction books. Nancy has won a number of prestigious awards, including the Hugo and Nebula awards for excellence in science fiction and fantasy. She is also the fiction columnist for *Writer's Digest* magazine. Nancy's two mystery/thriller novels, *Oaths and Miracles* and *Stinger,* introduced FBI agent Robert Cavanaugh. "Plant Engineering" is Cavanaugh's first foray into culinary crime.

Tamar Myers is the author of the Pennsylvania-Dutch Mystery Series and the Den of Antiquity books, including such fine novels as *Baroque and Desperate, Between a Wok and a Hard Place,* and *Eat Drink and Be Wary*. There aren't a lot of authors who can wield the gift of humor as effortlessly as Tamar Myers. She keeps a reader laughing longer and harder than anyone else we know, and manages to spin a splendid mystery yarn while she's at it. "Chicken Catch a Tory" is no exception, and we're pleased to be able to serve it to you in our anthology.

Sharan Newman is a medieval historian who prefers writing novels to grading term papers. She is the author of a series featuring Catherine LeVendeur. The first book, *Death Comes As Epiphany,* won the Macavity award. The fifth, *Cursed in the Blood,* won the Herodotus award for best historical mystery of 1998. Other books have been nominated for both the Agatha and Anthony awards. The most recent in the series is *To Wear the White Cloak.* Sharan tells us that her story for this collection is sprinkled with real historical figures, including Lord Milo, who died in 1147 crossing the Meander River in Turkey.

Mike Resnick is one of the finest storytellers we know, and certainly one of the most prolific. Since 1957 he has sold over two hundred novels, three hundred short stories, and two thousand articles. (The man has more pseudonyms than most authors have stories.) Mike has earned Hugo and Nebula awards for his work in science fiction and fantasy, as well as honors from Croatia, France, Poland, Spain, and Japan. In recent years Mike has begun to dabble in scriptwriting for Hollywood. His novel *The Widowmaker* was recently commissioned by Miramax. Mike's mystery novel *Dog in the Manger* introduces private eye Eli Paxton, and we're thrilled to print Eli's first appearance in a short story. As a point of interest, Mike has also collaborated on a number of short stories with one of the editors of this book (Nick DiChario), and their efforts have been published in a small-press collection entitled *Magic Feathers,* fall 2000, Obscura Press.

Elizabeth Daniels Squire is the Berkley Prime Crime author of the Peaches Dann Mystery Series, with such fine books to her credit as *Who Killed What's Her Name?,* *Where There's A Will,* and, most recently, *Forget About Murder.* Peaches is a delightfully forgetful sleuth, but Elizabeth writes with such charm and grace that you won't soon forget her novels, or the engaging story she submitted to this collection. Elizabeth has also won an Agatha award for her short story "The Dog Who Remembered Too Much."

Valerie Wolzien, in addition to some fine short fiction, has written a number of inviting mystery novels with a touch of suburban humor featuring Susan Henshaw, housewife and amateur sleuth. Among them are *Murder at the PTA Luncheon,* which was made into a Movie of the Week for CBS television. Josie Pigeon is another of her creations, a most clever carpenter. Other novels by Valerie include *Weddings Are Murder, Remodeled to Death,* and *Deck the Halls with Murder.*

> *Thanks for joining us in the fight against hunger!*
> —Nick & Claudia